M000275136

Other Novels by Buzz Bernard from Bell Bridge Books

EYEWALL

PLAGUE

SUPERCELL

Blizzard

by

H.W. "Buzz" Bernard

Bell Bridge Books

Bell Bridge Books
PO BOX 300921
Memphis, TN 38130
Print ISBN: 978-1-61194-593-5

Bell Bridge Books is an Imprint of BelleBooks, Inc.

We at BelleBooks enjoy hearing from readers.
Visit our websites
BelleBooks.com
BellBridgeBooks.com
ImaJinnBooks.com

10 9 8 7 6 5 4 3 2 1

Cover design: Debra Dixon
Interior design: Hank Smith
Photo/Art credits:
Snow texture (manipulated) © Malija | Dreamstime.com
Wolves (manipulated) © Kjetil Kolbjornsrud | Dreamstime.com
Atlanta cityscape © Buzz Bernard

:Lbnh:01:

Dedication

For my daughter, Vicky

Chapter One

Failure

American-International Systems Solutions, Inc. (AISSI)
North Metro Atlanta, Georgia
Wednesday morning, December 28

JONATHAN CARLTON Riggins, J.C. to his friends and family, stepped out of the elevator on the tenth floor of corporate headquarters. He checked his watch. Eight a.m. Right on time. He stopped at the desk of the CEO's assistant, Mary Hawthorne.

"Good morning, Mary. Hope you had a pleasant Christmas."

She nodded but didn't return the greeting. In fact, she appeared strangely dour.

"FedEx should be here around ten o'clock to pick up the proposal," J.C. said, deciding not to probe into Mary's personal feelings. "Eight copies. Mr. Billingsly will sign them out—"

"He'd like to see you." Something flashed in her eyes. A warning. A prophetess bearing a dire message.

Her tacit alert seemed so palpable J.C. actually glanced behind him, wondering if someone dressed as the Grim Reaper might be creeping up unseen.

"I just need to stop by corporate communications first—"

"Now," she said, her voice low. "He wants to see you now."

J.C.'s gut churned. The holiday bonhomie and sense of vocational optimism he'd harbored just seconds before fled like helium from a pricked balloon. Adding to his sudden angst, the smell of blackened toast and scorched eggs drifted in from the executive dining room three doors down. The term "burnt offerings" crossed his mind.

He tried to imagine what could have gone wrong, for surely something must have. He wasn't misreading the foreboding implicit in Mary's demeanor. At yesterday's final review, the wrap-up prior to the most important proposal in the company's history being shipped out, everything had seemed in order. The meeting had been brief and smooth. No gremlins lurking in a forest, no trolls hiding beneath a bridge.

All that remained was to print and bind the proposal documents and put them in the hands of FedEx who would deliver them to Rampart Aerospace & Defense Corporation in Durham, North Carolina, by the end of the day, a step ahead of an impending winter storm that had everyone on edge. It seemed as though the Southeast, in the over-the-top words of a major TV network, faced a once-in-a-millennium monster. A shutdown blizzard expected to cripple the region for a week, maybe two.

What had he missed?

He rapped on the door of Cyrus Billingsly, the CEO.

"Enter." A curt command from a retired Air Force major general.

J.C. stepped into Billingsly's lair. The man still appeared every bit a flag officer with his close-cropped gray hair, chiseled features, and laser-like gaze. While J.C. didn't mark him as a hard ass, he knew him to be demanding and blunt.

Billingsly didn't look up from a document he appeared to be studying. After a minute or so, he did. His gaze, something that could have withered a granite monolith, fell on J.C. with almost tangible intensity.

"Do you know how fucking pissed I am?" Billingsly said. His voice rumbled with volcanic undertones. His face, twisted into a mask of barely contained rage, gleamed lava-flow red.

J.C. had never heard the CEO use profanity before, so "fucking" became an immediate marker of the depth of the man's fury. J.C. chose not to respond to the question, understanding it didn't demand an answer. A wave of nausea swept over him. The strength in his legs failed, the muscles and tendons holding him upright deteriorating to a rubbery state. He grabbed the desk for support. Something cataclysmic had happened. On his watch. Under his leadership. His responsibility.

"Yesterday I was briefed everything was fine," Billingsly said. "Last night, I decided to make one final sweep through the proposal." He slid a stack of papers toward J.C. and raised his voice. "You just cost this company a billion-dollar project. A billion fucking dollars! Damn it to hell, J.C.! Damn it to hell!"

J.C. reached toward the papers, trying to camouflage the tremor in his hand.

"It's the test data," Billingsly snapped. "Here we are, the only company in the bidding with a working HDIRLLTAS"—he pronounced it hy-derl-tis—"a virtual shoo-in to win the job, and instead of entering working-model test results into the proposal, we entered the prototype evaluations. Two-year-old data. I know the differences are subtle, but when it comes to highlighting the effectiveness of the system, they're deal-breakers. Shit." He pounded his fist onto his mahogany desk with such force J.C. thought the CEO might have shattered the bones in his hand.

J.C. read the title on the top sheet in the stack of papers: TEST RESULTS: HIGH-DEFINITION, LOW-LIGHT TARGET ACQUISITION SYSTEM (HDIRLLTAS). The system, a high-tech blend of night vision technology and infrared detection capabilities, had undergone extensive modifications over the past two years. From a barely functional prototype, it had been crafted into a state-of-the-art, reliable, ruggedized military system. No other corporation, at least as far as AISSI's corporate intelligence could discern, had one. It was to have been the company's golden egg, the key to Fort Knox, their own Saudi oilfield. But now?

His hand visibly shaking, J.C. leafed through the papers.

"Don't bother," Billingsly said, his voice coated with rage. "I double checked, triple checked. It's not obvious, at least not until you drill down into the data, but it doesn't support our efficacy claims."

"We can fix it," J.C. said, his voice wavering and feeble.

"Sure we can," Billingsly said, his words derisive. "In case it escaped your notice, that data ripples through virtually every damn section of the document. Tech specs. Functional design. Applications. Maintenance. By the time we repair the damage, it'll be midnight."

"FedEx can still—"

"I already checked. They don't expect to be operating tomorrow. If the weather guessers are right, much of the Southeast may be non-op tomorrow. And Friday."

"Maybe they're wrong."

"Maybe pigs will fly, too," Billingsly snapped.

"Look, I'll talk to Rampart," J.C. said, his words hesitant, irresolute, "and see if they'll make an exception and let us email the document."

"Not a chance. You know how acutely sensitive the data is." Billingsly shook his head. "I don't believe it. I just don't fucking believe it. I trusted you. A billion-dollar opportunity. You assured me things were under control. No potholes in the road, you said. Jesus." He buried his head in his hands.

"Sir, let's at least try—"

"Shut up. Just shut up and get out. Pack your stuff. I want you out of this building in an hour. HR has your termination papers."

Another ripple of nausea coursed through J.C. A stream of bile erupted into his esophagus. He turned, made a desperate grab for a waste can, and vomited.

Dispassionate, Billingsly watched. "Same way I feel," he said. He nodded at the waste can J.C. held. "Take it with you when you leave."

Back in his own office, J.C. leaned over the foul-smelling waste can and loosed another volley of his barely digested breakfast. He wiped his mouth with a paper towel and shoved the can into a corner with his foot. He sat in his chair, stared blankly at a wall adorned with family photos and framed awards, and waited for his stomach and breathing to regain a state of relative normality. It took several minutes.

He attempted to analyze what had gone wrong, how his career had come to such a sudden and mortifying end. Somehow, as proposal manager, he'd lost control of the effort and allowed the corporate ship to founder on the rocks. A week ago, everything had seemed on course, smooth sailing ahead.

A Week Earlier
American-International Systems Solutions, Inc.
Thursday morning, December 22

J.C. SAT AT AN aircraft carrier-sized conference table in the executive meeting room of AISSI, a half-dozen key members of his proposal team flanking him on both sides. As team chief and Vice President of Systems Development, he carried the burden of heading the effort to put together the proposal to Rampart Aerospace & Defense.

If AISSI won the job—and there was every indication they had the inside track against a score of other companies—it would mean a billion-dollar project. A billion dollars. The company would move from being a minnow in the systems development world to being a whale.

The team members engaged in idle chatter, much of it centered on rumors of a major winter storm targeting Atlanta, sipped coffee, and nibbled on stale bagels and frosted doughnuts while they awaited the arrival of Cyrus Billingsly. J.C. knew Billingsly had called the meeting to make certain everything remained on track as the proposal's delivery date, December 30th, neared. With only eight days remaining, and Christmas in the mix, they had definitely entered the "no screw ups zone."

Jan Darleena, tasked with overseeing the Operational Applications section of the document, leaned close to J.C. "Do you think The General will be in a jolly mood?"

J.C. dabbed at his mouth with a stained paper napkin. "Is he ever?"

"It's three days until Christmas."

"My question stands."

Chastened by the reminder their boss wasn't exactly a hail-fellow-well-met or "one of them," Jan wrinkled her nose and slumped back in her chair. She folded her arms across her stomach, resting them on the front of a wooly black and white sweater adorned with leaping reindeer, and stared straight ahead.

J.C. patted her shoulder. "Don't worry. Everything's on schedule. I've reviewed all the sections. We're in excellent shape. No lumps of coal in our Christmas stockings."

The door to the conference room popped open. Cyrus Billingsly strode in followed by a rush of chilly air from an adjacent corridor. "Seats," he announced, though no one was standing.

J.C. understood old habits were difficult to break. Billingsly hadn't quite been able to take the stars off his collar, hadn't fully made the transition from military commander to civilian boss even after two years. When an Air Force two-star entered a briefing room, everyone stood until ordered to sit. Not here, not at AISSI, where employees worked in blue jeans and tee-shirts, at least during the warmer months, and called managers by their first names.

Billingsly lowered himself into a chair opposite of J.C. and his staff, flipped open the cover of an iPad, and tapped the screen. He looked up and spoke. "Good morning, ladies and gentlemen. I suppose I don't need to reiterate this, but the future of this company is riding on the work you're doing."

J.C. resisted an urge to roll his eyes. No, Billingsly didn't need to reiterate that, but just did. Everyone in AISSI, as professionals, knew very well what the proposal meant. It was the sort of opportunity on which careers and major corporations were built. It was, to be trite, an opening that comes along once in a lifetime.

The meeting went smoothly and quickly. Each member of the proposal team tendered a status report. Nothing seemed amiss.

At the close of the meeting, Billingsly snapped his iPad cover shut. "It sounds as if we're in excellent shape. But I want to make absolutely, dead-center certain this document goes out the door on December 28th. That gives us two-day's grace before it needs to be in Durham." He stood. "I don't want to get sandbagged by this so-called superstorm the media is screwing itself into the ceiling over. I understand it's probably the usual uber-hype, and that we'll end up with just a few raggedy-ass snow flurries, but I don't want to take any chances. This document is far too important for us to risk getting Little-Big-Horned by the weather."

He started to move toward the exit, but stopped.

"One more thing," he said, "just so we're clear. I know it sounds as if we're golden on this, so it's probably an unneeded warning, but I'm a guy who has zero tolerance for screw ups. If someone fumbles the ball, steps on his poncho, gets her tit caught in the ringer, don't expect absolution from me. What you *can* expect is that your next job will be stocking shelves in Walmart . . . if you're lucky. But like I say, it's probably an unneeded warning. Merry Christmas."

"Tit caught in ringer?" Jan mouthed to J.C., a smirk creeping across her face.

Billingsly executed a sharp pivot and strode from the room.

Chapter Two

Conflict

The Natural Environment Television Network (NE-TV)
Atlanta, Georgia
Thursday morning, December 22

SINCE NO ONE could pronounce Tomasz Przybyszewski's last name, he simply went by Tom Priz. He stood as his immediate superior, Sophie Lyons, the executive vice president of Operational Programming at the Natural Environment Television Network entered his cramped office. In her two-inch heels, she stood only a couple of inches shorter than his six foot one.

He understood it to be socially insensitive—she was, after all, his boss—but he often found himself appraising her more as a woman— well, to be honest, a sexual fantasy—than a network executive. Today, she looked particularly attractive with her raven hair pulled into a French braid and an Armani Collezioni business suit flattering her figure. In her early forties, a few years younger than Tom, the first faint signs of aging had crept onto her face: a trace of crow's feet near her eyes and thin threads of worry lines creasing her forehead. These early assaults by middle age had met their match; they'd been whipped into submission by her fair skin, subtle aquiline nose, and, he guessed, intense workouts at the gym.

He found himself attracted to her not only because of her physical assets, but because she came across as smart and authoritative, as well. Still, despite the fact she'd risen through the ranks in a rough and tumble business world, he sensed that underneath her frequent hard-shell bluster lay a certain vulnerability. Perhaps a lack of a "significant other" in her life? He didn't know, but he did know that on occasion their gazes had locked, albeit ever so briefly, with an intensity that hinted at something beyond a casual interest in one another.

More than once, Tom had found himself, after an encounter with

Sophie, sitting at his desk attempting to camouflage a woody and hoping fervently she wouldn't flounce into his office for one last word. There probably wouldn't be anything to hide this morning. Her intense blue eyes radiated welding-light intensity, a far cry from anything sexual. Tom decided he'd better sit and motioned for her to do the same.

She glanced at the chair he'd gestured toward, essentially an ad hoc table littered with meteorological journals, research papers, and *National Geographics*, and declined. "This won't take long." She clenched her lips as if sucking on a pipe.

Tom wondered if he should be looking for a foxhole. She wasn't referred to, at least behind her back, as "Her Highness, the Lyoness," a play on her last name, for nothing.

"Network Chief of Meteorology," Sophie said, "that's what you are?"

A rhetorical question? She seemed to be waiting for an answer, so Tom decided it wasn't. "Unless I've just been demoted," he said.

"Don't tempt me."

"Where the hell is this coming from?" Tom said, his voice firm but defensive. "Why am I suddenly on your shit list?"

A rising tide of red enveloped her face, a reflection of anger held barely in check. "Because I don't want to get taken to the cleaners by some other private forecasting outfit on this winter storm," she snapped.

"What winter storm?" He realized his tone of voice had risen in sharpness proportional to hers.

"The one that's all over Facebook, Twitter, the blogosphere, and a gaggle of TV talk shows. Rumors of a foot of snow in Atlanta."

"Jesus, Sophie, it's a fantasycast."

"A what?"

He rose from his chair, removed the stack of papers and magazines from the other chair, and told Sophie to sit. This time she did.

Tom stared out his window for a moment at the traffic edging along I-285 at ice floe speed through a cold, gray dawn. "Fantasycast," he said. He returned to his chair. "That's what forecasters call a numerical model forecast of a major weather event eight or ten days in the future. It rarely happens. It's a fantasy."

"You said rarely. Meaning every once in a while one of your fantasycasts, as you call them, must hit the nail on the head?"

Tom tapped his forefinger on his desk to emphasize a point he wished to make. "The skill of longer-range predictions diminishes to virtually zero after about six or seven days." *Tap, tap, tap.* "The storm mongers right now are hyping a *blizzard*, I think I heard that term used, based on a two hundred forty-hour forecast. Absurd."

"There's talk of a foot of snow in Atlanta."

"Oh, sure. When was the last time you saw a foot of snow in Atlanta?"

She remained silent.

"When do you *think* the last time was that Atlanta had a foot of snow?"

"Superstorm 1993?"

Tom had to admit, she at least had awareness of significant historical weather happenings. "No. Some of the northern suburbs might have picked up ten inches in that storm, but officially, Atlanta had only a little over four inches."

"So when *was* the last time we had a foot?"

"Never."

"Really?"

"In January 1940 the city had an eight-inch storm. Well, a tad more than eight inches, but we've never come close to a foot."

"So what are people seeing that's got them bouncing off the walls?" The crimson had drained from her face. She appeared ready to listen to reason.

"One of the models we look at regularly is showing the evolution of a storm very similar to Superstorm '93—"

"Whoa, whoa," Sophie interjected. "So we're just gonna sit on our thumbs and ignore that? I don't think so. If there's even a remote—"

"Let me finish, Sophie. Please."

She exhaled audibly. "Yeah, okay. Convince me NE-TV shouldn't be all over this." She sat back, crossed her legs—shapely legs, he noted—and brushed a strand of hair from her forehead.

Outside, the wind had picked up. A skeletal bush tapped against the office window. "I mentioned earlier that forecast models beyond about a week have very little skill. So what forecasters like to look at instead is an ensemble forecast."

"Which is?"

"In simplest terms, it's an average of a bunch of individual model runs, each using slightly different initial conditions. In other words, the parameters going into each iteration of the model run are tweaked slightly to account for our uncertainty about what's really going on in the atmosphere."

"You mean you don't know?" Her words bore a slightly accusatory tone.

"Not with pinpoint, one-hundred-percent accuracy. I mean, what if a storm system far out over the Pacific Ocean is actually stronger than our limited observations in that region suggest? What if a cold air dump over China isn't quite so cold as we were led to believe? What if the jet stream over the Himalayas is blowing at two hundred knots instead of one eighty?"

"Your profession comes with built-in excuses, doesn't it?"

He glared at her but held his tongue.

"Relax, Tom. I'm yanking your chain. Go on about ensembles."

He drew a slow breath and continued. "Well, for instance, with the European model, or Euro as we call it, fifty different runs are generated every twelve hours. The average of those runs beyond about five or six days turns out to have more validity than the primary forecast generated by what's known as the operational or deterministic run."

She nodded. "Okay. So what does the ensemble average suggest is coming up next week?"

"A modest snowstorm, maybe for Tennessee."

"And the . . . what did you call it?"

"The operational run?"

"Yeah. What's it showing that's giving everybody—well, everybody but you—wet dreams?"

He drummed his fingers on his desk, suddenly thinking about wet dreams, Sophie, and what to say next. He wondered if her choice of words, "wet dreams," had been deliberate, meant to titillate him. Or was she just being the slightly bawdy, "one-of-boys" boss she liked to portray herself as?

He found himself unable to focus, unable to articulate a response, her nocturnal emission reference catching him off guard. Though both divorced, they'd maintained their relationship at a strictly professional level. He supposed her remark wasn't out of bounds—it's something guys often said—yet he'd on occasion wondered if there might not be a reciprocal attraction. After all, she had a way of standing tantalizingly close to him during their talks, though that could be just her style.

"Tom?" she said, snapping him back to the moment, back to her question.

He blinked. "You mean, if you took its forecast literally?"

She hung her head in mock dismay. "Am I not speaking clearly?"

"It's nothing cast in concrete, Sophie. Haven't you heard anything I've said?" He struggled to keep a civil tone, stood, and faced her. "It would be irresponsible to go on the air a week in advance and trumpet something like what the operational model implies is coming."

"Which is?" she said. "Look, I want to be leading the charge on this, not eating someone else's dust." She stood and approached him, moving close enough for him to inhale the heady sweetness of her cologne and sense the heat radiating from her body.

His resolve faltered, but he opted for a last-ditch stand. "We can't go on the air like Chicken Little and scream 'The sky is falling.' If we do, I'll guarantee you that within twenty-four hours every grocery store in the metro area, every Lowe's, every Home Depot, will have shelves that look like they've been attacked by piranhas."

"Oh, for shit's sake. All you have to do is mention *flurries* in Atlanta and that happens. Well, except for 2014 when an inch or two was forecast and everybody went to work instead of Kroger. Then everybody *left* work at the same time when the snow started, and the city crashed and burned. Anyhow, I don't want to become known as the network that blew the biggest winter storm in Southern history. Give me something to work with."

"I'm trying to give you a little sage advice. I understand you don't want the reputation of blowing a forecast for a major storm, but I'm trying to keep us from becoming the outfit that cried wolf when all that was out there was a fuzzy puppy."

"Cute, Tom." She moved even closer to him, the cool freshness of her breath a curious counterpoint to the warmth of her nearness.

He stood his ground.

"Tell me what the model suggests," she whispered.

"Is that an order?"

She waited, not responding.

"Then I'll take it as a command." He paused, then forged ahead. "Perhaps as much as ten inches of snow and forty miles per hour winds."

"My God," she said, stepping back from him, her voice harsh. "You expected the network to sit on that?"

"Emphasis on *perhaps*, not ten inches," he snapped.

"Tom, maybe you need to consider a new line of work. Something where you can find shelter in ivory towers behind ivy-draped walls." She turned, exited his office, shut the door.

"Thank you, Your Highness ... the Lyoness," he said to the

closed door. He sank into his chair, attempting to analyze Sophie's words, trying to divine if his job had just been threatened.

His door reopened. Sophie reappeared. "I'm not over-the-hill yet. My hearing is fine." She backed out and shut the door once more, this time with particular firmness.

He sat staring at the closed door, wondering if he'd just managed to punch his ticket for a pink slip. He knew Sophie to be quick and smart and not liking to be second-guessed, but she'd never seemed vindictive. All he'd been doing was standing his professional ground. Still, he decided he'd probably ventured into a minefield and should move forward with extreme care.

The idea of beating the drums for a major snow dump on North Georgia a week in advance seemed meteorologically irresponsible. But he realized Sophie viewed things through the prism of a broadcast network and thus saw most things in terms of headlines and hooks. That shouldn't absolve her from exercising a modicum of circumspection, especially when it came to sounding an alarm for an event that occurs about as often as a rabbi appearing in a mosque.

Time for a visit to Gandalf. Tom stood, peeked out his office door to make sure Sophie wasn't lying in wait for him, then walked toward the forecast center, a glass-enclosed anteroom just off the production area. A half-dozen workstations for forecasters occupied the back wall of the center. Usually only two or three of the positions were filled, and today proved no exception.

A large-screen HD TV exhibited a series of the latest forecast maps out through forty-eight hours. The maps displayed both meteorological features, such as highs and lows and fronts, and sensible weather, like rain, wind, and snow.

An elderly gentleman sporting an "old man's belly," unruly white hair, and a shaggy beard, thus the Gandalf moniker, sat at the far end of the room scratching with a pencil at something antiquated—a paper copy of a weather map. The nameplate on top of his computer proclaimed: Alfred R. Tillman, Special Consultant. As Tom approached, he looked up.

His clear gray eyes sparkled through tiny round spectacles. A bulbous nose threaded with blue veins suggested he'd perhaps been close friends with the Daniels or Beam family in the past.

"Morning, Al," Tom said.

"Jesus, kid, I hope you come bearing Celebrex."

"Arthritis acting up?"

"I should have moved to Tucson when Maggie wanted us to, a few years back."

"You still could, you know."

"Not much point now . . . now that she's gone. It just seems like too much effort." He kneaded his left shoulder with his right hand.

Tom sat in a chair adjacent to Al and scooted close to him. "Maybe you'll find a new lady in your life someday."

Al issued a phlegmy laugh. "I hate to break this to you, but I'm old. Not to tarnish anyone's rosy outlook for the Golden Years, but you reach a stage in your life where a good dump is better than a good hump."

"Well now, *there's* something to look forward to."

"Yeah," Al growled, "that, and the fact that things which should be soft get hard like arteries, and things which used to get hard—"

Tom cut him off. "Stop right there, or I may commit suicide before I'm Medicare-eligible."

"Might not be a bad idea." Al arched his back, a careful movement, and groaned. "Did I mention arthritis?"

"Maybe there's a storm coming," Tom said. "My ex used to say that every time her joint pains flared up."

Al narrowed his gaze at Tom. "A storm? Ah, I'll bet Her Highness paid you a visit. Added some extra octane to your testosterone, did she?"

Tom laughed. "After she got through with me, even Viagra wouldn't have given me a lift."

"So, I'm assuming she was on the warpath, beating her snow tom-tom and getting ready to scalp the first person who doesn't kowtow to her 'let's-get-a-blizzard-warning-on-the-air-right-now' party line?"

"Something like that. Look, I'd like your opinion on what's brewing. I warned her we could be crying wolf if we blow the air raid siren now. What's your take on things? Dog sleds and mukluks for the Deep South?" He placed his hands in a prayerful position under his chin and bowed toward Al. "Lay some wisdom on me, O meteorological Maharishi."

"Real wisdom? I'm still waiting. I think what passes for sagacity in us old farts is just the fact we become less stupid. Whaddaya wanna know?"

"Maybe how not to grow old."

Al chuckled, but it morphed into a cough, stirring up something watery deep in his lungs.

"Look, put yourself in my shoes for a moment," Tom continued. "What would you argue should be the network's position on this storm . . . alleged storm?"

Al wiped his mouth with a handkerchief and stuffed it into his pants pocket. "When I was on active duty with the Air Force, we had a saying, and this, my friend, *is* genuine wisdom: 'Never pass up a chance to keep your mouth shut.'"

Tom considered the old man's words. "Sooo"—he drew out the word—"what you're saying is we go on the air and just ignore all the chatter about the possibility of a historic Southern snowstorm? Don't even reference it?"

"Exactly. At least for now. You know as well as I do that at this range the models are going to be bouncing back and forth like a Ping-Pong ball with every run. Every twelve hours they'll spit out a new solution. Big storm. Little storm. Big storm. Wait, no storm."

Tom cracked his knuckles. "But, if it comes to fruition?"

"We will have figured things out long before then. Look, we wait until we're certain, as certain as we ever can be in this business, then we play up whatever the forecast ends up being; like it was the Second Coming. It's win-win for the network."

"How so?"

"If what's flying around in cyberspace now turns out to be the usual model make-believe, then we come out looking really good and remind everyone it wasn't us crying wolf. If, on the other hand, a blockbuster does materialize, we jump on it when we're sure and forecast the hell out of it. Everyone will have forgotten we weren't out there baying at the moon like all the others a week in advance. People have short, non-discriminatory memories."

"Beautiful theory."

Al spun on his chair like a little kid. "It is, isn't it?" He sounded pleased with himself. He braked his spin. "But it's not gonna happen, is it?"

"Her Highness has spoken."

Al sighed. "Must be tough."

"What?"

"Having to kowtow to a woman who isn't even your wife."

"Bite me, Al."

Al choked out a laugh. "Okay, maybe you'll be right. Then you can lord it over *her*. On the other hand, if you're not, maybe somewhere in the world a village is short an idiot, and you'll still be able to find a job." Al grinned, a geriatric Cheshire Cat.

Tom tipped his head back and stared at the ceiling. "Thanks for your encouragement."

"Look, junior, if you're gonna have your ass run out of town on a rail, it might as well be by a chick in a tight pantsuit, right?"

"Good night, old man." Tom stood and departed.

Chapter Three

Cole

**Magnolia Heights Subdivision
North Metro Atlanta, Georgia
Thursday evening, December 22**

J.C. ENTERED HIS sprawling McMansion, as some people derisively called it, on Bankside Drive overlooking an ice-fringed lake. His six-year-old son, Cole, sprinted into his arms.

"Daddy," he yelled.

"Hey, Big Guy." J.C. lifted him into the air and swung him around, but only once, since Cole remained prone to bouts of nausea. He had just completed a month's worth of chemotherapy for his acute lymphocytic leukemia.

"Santa Claus is coming," Cole said, clinging to J.C.'s neck.

"Yeah, I know. I'm excited. Are you?"

Cole bobbed his head in affirmation.

From the kitchen, the aroma of pork roast, sweet corn, and baked potatoes wafted into the foyer. "Let's go find Mommy," J.C. said. He set Cole down and followed him through the living and family rooms into the kitchen.

In the family room, flames swayed and pirouetted from almost real-looking logs in a gas-fed fireplace. Garlands of greenery freckled with red holly berries draped the mantel. Adjacent to an expanse of sliding glass doors overlooking an outdoor deck, a real Fraser fir twinkled with hundreds of tiny white LEDs.

The house, in fact, appeared more like an overstocked Christmas decoration shop than a home decked out for the holidays. But J.C. and his wife, Ginny, had done that deliberately, wanting to make this Christmas a memorable one for Cole. He'd just spent forty-two days at the MD Anderson Center in Houston undergoing debilitating treatments. Ginny had spent most of her time with him. J.C. had flown back and forth, splitting his time between Houston and Atlanta, while simultaneously attempting to remain focused on the billion-dollar proposal effort at AISSI.

But now that they were all home for Christmas, it needed to be special.

As J.C. and Cole entered the kitchen, Ginny wiped her hands on a paper towel and greeted J.C. with a vigorous hug.

"Smells good," he said.

"Me?" Ginny asked.

"That, too."

"Hard to rid myself of that charwoman's odor, huh?"

"You're hardly that. I don't suppose you've noticed the guys at the club giving you surreptitious glances every time we walk in?"

"Some aren't so surreptitious." She winked at him.

She still looked "hot," as teenagers say, although a tinge of weariness had crept in around her eyes and lips; Cole's illness had taken its toll. Both she and J.C. knew additional challenges lurked in the future.

"So," she said, "all went well at the meeting today?" She turned to Cole. "Go wash your hands. Dinner's almost ready."

Cole scampered away.

"Really well," J.C. said. "I think everything's in great shape. Maybe better than I could have expected."

Ginny smiled and stuck a fork into a baked potato, testing. "Well, you know the old Murphy's Law corollary, right? The one about 'if everything seems to be going well, you've obviously missed something'?"

"Mmm, never heard it," he lied. "No, really, I think we're dead center on the glide path. All the proposal parts are in place, everyone's done their job, and the boss is happy."

"Good. Maybe you can kick back and relax and enjoy Christmas now. I know the last few weeks have been a real goat rope for you, between the proposal, Cole being home, and getting ready for the holidays."

Cole ambled back into the kitchen.

"Let's see 'em," J.C. said.

Cole showed him his hands, backs then palms.

"You're good to go, kid. Grab a seat."

J.C. walked to the oven, pulled out the pork roast, and set it on a trivet. "Want me to carve it?"

Ginny handed him a knife.

"The proposal has been a huge time suck, I know," he said as he sliced. "I just hope I haven't short-changed Cole. I've tried not to, I really have."

Ginny draped her arm across J.C.'s shoulders and kissed his cheek. "You've been a great dad. I know how much he means to you. Honestly, I don't understand how you've done it, how you've been able to concentrate on everything. Work, Cole, home." She shook her head, kissed him again, and whispered in his ear, "Pressure's off."

As Cole poked at his food with a fork at the dinner table, he said, "Will Santa bring what I asked for?"

"Well, you asked for a lot of stuff," J.C. said. "I'll bet you get most of it."

"Yeah," Cole said, his tone suggesting *most of it* wouldn't cut it. He stuck a small piece of pork into his mouth and chewed on it without enthusiasm.

"What do you want most of all?" Ginny asked.

J.C. already had a pretty good idea what that might be and knew that neither he nor Ginny, nor even Santa, would be able to deliver it.

"My hair to grow back," Cole said softly.

"It will, Big Guy," J.C. said, a slight catch in his voice. "But it will take time. So, you know what I'm going to do tomorrow?"

Cole looked up.

"I'm going to get a haircut just like yours. Father and son chrome domes for the holidays."

Cole laughed. "Cool." Then he mumbled something.

"What?" J.C. asked.

"Do I have to go back to the hospital?"

J.C. looked at Ginny, who nodded.

"Yes, after New Year's, but you probably won't have to stay overnight. We'll rent a nice place to stay somewhere near the hospital, and GaGa and PaPa and Grandma and Granddad will come visit."

"I like the doctors and nurses at the hospital," Cole said, "but sometimes I get scared when I have to stay there by myself."

"We'll try not to let that happen, son."

Most of Cole's follow-up chemo, known as consolidation therapy, would be on an outpatient basis. But there remained concern a stem cell transplant might be necessary. That left J.C. weak-kneed and feeling gutshot just thinking about it.

What the family faced would be traumatic, but he had abundant faith in the staff at MD Anderson, and Cole felt comfortable there, calling the doctors by their first names. It would be expensive, too:

renting an extended-stay suite, shuttling between Atlanta and Houston, covering the travel expenses of the grandparents, and picking up whatever medical costs insurance didn't.

Thank God for a six-figure salary and gold-standard health insurance at AISSI.

The English carol *I Saw Three Ships* floated from the home's integrated sound system. In the family room, the flames in the fireplace gamboled in a lively jig, their transient warmth a nostrum to the chill lurking outside.

For a fleeting moment, J.C. allowed himself to believe all was well in the world. That children didn't get sick; that hospitals were for the elderly; that Christmases with him and his son and wife would come and go forever. But he knew that was only a December daydream, a winter will-o'-the-wisp.

On a muted TV, a red-lettered headline crawled across the bottom of the screen: HOLIDAY BLIZZARD FOR ATLANTA?

Chapter Four

Chaos

The Natural Environment Television Network
Friday morning, December 23

HOLDING TWO cups of McDonalds coffee, steam leaking from drinking holes in their plastic tops, Tom used his foot to push open the door of the forecast center. The meteorologists on duty, three today, acknowledged his arrival with subdued good mornings.

Al, as usual, sat by himself at the far end of the facility. He nodded a greeting to Tom who extended one of the cups to him. He accepted it, popped its cover off, and sniffed. "Something's missing."

"Mickey D's doesn't serve liquor before noon."

"My loss. Well, have a seat and prepare to feel vindicated."

"The Euro has backed off on the Blizzard of the Century?"

"Yeah. For now. Several of its ensemble members still suggest some Currier and Ives follies next week, but the ensemble mean and operational model are advertising only typical wintertime dreariness for Atlanta—a cold rain, maybe a bit of sleet at the onset, then some post-cold frontal snow flurries. No big deal."

Tom sipped his coffee. "So, has that reined in the snow hounds on Twitter and Facebook?"

"Not all of them. A few still have their noses to the ground, searching for new scents. And who knows, when the next model runs come out this afternoon, they just might find them."

"And all the blather will get reenergized," Tom interjected.

Al took a long drink from his cup. "Sure you don't have some of Kentucky's finest hidden in your desk?"

"No. I finished it last week."

"You kids." Fake exasperation.

"Check your Christmas stocking. You might get lucky."

"Yeah, that's about the *only* meaning that phrase has anymore."

Abruptly, Al set his cup on the table and stared into the production area. "Uh, oh."

"What?"

"Dragon Lady warning."

Tom followed his gaze. Sophie, on a course for the forecast center, glided through the production area, nodding to a few of the staff and stopping briefly to chat with others.

"A queen recognizing her court," Al noted.

Dressed more casually than yesterday, perhaps in deference to the approaching holiday weekend, or maybe in an effort to ward off the outdoor chill, Tom had to admit Sophie still looked elegant, adorned as she was in a white silk blouse, red cashmere cardigan, and black slacks.

Al caught his appraisal. "Better to think how she might be sizing *you* up for your annual review rather than fantasizing how *she* might be in bed," he whispered.

"Jesus, Al."

"What? You think just because my testosterone tank is empty my daydream locker is, too? It's okay, junior. You're normal. The hormones still flow. You wonder if she might be a lioness in some other environment than the office." He elbowed Tom softly in the ribs. "Right?" He broke into one of his patented hacking coughs.

Sophie entered the room, a concerned look on her face. "Everything okay, Mr. Tillman?"

Al ceased coughing and cleared his throat. "There, that's how you know you're over the hill. *Mister* Tillman. I'll bet she doesn't call you *Mister* Przybyszewski, does she? But to answer your question, my dear, I'm fine. Just giving Tom a little adult guidance."

"I approve. He needs it. Good morning, Tom." She stepped close to him and allowed a smile to unfold in slow motion across her face. "Your Highness, the Lyoness? Really?"

He shrugged but didn't offer an apology.

She eyed the McDonald's coffee. "None for me?"

Tom slid his cup toward her.

She rolled her eyes.

"So what brings you to the salt mines, young lady, other than our scintillating company?" Al asked. He pushed a chair over to her, and she sat between the two men.

"A couple of the on-camera meteorologists tell me our big storm is kaput."

Tom forced himself not to smile—stifled smugness. "It never was un-kaput."

"Meaning?"

"It never was real."

"It was imaginary?"

"In a way. It was just the product of a bunch of mathematical calculations used to simulate the atmosphere. The key word being *simulate*. Throw in natural chaos, or the propensity of tiny differences in initial conditions to lead to widely diverging outcomes, and you're swimming upstream when attempting to forecast the weather a week in advance."

Al piped in. "Professor Edward Lorenz was a pioneer in chaos theory. He defined chaos this way: 'When the present determines the future, but the approximate present does not approximately determine the future.'"

"Wow," Sophie said, "you were right about scintillating company." She grabbed Tom's coffee cup and took a swallow. "Ugh." She held the cup at arm's length and stared at it. "Something's missing."

Al smiled at Tom. "Told ya."

"Anyhow," Tom said, ignoring Al and focusing on Sophie, "now that you understand chaos, you understand why we use ensemble forecasting."

"And the ensembles are still suggesting no big deal?"

"The ensemble mean is," Al said, answering for Tom, "but there are still two or three individual members clinging to the idea of a snow jam for Atlanta."

"So the threat isn't dead?"

"Comatose," he said.

Sophie expelled a long breath and tilted her head toward the ceiling. "So, what do we say on the air?"

Tom looked away from her. *We? Why didn't she listen to me in the first place?*

Al spoke up. "In the Air Force, we had a saying—"

Tom cut him off. "Well, we want to avoid pinballing all over the place every time a new model run comes out. But, since we've already committed ourselves publicly, we need to *ease* back from that stance, not leap."

Sophie stared at him. She pinched her lips together as she had yesterday when she'd entered his office.

"I think what we, well, the on-camera people anyhow, should do at this point," Tom continued, "is a little soft-shoe routine. Just give lip service to the fact we're keeping an eye on the *possibility* of a snowstorm, no adjectives, and let it go at that. No elaborations. No explanations. Then, depending on what subsequent model runs indicate, we can shuffle either way—back off further, or sound the Klaxon."

"What time do the next model outputs come in?"

"Midafternoon."

Sophie stood. "I'll drop by then." She took a step toward Tom who remained seated. "Thanks," she said softly. She touched him on the shoulder and left.

Again her face had been disconcertingly close to his, and he wondered whether that had been deliberate or casually unintentional. He decided he'd better settle on casually unintentional; it was better for his peace of mind. Deep down, he sensed "deliberate" might have been truer.

The Natural Environment Television Network
Friday afternoon, December 23

TOM, AL, AND SOPHIE gathered in the forecast center.

"What've we got?" Sophie asked.

"Nothing that's gonna sell snow shovels," Al responded.

"The soft shoe continues, huh?" She stared at the floor.

"If it will make you feel any better, a couple more ensemble members have jumped on the superstorm bandwagon again," Tom noted.

Sophie nodded. "But the consensus remains 'no big deal'?"

"Pretty much."

"Still, the monster lives?"

"On life support."

"So we'll see where we stand tomorrow then?"

"Even though it'll be Saturday, I'll come in and check the models," Al said. "Nothin' else to do."

"I'll be in Philly visiting my mother for Christmas," Sophie said. She took a piece of paper from a table, wrote on it, then handed it to Al. "That's my cell number. Give me a call if you see anything that gets you excited."

"That'll be the day," Al muttered.

"Give me a call, too," Tom said. "I'll be at home. The kids are coming over to spend Christmas Eve."

Sophie stood. "Well, then, Merry Christmas to both of you. I'll be back on Tuesday. Oh, and I almost forgot, there'll be a reporter from the *Atlanta Journal-Constitution* dropping by on Tuesday. He wants to find out what goes on behind the scenes here when a big storm is approaching."

"He might not have much to write about," Tom said, "but I'll take care of him. Happy travels, Sophie."

She nodded slightly. An unusual warmth seemed to radiate from her eyes.

A reflection of the season? Or something else? As usual, she exuded ambiguity. He never knew whether he was on her naughty or nice list.

Chapter Five

Blue Light Special

Windy Hill Towers
Northwest Metro Georgia
Saturday afternoon, December 24

TOM PRIZ AND his two children, Billy, ten, and Bonnie, seven, stood at a south-facing picture window of his seventeenth-story condo in Cobb County.

"This is so cool, Dad," Billy announced. "You can see downtown Atlanta from here." He studied the cityscape. "What's the tall building that looks like a pencil?"

"The Pencil Building."

"Really?"

"No, not really, you little dufus." Tom ruffled Billy's curly red hair. "It's the Bank of America Plaza."

"It doesn't look like a plaza. It looks like a skyscraper."

"True. It's over a thousand feet tall, but I forget the exact measurement."

"What's the flashing red light on top for?" Bonnie asked, pressing her face against the glass.

"It warns airplanes there's a big building there."

She pondered the statement, then, with her face screwed into a mask of concern, turned to her father. "And Santa Claus, too? So his reindeer won't bump into it?"

"That's stupid," Billy piped up. "There is no—"

Tom clamped a hand over Billy's mouth and flashed him a warning look. "There is no chance of that, is what your brother wanted to say," he said, kneeling in front of his daughter, already a dark-eyed temptress, like her mother.

Tom's cell phone "rang," playing the tune *Stormy Weather*. He answered.

"Gandalf here," the voice on the line said. "I think you'd better drop by work. The afternoon model runs are in."

"Bad news?"

"Come see for yourself."

"My kids are here, Al. It's Christmas Eve, and I don't have that much time to spend with them. I've got to get them back to their mother's by 10 p.m. And I promised I'd take them to see the lights at Lake Lanier this evening."

Al paused, then responded. "Pull up the Global Forecast System on your laptop. You won't have access to the Euro yet, but it's even more extreme. Look things over out through a hundred sixty-eight hours. Try not to wet your pants, then call me back."

Tom agreed, then disconnected the call.

"Hey, kids. We'll leave for Lanier in about an hour." He checked his watch. "Billy, about a quarter to five, gather up your jackets and gloves for you and your sister. I've got a little work to do until then, but we'll hit the road as soon as I'm done."

"Gloves, Dad? It's not that cold."

"Okay, macho man. At least get them for Bonnie."

"Whatta we do until then?"

"Watch football." Tom nodded at the fifty-five-inch plasma set in the living room.

"No football." Bonnie stamped her foot on the hardwood floor.

"Cartoons, then."

"Daaad," Billy protested with total exasperation.

"Guys, work it out with no yelling or fighting, or forget about Lanier." He attempted a stern look but probably came up short. He exited the living room and entered his study.

On his laptop, he called up the US Global Forecast System model, the GFS, and clicked through its graphical output. Over and over, he ran through maps showing various parameters: surface, mid-levels, upper air. After twenty minutes, he swallowed hard and sat back in his chair.

The sound of the TV floated in from the living room. Apparently Billy and Bonnie had reached some sort of détente, as the muted noise alternated between football-stadium cheers and laugh-track guffaws. The odor of microwaved buttered popcorn also wafted through the condo. Peace on earth.

On his cell, he punched in the number of NE-TV's forecast center.

"I didn't wet my pants," he said when Al answered.

"Yeah, but I bet you came close."

"I'll tell you one thing, I've never seen a pattern like what the models are showing."

"Yes, you have."

"I have?" He had a feeling he was about to witness a manifestation of Al's half-century of experience trumping, as it often did, his academic background rooted in the University of Chicago and MIT.

"Think hard. You saw this pattern in 2012."

Tom drummed his fingers on his desk and stared out a small window at the brown, bleak winter landscape of Atlanta. He still couldn't recall seeing an atmospheric arrangement in 2012—or ever, for that matter—like the one currently depicted by the GFS.

"Need a hint?" Al asked.

"Apparently."

"Sandy."

"Hurricane Sandy?"

"That MIT education paid off."

"Sandy was a Northeast storm. New York, New Jersey."

"You gotta think outside the box, junior."

A ruckus arose from somewhere in the condo. Billy shouting, Bonnie crying.

"Hold on, Al, I'll be right back." Tom placed the phone on his desk and stalked into the living room.

Billy, red-faced, spoke first. "It's the fourth quarter, seven to seven, two minutes to go, and she wants to watch some stupid girly show." He pointed an accusatory finger at his sister.

Bonnie darted to Tom and threw her arms around his legs, sobbing into his trousers. "It's my turn to watch my program, and he won't let me."

Resting his hand on his daughter's shoulder, Tom spoke, trying for firmness. "So, do you guys want to go to Lanier or not? If you do, here's what I suggest." He tipped Bonnie's face toward his. "Let your brother finish watching his football game, then he'll let you watch whatever you'd like until we leave." He looked at Billy. "Right?"

"Yeah, sure," Billy mumbled.

"And you, young lady, remember Santa's helpers are around keeping an eye on you."

"You'd *better* let me watch," Billy interjected, aiming his invective at his sister, "or I'll get that light on the Plaza tower turned off, and

Santa's sleigh will have a midair—"

"Billy!" Tom snapped.

Billy fell silent.

Geez, kid, learn to shut up while you're ahead.

Tom returned to his study. He put his cell phone on speaker. "Trouble in the DMZ," he explained.

"A wooden paddle ended most problems when I was growing up," Al said.

"We can't do that anymore."

"That's worked well, hasn't it?"

Tom ignored the bait, wanting to stay on-topic. "So, Sandy, outside the box." On his laptop he brought up the GFS images again.

"Remember the upper-air pattern when Sandy hit?" Al said.

"Deepening trough along the east coast. Anomalous blocking high east of the Canadian Maritimes."

"The blocking high is what turned Sandy to the northwest, into New Jersey."

"Instead of allowing it to plow out to sea, into the Atlantic, like most good hurricanes," Tom offered.

"Okay. Now picture that pattern displaced south and west. Remember, it's wintertime now, not autumn, like when Sandy blustered around. The jet stream, everything, is climatologically displaced southward."

Tom studied the GFS model images more closely. He picked up his cell and shut off the speaker feature. "I see what you mean. A blocking high predicted over Pennsylvania. But you're not suggesting this storm—potential storm—is going to come up out of the Gulf and spin westward, are you?"

"No. But I think it's going to be a slow mover."

"If it forms."

"Yes, if it forms. My point is this: most storms that form in the Gulf scoot through southern Georgia or northern Florida pretty rapidly, then lumber up the Eastern Seaboard. Their rapid movement through the Southeast is what precludes big snow dumps in Atlanta, on the rare occasions when there's enough cold air around to even make snow a possibility."

From the living room, Billy's enthusiastic yells punched through the study's door. Apparently, the team he was rooting for had done something good.

"So," Tom said, "what are you suggesting?"

"That maybe we think about reviving the ten-inch, forty miles per hour scenario."

"You're talking blizzard, near-blizzard?"

"Humor me. Look at the pattern objectively, and forget for a moment the target is the Deep South. What do you see?"

"Al, damn it, Atlanta hasn't measured more than eight inches of snow in almost ninety years."

"Technically true."

"What do you mean 'technically'?" Tom stood, walked to the window, and peered into the fading winter light. A string of pearls, headlights, and a necklace of rubies, taillights, marked the northern arc of the "Perimeter," the eight-to ten-lane interstate encircling Atlanta.

"The city has had close calls," Al responded. "Maybe we've just been lucky. For instance, while the 'official' snowfall for Superstorm was just over four inches, some spots in the northern suburbs reported ten."

"I know. I would also add a caveat. People around here don't know how to measure snow."

"That's possible, but there were reliable reports from far northern Georgia of a foot and a half with eight-foot drifts."

"Not exactly a near miss for us. That's fifty or sixty miles north of the city."

"You're a hard sell, aren't you?"

"I'm trying to keep things in perspective. In the end, the forecast is my responsibility."

"Okay, how about fifty to sixty miles *south* of the city then? February 1973. A storm center marched across northern Florida and unloaded a swath of well over a foot of snow from Columbus, Georgia, to Augusta and on into Columbia, South Carolina. Shift that track fifty or sixty miles north, kind of like what the models are showing now, then what?"

"Armageddon?"

"Yeah, more or less, for the ninth most populous metro region in the nation, for the biggest travel week of the year, and for a city where three major interstates intersect. And . . ." He paused, seeming to toss the narrative to Tom.

Tom picked up the thread. "And the busiest airport in the world."

"Yep. And all of that," Al continued, "in a city that can't handle a few *inches* of snow, let alone a foot."

"It's still four to five days in the future. I'm not ready to send up flares yet."

Al cleared his throat, a sound like a toilet flushing. "I agree. Here's the thing, though. Enough of the ensemble members are saber rattling now that we can't ignore the possibility. I think you'd better call the Dragon Lady, wish her Merry Christmas, and tell her she was right to begin with."

"You call her. You're the one she gave her cell number to."

"I'm just a consultant. You're in her chain of command, not me. Besides, you're the guy who gets a pocket rocket every time she comes close to you."

"Al, for Christ's sake!"

"Rejoice, junior. At my age, that's just a fantasy. Anyhow, Merry Christmas. See you Tuesday." He disconnected the call.

A sharp knock on the door drew Tom's attention back to the moment. "Yeah?" he said.

Billy poked his head into the study. "It's almost time to go." He held up his iPhone and pointed at the time.

"Give me ten minutes, please. I've got one more call to make, then we'll be off to the lights."

Bonnie's head appeared beside Billy's. "You have to buy us hot chocolate up there. Mom said so."

"I might, if little girls ask politely."

Bonnie sighed theatrically. "*Please*, then."

"Ten minutes."

Tom punched in Sophie's number. When she answered, he said, "There've been some changes, Sophie." He explained.

"So, can I light up the airways now? The Great Post-Christmas Snow Jam in the offing and all that?" She sounded almost gleeful.

"Let's just say the possibility is looking stronger."

"No, I want to hit it harder than that. From what you're saying, this could be the biggest weather event in Atlanta's history."

"There's still time to go whole hog, but not yet. We don't want to end up with egg all over our face. What if the next model run backs off on the idea again?"

"That doesn't sound like the trend. Look, I just don't want to get caught with our pants down. Sorry, I guess that's a male metaphor. I mean, I want to be out front on this. I want to be screaming 'city shutdown,' 'travel nightmare,' 'air traffic catastrophe.' Nobody else, National Weather Service included, is gonna eat our lunch on this one."

Tom tightened his jaw, ground his teeth, didn't respond.

"Tom, you still there?"

"Yes. Look, I've tried to explain this before. Forecasting weather is an exercise in probabilities. Nothing is ever certain. We can't produce yes or no, black or white answers. We can't *precisely* replicate the atmosphere with equations. We can only approximate it and generate statistical outcomes. Which we try to translate, much to our own detriment at times, into absolute-sounding predictions."

Sophie issued a soft, ladylike snort. "You need to live in my world for a while, Weather Boy, where success *is* measured in black and white. You're either getting a scoop, or you're scooping poop. You're either out front on a story, or you're sucking wind to catch up. You're either breaking news, or you're breaking out a new résumé. Get the picture?"

"I—"

"Good. You know, the problem may be you don't have a dog in this fight, as they like to say in the South. Sure, you can hunker down in your Ivory Tower, hide behind your statistics, and feel like you've done your job and been faithful to your scientific credo, but it's all make-believe." Her words carried the hardness of an icicle.

"Sophie—"

"Tell you what. Let's make this interesting. I'm going to let you walk a mile in my shoes, let you toss a pit bull into the ring. You're gonna make the call. Do we play it conservatively, cautiously? Or do we become Paul Revere screaming, 'A blizzard is coming, a blizzard is coming!'? Except we're riding the airways, not a horse. Sound okay?"

"Sophie—"

"Here's the best part, the real stakes. If you make the wrong call either way, if you say 'back off,' and we end up eating shit, or you say 'balls to wall,' and we end up like Wile E. Coyote flattened by an Acme safe, you pay the consequences. Well, I probably will, too, but at least we'll share the misery, pounding the pavement together come the new year."

"That doesn't sound quite fair, Sophie," he shot back, sensing a rug being yanked out from underneath him. "The nature of your job is that you take the broadcast risk. I take the scientific risk."

"Without consequences, where's the risk?"

"Not in my job description," he snapped.

"It is now."

What the hell, Sophie. Why are you busting my balls?

Another rap on his door. "Dad, it's time to go."

He muted his phone. "Just a minute. I'll be right out."

"I need an answer," Sophie said. "What do I tell the on-camera presenters? Hit it hard, Blue Light Special? Or back off, pull down the blinds, nobody home? Take a minute."

Ire bubbled through Tom's psyche. He struggled to focus on the evidence. Historically, a big snow was a bad bet. Yet the models seemed to be suggesting otherwise. Still, the event remained five days in the future. At that range, the downside loomed huge. He'd been burned before. On the other hand, the ever-improving models, especially the Euro, had proved adept at handling highly anomalous events, Sandy being the shining case in point. Further, he knew the clamor on social media and television for the Great Southern Snowstorm would be deafening.

Deep down, scientifically, he knew he held the high ground, that his position, from a meteorological and probabilistic standpoint, remained unassailable. He also understood that probabilities didn't cut it with the public. Or Sophie.

He un-muted his phone. "Blue Light Special."

"Merry Christmas, Tom. See ya on Tuesday. Keep me posted."

"Sure. Goodbye." He didn't wish her a Merry Christmas. Instead, he jabbed his middle finger into the air of the darkening study.

"Dad!" Billy stood in the doorway, backlit by illumination from the living room.

"Extra hot chocolate if you don't tell Mom."

Chapter Six

Christmas

Magnolia Heights Subdivision
Sunday afternoon, December 25

THE MESMERIZING flames in J.C.'s massive stone fireplace leapt and weaved, almost as if in touch with the spirit of the season. Appropriate crackles and pops, courtesy of special vermiculate "pine cones," accompanied the blazing warmth. A nonstop concert of Christmas music from FM radio filled the house.

Outside, a stiff breeze bore a touch of the Yukon. The lake, that just a few days ago had been edged in ice, now sported a thin glaze over most of its expanse. Only a small circle of dark, open water remained at its center. Overhead, scudding clouds, amorphous gray dhows sailing on an inverted ocean, appeared to flee the polar invasion.

The setting, both inside and out, sparked childhood memories in J.C.: Christmases spent at his grandparents' hardscrabble farm in northern Vermont, roaring blazes in a smoky, wood-burning fireplace, the Polar Express sighing through cracks in a sagging, century-old house, and deep snow slathered over a taiga-like landscape. He wondered if Cole would remember *this* Christmas forty years from now. He wondered if Cole would even. . . . No, J.C. didn't want to go there. He swallowed hard, checking his emotion.

J.C. and his wife, flanking Cole, sat on a couch in front of the fire. Between them and the fireplace, the aftermath of Christmas morning—shredded wrapping paper, torn ribbons, and wounded cardboard boxes—littered the floor. Immediately in front of them, a marble-topped coffee table boasted a multitude of holiday treats: snowman cookies, German stollen, peppermint bark, chocolate trees, and the rubble of an imploded gingerbread house.

"You look funny, Daddy," Cole said.

J.C. ran his hand over his shaved head. "I *feel* funny." He rubbed

Cole's head. "But so do you."

"Thanks for all the stuff, Dad, Mom." Cole's eyes sparkled, something J.C. had rarely seen of recent.

Stuff. Computer games. An iPod. An iPad mini. A new cell phone. Neon-bright red and black Nike shoes. Stuff.

"There's one more thing, Big Guy." He draped his arm over Cole's shoulder. "And it's from your mother, too."

Ginny's eyes glistened, filmed over by a sheen of tears.

"It's a commitment," J.C. said. "Do you know what that is?"

"Uhhh . . ."

"It's a promise," Ginny explained.

Cole swiveled his head, first looking at Ginny, then J.C. A wide-eyed, expectant mien countered the pale fatigue that had begun to creep into his face during the course of the day.

"The promise is this," J.C. said, a slight catch in his throat, "that we'll get you well, that we'll spend whatever it takes—however much money, however much time, however much prayer—to bring you back to full health. For instance, now that the big job I've been working on is almost finished, I'll be able to spend a lot more time with you in Houston, especially next month."

"You'll stay with me overnight, if I have to sleep at the hospital?"

J.C. pulled his son close and nuzzled his head. "Absolutely."

"Cool. Mom, too?"

"Of course. Nothing is more important to us than you, Big Guy. Nothing."

Ginny, with orphaned tears sliding down her cheeks in a slow-motion glide, didn't speak, but leaned toward J.C., and Cole hugged them both.

"Everything will be fine, honey," J.C. whispered. "Everything will be fine."

AFTER A LIGHT supper, J.C. and Ginny sat in the family room watching the evening news while Cole busied himself experimenting with his iPad.

The local news kicked off with the usual grim holiday headlines: a house fire had killed three people; a crash on I-85 had wiped out a family of five; a robbery had left a poor family with no gifts for their children.

"It's the same every Christmas, isn't it?" Ginny said.

"Joy to the world," J.C. responded. He pulled Ginny close to him. The weather girl came on, Ashley something or other.

"Always blond with long legs and big tits," Ginny groused.

"Not always."

"Yeah?"

"Sometimes they're brunette with long legs and big tits."

"But do they know anything about weather?"

"Who cares?" J.C. smiled and leaned away from Ginny, already knowing what was coming.

In mock anger, she popped him lightly on his ear with her right hand.

"Hold it," he said. "I think she's saying something important."

"Unlikely," Ginny muttered.

"No, listen."

Ashley something or other gestured at a map of the Southeast. "Meteorologists call this a cold air 'wedge,'" she said, sweeping her hand from the Carolinas across Georgia into Alabama. "And it's a frigid one, likely to bring North Georgia the coldest weather in two decades. Some spots in the mountains could be below zero by Tuesday morning." She stopped, drew a deep breath, and walked toward the camera.

"But there's more," she said.

"If you act now," Ginny interjected, "for just $19.95 you can get—"

"Shhh." J.C. placed a hand over her mouth.

"The National Weather Service has issued a Winter Storm Outlook. Now, that's not a watch or warning, let me emphasize. It just means that storm conditions, with significant snowfall and strong winds, are possible here in Atlanta and North Georgia by later in the week. We'll keep you abreast of the situation here on Channel—"

Ginny muted the sound. "She had to say 'abreast,' didn't she?"

"You're hardly one to speak disparagingly of big tits," he said.

"They aren't big."

"No, better than that."

She stared at him. "Go on."

"You've got a Goldilocks rack."

"A what?"

"Not too big, not too small—"

"Okay, I've got it, you pervert." She pulled him close and kissed him.

Something stirred within him he hadn't felt in a long time, not since Cole had become sick, and he nestled into her arms.

"Ummm, if I'm not mistaken," she whispered, "I think there's an ICBM ready for launch."

"Hey, you guys," Cole yelled. "Cut out that mushy stuff."

They broke their clinch.

"Later," J.C. said, keeping his voice low. "Missile launch into the Promised Land."

Ginny face's turned fifty shades of crimson. She fanned herself with her hand. "Is it just me, or is it hot in here?"

"Take a guess."

"Serious for a minute," she said. "If there's a snowstorm this week, that won't affect getting the proposal out, will it?"

"The weather babe said later in the week, so I assume that means Thursday or Friday. I've got FedEx on the hook to pick up the document early Wednesday. That means it'll be in Durham by late afternoon. We're good to go."

"Maybe we'll get trapped at home." She snuggled into him again.

"But first, my buxom lady, we must don our scabbards and swords and go forth with the Huns to pillage and loot the peasant granaries tomorrow." He sat back from Ginny. "You know darn well that by noon tomorrow the shelves at Kroger and Publix will look like Old Mother Hubbard's cupboard."

Ginny smiled. "It's good to see you relaxed," she said. "You've been uptight for so long."

"We both have been." He glanced at Cole, who looked up from his iPad and grinned.

"It's been a good Christmas," Ginny said. "Good to have Cole home."

"It'll be a good week. A day off tomorrow, wrap and tie the proposal on Tuesday, out the door Wednesday. And then, for all I care, let it snow, let it snow, let it snow."

"Everything's under control?"

"Everything's under control."

Outside, a gust of wind rattled a screen door as though a host of winter demons were attempting to claw their way into his life.

Chapter Seven

Sophie's Rules

**The Natural Environment Television Network
Tuesday morning, December 27**

SOPHIE, ROSY-CHEEKED and looking refreshed, knocked on Tom's office door, already open.

"Yeah, come in," he said, not particularly happy to see her after her ultimatum to him on Christmas Eve.

"And good morning to you, too."

"Sophie—"

She held her hand up, a signal for him not to talk. She motioned for someone behind her to enter the office.

A disheveled, gray-haired man with bifocals perched crookedly on his nose stepped through the doorway. He wore a parka embroidered with the initials AJC. Sophie introduced him.

"Mr. Hemphill, this is Tom Priz. He's the network's chief meteorologist. Tom, this is Don Hemphill from the *Atlanta-Journal Constitution*."

Tom stood and shook hands with the man.

"Welcome, Mr. Hemphill." He paused, something about that name. . . . "Hemphill? Hey, you were the guy who wrote about the network and your adventures with the Hurricane Hunters, right? What a wild story. You were there when St. Simons Island went underwater a few years back."

Hemphill nodded.

"And the stuff that went on here at the network during the hurricane, the battles between Dr. Obermeyer and Robbie McSwanson. Just unbelievable."

"All in the past," Sophie said, motioning for Tom to sit. "Mr. Hemphill—"

"Don, please," Hemphill said.

"Don wanted to return to the network now that it's recovered the panache its predecessor, The Weather Channel, once laid claim to. You know, actually focusing on the weather."

"That, my dear lady, is largely due to you, as I understand it." Hemphill made his declarative sentence sound like a question.

"I had the support of the network," she said, not denying the accolade tossed her way, but at the same time maintaining a facade of modesty. "Anyway, Tom, before I forget, and not trying to capitalize on the old Johnny Carson-Ed McMahon shtick, but just how cold was it this morning?" She gave a little shiver, perhaps an unconscious movement, as though the brittle cold had pursued her into the building.

"Seven above at the airport, a record low for the date. Two below in Blairsville up in the mountains."

"Colder than a witch's . . . whatever," Sophie responded.

Hemphill jotted a note on his iPad.

"So," Sophie said to Tom, "I'd like you to take Don under your wing today, show him around the operations area, let him sit in at the forecast center for a while, maybe give him a little inside dope on this impending—can I say 'blizzard' yet?"

"You might as well," Tom said. "Everybody else is."

"Apparently, everybody else but my chief meteorologist."

"When I say it, you'll know it's for real."

She motioned for Tom to step into the hallway, out of earshot of Hemphill.

"You already said it," she said.

"No, you challenged me, told me to make an up or down call for our on-camera mets, so I did."

"But you didn't really believe what you told me?" She threw him a stare that matched the iciness outside. Again, she stood uncomfortably close to him, as she had a few days previous in the forecast center. Violating his personal space. Well, maybe not *violating*. That was too strong a word. He didn't feel threatened by her close proximity. No, he sensed something else: an amalgam of arousal and provocation.

Instead of backing away, he leaned a fraction of an inch closer to her. "I believed what I told you," he said, keeping his voice low, "to the extent the preponderance of evidence was *slightly* on the side of a big storm, maybe fifty-five to forty-five. Far from a slam dunk."

She folded her arms beneath her breasts—nicely highlighted, he metaphorically kicked himself for noticing, by a tad-too-tight Ralph Lauren sweater—and cocked her head at him, a sort of disciplinarian schoolmarm stance. "So where are we this morning?"

"The GFS operational model is waffling again, backing off on the blockbuster storm scenario."

She nodded, looked at the floor, then back at Tom. "So come January, we both may be updating our résumés, huh?"

"If we're playing by *your* rules, yes."

"We are." She pivoted and strode away.

He clenched his jaw and bit back his defense.

AFTER GRABBING a cup of coffee in the cafeteria, Tom escorted Hemphill to the forecast center. Al, squirreled away in his usual corner like a monastic hermit, plotted ship and upper-air reports by hand on a large paper chart. He didn't look up as Tom and Hemphill approached.

"Now there's something you won't see anymore," Tom said, pointing at Al. "That's classic old school. These days, plotting and analyses are all computerized."

"Yeah, and you lose any feel for what's going on," Al muttered, as much to himself as to Tom.

"Twelve-Z reports?" Tom asked.

Al nodded. "Ya bring me some coffee?"

"Nothing to mix it with. They were all out of bourbon."

"Twelve-Z?" Hemphill asked.

"Z used to stand for Greenwich Mean Time. Now it's called Coordinated Universal Time. Same thing. Translated, 7:00 a.m. EST."

"Okay." Hemphill set his coffee on a nearby desk and poked on his iPad.

"Al," Tom said, "this is Don Hemphill from the AJC. He's here to get the inside scoop on the storm. See how we go about business."

Al grunted but didn't otherwise acknowledge Hemphill. He began drawing lines on the map, carefully sketching, then erasing, re-sketching, erasing again, then, with an artist's practiced eye and steady hand of a surgeon, finally firming up the arcs and loops he'd delineated.

Tom and Hemphill watched in silence.

Finished, Al jammed his pencil into a Hurricane Hunters coffee mug already overstuffed with pens, pencils, and highlighters. He leaned back in his chair and swiveled to face the two men. He raked his fingers through his scraggly beard as though expecting to encounter something small and perhaps living. He cleared his throat, a grating, hydrous effort. "A storm is forming in the Gulf," he announced. "And, like the Euro has been advertising all along, an upper-air trough is digging like a badger toward the central Gulf. This thing is going to bomb out."

Hemphill looked at Tom, seeking a translation.

"What he's saying," Tom said, "is that the European model, the one that's stayed the course on predicting a big snowstorm, looks like it's going to be right."

"So, are you guys going to post a winter storm watch?" Hemphill asked.

"Not us. Only the National Weather Service can do that." He looked at the chart Al had created. He had to admit, finally, that his conservatism, at least in this instance, had probably been misplaced. "And they will."

"Mr. Tillman," Hemphill said, "you used the term 'bomb out.' What's that mean?"

"The storm in the Gulf of Mexico, the one that's a mere embryo now, is going to strengthen explosively. Probably like the '93 Superstorm. Boom!" Al spread his arms dramatically. "From sperm and egg to Tyrannosaurus rex in twenty-four hours."

"Blizzard?" Hemphill ventured.

Al nodded at Tom. "I'll let our chief of meteorology handle that." A benign smile crept over his face.

Tom swallowed, a nervous reaction. *Jesus, does Al know about Sophie's threat? Has he gone over to the Dark Side?*

"I'm not ready to use that term yet," Tom responded, grasping at the last vestige of a cautious approach. "Let's see what the twelve-Z model runs show."

"Look, I gotta ask you gentlemen something else." Hemphill seated himself between Al and Tom and plunked his iPad onto a table. "There seems to be little doubt these days that global warming is a fact. Although some skeptics argue the upward temperature trend has flattened out recently—"

"They aren't genuine skeptics," Tom interjected, "they're just naysayers and contrarians. If you break out any short-term period, let's say fifteen years, for example, from any long-term trend, you may often find leveling or even reversals in the overall tendency. Worldwide warming during the course of the twentieth century and into the twenty-first is well established, but that doesn't mean natural variability disappears."

"You've done some work in this?" Hemphill typed on his iPad.

"Postgrad study at MIT."

"Okay, help me out here. The earth is warming, yet we're sitting here during a record-breaking cold snap talking about the possibility of a historic snowstorm. That doesn't compute for most people. What the hell is going on?" He reached for his coffee, dribbled a few drops on his unzipped parka, brushed them off, and took a long swallow from the cup.

Tom stood and began pacing the work area. "As I said, natural variability, the ups and downs of weather, don't take a powder just because the globe is heating up."

Al joined the conversation. "Wasn't there a guy at The Weather Channel, before Asian-Pacific renamed and gutted it, who did a lot of research on the subject?"

"Yeah, there was," Tom said. "I can't remember his name, but he was one of the first to realize that global warming was beginning to influence daily weather events."

"How so?" Hemphill asked.

"What he discovered," Tom answered, still pacing, "is that the frequency of blocking highs in the atmosphere, like the feature that kicked Sandy into New Jersey instead of letting it skedaddle into the wilds of the Atlantic, was increasing in lockstep with global warming."

"So that's what we're looking at today," Al chimed in. "A block developing over the mid-Atlantic region. That, in turn, traps an anomalous pool of very cold air aloft to its southwest, over us, and voila, you've got the ingredients for a slow-moving, kick-ass storm."

Hemphill typed furiously on his iPad. "Define 'kick-ass.'"

"Let's wait 'til the winter storm watch hits the street," Tom said.

Al shrugged.

"Okay, we'll pass on that temporarily," Hemphill said. "Again, just so people understand, what's the difference between a watch and a warning?"

"A winter storm watch is meant to alert the public there's a decent *possibility* of nasty winter weather within roughly forty-eight hours," Tom said.

"Seems to me that's already happened," Hemphill responded, "with all the chatter on Facebook, Twitter, and TV."

"Not officially. But nobody seems to care, or even know any more if stuff is 'official.' Social media and instant communications have pretty much obliterated the distinction between officialdom and rumor."

Hemphill shrugged. "Yeah, kinda, I guess. So, tell me about warnings."

"A warning means hazardous winter weather is occurring or imminent. Ideally, warnings are posted twelve to twenty-four hours prior to the onset of ice or snow."

"Got it," Hemphill said. "So now we're just waiting for a watch to be issued, right?"

"Like waiting for a blessing from the Pope," Al muttered. "Once that happens, everyone will know all is right with the world."

"Sarcasm?" Hemphill asked.

"Look, my friend, Atlanta's gonna get buried. Waiting for the NWS to promulgate that doesn't change anything." He stood, a laborious effort, and took an unsteady step. "Gotta take a pee," he said. Then more softly, "Damn prostate."

"Buried?" Hemphill exclaimed. He looked at Tom.

Tom lowered his head. It seemed he had no allies for caution left. First Sophie, now Al, had abandoned him. "Later," he said to Hemphill.

AT PRECISELY 2 P.M. Tom knocked on the door to Sophie's office.

"Come on in," she said, sounding a bit weary, or perhaps resigned to the fact she was about to go another round with her chief of meteorology.

He placed a sheet of paper on her desk. "A winter storm watch has been issued for Atlanta and northern Georgia," he said.

She didn't look at it. "Summarize it." She leaned back in her chair and aimed a hard stare at him.

"It says, 'Conditions are favorable for substantial snowfall and high winds on Thursday and possibly Friday. Severe disruptions to travel are likely.'"

"How much snow are we expecting?"

He drew a deep breath. The battle, once more, appeared about to be joined. "As the text says, a substantial amount."

"Oh, for shit's sake, Tom. What the hell does that mean? A substantial amount for Atlanta is two inches. A few years ago, four inches shut down the city for the better part of a week. Are we talking four inches or two feet?" Her voice carried the spring-loaded tension of an armed crossbow.

He stared past Sophie, looking through the panoramic window behind her into a barren winter landscape. Patches of ice reflected the low-angled rays of the sun into diamond bursts of cold brilliance.

"Let's stick with the NWS terminology for now. We can refine things later. We're not in competition here."

"*I* am, damn it." Sophie stood and pounded her desk. "I'm in competition every single time we go on the air. With CNN, with FOX, with NBC, with all the other networks, even Al Jazeera. Jesus, Tom, we're supposed to be the premier private weather service in the world, and we can't even tell people how much friggin' snow is gonna fall forty-eight hours in advance?"

"They've been alerted—"

"You don't get it, do you? We're at the height of the holiday travel season. The city sits at the crossroads of three major interstate highways. A quarter-million people per day are elbowing their way through the airport which, by the way, if it shuts down, carries international implications for air travel. And, we've got the Peach Bowl coming up on Saturday."

He started to respond, but Sophie held up her hand like a cop stopping traffic. She spoke deliberately, clipping her words into sharp little blocks of ice. "You think people might want to be apprised about *how much* snow is going to fall?"

He remained silent, rooted to the floor by the intensity of her response.

"I do," she continued, almost shouting. "I think they might like to know. I think city and state officials might like to know whether it's going to be a few inches or, like Gandalf suggested, a foot. I think they might like to know if the wind is going to push the snow into drifts that make the Perimeter expressway look like Donner Pass, if Hartsfield is going to end up buried like Bismarck in a blizzard. If *we* don't know, who does?"

She remained standing, her palms flat on the desk, her cheeks flaming, her chest heaving. She pinched her lips together, which, Tom had learned, wasn't a good sign. He waited for her to speak again.

"Get out, leave," she said softly.

"I'm fired?" Probably not a wise question.

She didn't answer. Instead, she stepped from behind her desk and walked to Tom. She stood directly in front of him, still breathing heavily. Her anger appeared to have dissipated, replaced by something else, something that grabbed him by surprise, stole his breath. He inhaled her fragrance, an essence of honeysuckle that carried him off to lazy spring days, warmth, and sunshine. She edged even closer to him, her hips almost touching his, the tips of her breasts resting against his chest. She reached up and stroked his face.

"Sophie—"

She raised her forefinger to her lips, signaling him not to speak. "You aren't a bad-looking guy, you know." Her words came out soft and measured. "But that's not it. Maybe I'm just attracted to men who will stand up to me without being condescending, without using the B-word, without viewing me as a conquest. You're a decent guy, I think. And if my woman's intuition hasn't gone off-line, I sense the attraction might be mutual." The statement sounded more interrogative than declarative.

He nodded. He felt himself growing hard. He flushed and tried to back away from her without being obvious. Maybe the macho thing to do would be to take her, right here, right now, in her office, but he tossed the impulse aside. She *was* still his boss, and she'd expressed only an interest in him, not dropped her panties.

"That's a relief," she whispered and leaned into him more firmly, the hand that had stroked his cheek resting on his shoulder. "Otherwise, you'd have me on sexual harassment."

Her hips pressed into his now. He had no chance of hiding his "male reaction." Their gazes met and held. She grazed his lips with hers and backed off.

"This didn't happen," she said. She brushed her hands over her sweater, smoothing it. "Well, it did happen, but we're the only ones who need to know about it. I think, from both a business and personal standpoint, you should take a leave of absence, okay? We both need to get a handle on our emotions. Take the rest of the week off. See me after New Year's." She shooed him away with a flick of her hand.

Semi-stunned, he gestured in the direction of the forecast center. "What about the storm? We'll need all hands on deck."

"We'll handle it without you."

"We're going to need all the bodies we can—"

"For God's sake, Tom, just go, please." She directed her gaze at his crotch. "And maybe you'd better stop in the men's room, step into a stall, and take care of that before you do anything else." Her eyes danced in wicked merriment.

He turned to leave, but Sophie had one last word for him. "I'm still going to be all over your case, you know."

"I know, Sophie. I wouldn't have it any other way." He shut the door and returned to the forecast center.

Feeling a bizarre mix of sexual excitement, emotional confusion, and subdued anger, he confronted Al. "You went behind my back?" he growled. "Told Sophie we were looking at a foot of snow? A blizzard? What the hell were you thinking?"

"Of telling her the truth, junior, in case you missed it."

Several of the forecasters working at their computer stations turned to watch the verbal exchange.

"We're supposed to be singing from the same sheet of music," Tom said, his words curt. "Instead, you're off yowling solo to the boss."

Al rolled his eyes. He stood and took a step toward Tom. "Just for the record, Sophie came to me, I didn't go sniffing her out. She asked me what I thought. I told her. In case it slipped your mind, I'm a contract employee here, lured out of retirement. I don't have an agenda. I don't give a shit about impressing anyone or storming the corporate ramparts. If somebody wants my opinion, I give it. Otherwise, I'm content to sit on my ass and take home a check."

"Well, you're not only sitting on your ass, you're stomping on mine."

Al cleared his throat and hitched up his pants which had crept southward beneath his prominent tummy. "The only reason you're getting your ass stomped on is because you're tangled up in your academic robes. You're enamored by the idea that weather forecasting is an exercise in uncertainty, cloaked in probability. That doesn't play well with the public, or Sophie. I know you know that. Why in the hell can't you act on it?"

"The models are a long way from barking about a foot of snow," Tom said.

"Forget the damn models. Let me tell you something, and the rest of you, too." Al inclined his head toward the small audience of forecasters the skirmish between him and Tom had attracted. "Pay attention to pattern recognition, not some numerical simulation of the atmosphere."

"Pattern recognition?" Tom said, his mind only half on Al's pontification, the other half still dwelling on his encounter with Sophie. At least his "maleness" had shrunk back to normalcy, on its own.

Virtually gasping for breath, Al lowered himself into a chair. "In other words, let me lay a little experience on you. All of the blockbuster winter storms I've dealt with—New York's Lindsay storm in '69, Boston's Blizzard of '78, Superstorm, the Blizzard of '96—all of them had features exactly like what's shaping up with a strong, cold high beneath a cut-off low pressure system aloft. At least the models are good about telling us that."

"This is the Deep South, not the Northeast," Tom said.

"That's my point. You're wound around the axle because we've never had a foot of snow in Atlanta. But, as I pointed out earlier, we have had that much not too far to our north and not too far to our south. Near misses. Look at the pattern and think about Boston in '78: a big arctic high, a cut-off low aloft, a stalling surface storm, hurricane-force wind gusts, and over two feet of snow in the city. Closed it down for a week. Boston, a city used to dealing with that stuff. This is Atlanta, probably no more prepared for a big winter whopper than Kuala Lumpur."

One of the forecasters snickered. Tom glared at him, and he fell silent.

"Well," Tom said, turning back to Al, "good luck with your twelve-inch forecast."

"*My* forecast?"

"I don't have any say in the matter any longer."

A stricken look etched its way across Al's face. "Jesus, the Dragon Lady fired you?"

"Not exactly."

"Not exactly?" Al stood again.

"I think I'm under house arrest. Which means, I'll get to watch things evolve on my Sony at home."

"Hey, it wasn't my intent to—"

"I know. It wasn't your fault. Something didn't click between Sophie and me." Not true. Something had clicked, big time. He moved closer to Al and lowered his voice, whatever anger he had had, spent. "So, really, a foot? Is that what you honestly think?"

"No," Al responded, his voice thick and watery.

Tom smiled, a hollow victory.

Al smiled, too. "I think it'll be a hell of a lot more than that."

Chapter Eight

Not on My Watch

American-International Systems Solutions, Inc.
Wednesday afternoon, December 28

J.C. SAT SILENTLY in his office, his throat raw from his earlier vomiting, his stomach still knotted from the verbal assault and summary dismissal by his boss.

It really wasn't difficult to figure out why he'd stumbled, why he'd failed, why he'd gotten the ax. In fact, it was ridiculously easy. He'd lost focus; he'd been distracted by all that had happened with Cole. The leukemia, the diagnostic tests, the spinal taps, the chemo, the frequent trips to Houston and back, the long stays in the hospital, and on and on and on. Then finally, a Christmas reprieve with Cole home for the holidays and deserving his father's full attention.

J.C. understood that his family responsibilities, as demanding and gut wrenching as they had been, offered no excuse for screwing up the most important bid in AISSI's history. The cross lay on his shoulders and his alone. When Cole got sick, perhaps he, J.C., should have handed off the proposal management to someone else. But things had been going well—not smoothly—but well. And he thought he could handle the challenges presented by both Cole and the proposal effort. That decision turned out to be a costly mistake, costly beyond anyone's comprehension.

Not only did the company face a huge loss of income, but probably layoffs as well. Of course, nothing is guaranteed in bidding wars, but AISSI was generally acknowledged to have had the inside track on this one. Now, without even a horse in the running, defeat seemed assured.

And what would the consequences be for Cole? The company-subsidized health insurance, a "Cadillac" policy, had covered virtually all of Cole's medical expenses so far, costs approaching $100,000. J.C. had been warned that if his son needed a stem cell transplant, they could be looking at something in the neighborhood of a half-million. Further, none of those tallies included the extensive travel to and from Houston and the often lengthy hotel stays required.

Yes, health insurance policies could be purchased on the open market, but premiums to get the same coverage as he had now, if that were even possible, would be astronomical. And yes, Cole's care could always be shifted closer to home, but that wasn't an option J.C. wished to consider. The rapport his son had developed with the doctors and staff at MD Anderson was, no doubt, integral to his treatment. There was no way he would yank that out of Cole's life.

J.C. acknowledged, too, that there came significant personal impact with his dismissal from AISSI. He'd join the millions of middle-aged executives shuffling through corporate America in search of jobs that had evaporated like dew on a summer morning. In addition, he'd bear the stigma of having blown a billion-dollar opportunity.

What a waste. Fifteen years of scaling the corporate ladder in the dumper. He'd been recruited by AISSI immediately after coming out of the University of Virginia with an MS in Systems Engineering. He'd made it to vice president within a decade and developed a reputation as a reliable, can-do kind of guy, always busting his ass to get the job done. He knew, as in any job or sport, you were only as good as your latest success, but he never expected to be a poster boy for the old saying that it takes only one "aw shit" to cancel out ten "attaboys."

Goodbye McMansion in Magnolia Heights. Goodbye country club. Goodbye his and her Mercedes. Goodbye good life. Minor stuff compared to Cole's health and welfare.

He folded his arms across the top of his desk and lowered his head onto them. He considered weeping, but that, he knew, would only exacerbate the depression that seemed on the verge of breaking over him like a rogue wave in a storm. He sat upright in his chair, swiveled it, and gazed out into the gray morning, at an airliner descending toward Hartsfield-Jackson, at traffic sweeping along a nearby four-lane, at songbirds huddled in the bare branches of hardwoods. He tried to imagine what the landscape would look like tomorrow, buried in silent whiteness . . . much like his life.

"No," he whispered to himself, then out loud, "Not on my watch." He fumbled through his desk drawers, found a bottle of mouthwash, took a swig, swirled it in his mouth, and spit it into an empty Styrofoam cup. He stood, straightened his suit jacket, adjusted his tie, shot his cuffs, and strode out of his office.

Thirty seconds later he reached Billingsly's outer office.

"He doesn't wish to be disturbed," Mary announced officiously, no longer deferring to J.C.'s now-former position of vice president.

"Tough shit," J.C. said.

Mary covered her mouth. "Tough shit" was not the response she expected. She reached for her telephone.

"I'm not here to assault anyone, Mary," J.C. said. "No need to call security. Sorry about the language, but I'm a little pissed off." He knocked once on Billingsly's door and pushed it open.

Billingsly leapt to his feet. "What the hell, J.C.?"

Not Mr. Riggins? Similar to what Mary had done, Billingsly reached for his phone.

J.C. took a seat in front of his boss's—former boss's—desk. "Relax, sir. I'm not here to hurt anyone or bust up the place."

Billingsly held the phone for a moment and studied J.C. with the analytical eye of a former military commander. Satisfied J.C. presented no threat, he replaced the handset in its cradle and sat. "I fired you, you know," he snarled.

"Un-fire me."

Billingsly snorted. Derision. "You just blew a billion-dollar opportunity for this company, my friend. Do you think I'm out of my frigging mind?" The words came out harsh and clipped.

"No, of course not. Look, it was a massive screw-up. I accept full responsibility. I'm the one who stepped on my dick. I lost focus. No excuses. But let's not throw in the towel. Let's repair the damage, and I'll get the proposal to Durham before the deadline, before close of business on Friday."

"Don't blow smoke up my ass, J.C. You know damn well that ain't gonna happen. Life doesn't imitate fairy tales with happy endings and all that crap. From the hue and cry on TV and social media, you'd think the End Time was upon us."

J.C. attempted to respond, but Billingsly cut him off with a curt hand signal.

"We're pressing ahead with amending the document, just in case the weather doesn't turn out to be as bad as advertised." He leaned forward and stared hard at J.C. "But quite frankly, things sound pretty damn dire. There are rumors that Hartsfield could be shut down for days and that the interstates from Alabama to the Carolinas will be closed through the weekend." He shook his head, a gesture of either disbelief or disappointment. Maybe both. "So don't tell me you've got some half-assed secret plan to get the proposal to Durham."

J.C. stood, placed both his hands on Billingsly's desk, and leaned toward him, their faces only a foot apart. "I don't. But I *will* get it there, even if I have to do it by dog sled. Let's just say I'm a highly motivated employee . . . former employee."

"Not gonna happen!"

"Come on, Cyrus," J.C. snapped. "Neither one of us, nor the company, has anything to lose at this point. So what if I fail? You can fire me. Again." J.C. paused, searching for the right words to convince Billingsly. "Look, I heard you're an ex-fighter pilot. Since you rose to the rank of general, I'm gonna guess you didn't get there by turning tail, lighting the afterburners, and bugging out when the going got tough. Let's at least go down fighting. But just to re-emphasize my point, I have no intention of going down."

Billingsly expelled a long breath, sat back in his chair, and didn't say anything for a long time.

J.C. waited.

Finally Billingsly said, "Pick up the document at 10 p.m."

"Yes, sir." J.C. turned and walked toward the door.

"One more thing."

"Yes?"

"You're rehired. As a probationary intern."

BACK IN HIS OFFICE, J.C. watched with growing apprehension the midday news reports on local TV. The accounts seemed nothing short of apocalyptic, at least in terms of the weather. The NWS had issued a blizzard warning, virtually unprecedented, for all of North Georgia, including Atlanta. Forecasts varied from channel to channel, but the consensus seemed to be for a foot of snow with fifty miles per hour wind gusts.

Accompanying stories warned of impending airport and road closures, likely power outages, possible postponement of the Chick-fil-A Peach Bowl, and cancellation of New Year's Eve festivities including the famous "Peach Drop." But it was the looming airport and road closures that worried J.C. Nothing else mattered.

He went to work on his desktop computer, calling up airline schedules between Atlanta and the Raleigh-Durham airport. If he could hand-carry the proposal and get out of Atlanta before flights were canceled or the airport closed, everything would be fine. The snow wasn't expected to start until the wee hours of Thursday, so if he could secure a red-eye or early morning flight . . .

But his hopes spiraled down in flames almost immediately. The last two flights out of Hartsfield-Jackson to Raleigh-Durham in the evening departed prior to 11 p.m. No way could he make either if he didn't get the document until 10 p.m.

Early morning then. Several flights leaving around 7 a.m. offered hope. He called the airlines directly—Delta, Southwest, US Airways— but to no avail. Flights had already been canceled and aircraft dispersed. A reservationist at Southwest told him, "If it's any consolation, sir, you probably wouldn't have gotten on the flight anyway. You know, it's the holiday season to begin with, and now with the storm coming, people are scrambling to get out of town early. It's a zoo."

He investigated flights to other destinations: New York City, Chicago, Miami, Houston, Philly, all with the thought of just getting out of Atlanta, then beating his way back to Raleigh-Durham any way he could. Every time, he met the same schedule roadblocks. The flights left too early in the evening to be of any help, and the dawn flights had already been scratched.

J.C. took a break, stood, and paced his office. Outside, the sun had dimmed to a faint yellow smudge hidden behind a gauzy overcast the shade of a mothballed battleship. The traffic on the nearby thoroughfare appeared denser than one might expect during Christmas vacation week. It probably consisted, J.C. surmised, primarily of family raiding parties on their way to loot and pillage whatever grocery stores had not yet been stripped clean, or maybe people fleeing the looming "Snowmageddon" as coastal residents might an approaching hurricane.

He sat again at his desk and stared into nothingness. He realized he'd signed on for a fool's errand by suggesting he could somehow overcome the forces of nature and deliver the proposal on time through a once-in-a-century—some commentators had suggested a once-in-a-millennium—Southern blizzard.

He swiveled his chair toward the window and watched another airliner on approach into Hartsfield. A second, smaller plane, a corporate jet of some sort, followed it, but then broke off toward the west, apparently headed into Charlie Brown Field or, more formally, Fulton County Airport.

"Yes," J.C. said aloud, "*that* could be the answer." It would be an expensive solution to his dilemma, but worth every dollar he might have to shell out. He Googled "Atlanta charter aircraft," and a dozen entries popped up. He called them in order. But, as with the commercial airlines, discovered he was too late. The charters, both fixed wing and rotary, were either already booked or lacked sufficient crews (many were on vacation) to cover the sudden, storm-driven spike in demand.

An hour later, J.C. phoned his wife and fought back sobs as he told her what had happened. He'd screwed up, failed her, Cole, and the company and, for all practical purposes, had probably committed professional hara-kiri.

Ginny met his labored confession with an extended period of silence.

"Ginny?" he said.

"I'm sorry. I know it wasn't your fault. You've been so wrapped up in Cole."

"It's still my fault. You don't get a pass because things are tough at home. It's an all or nothing deal. You either perform or you don't. All that counts is whether or not you deliver for the corporation. I didn't."

Again silence, deep breathing on Ginny's end of the line. Then, "The game isn't over."

"You think? In case it escaped your notice, a blizzard warning is in effect for us. A *blizzard* warning, and there's talk of extending the warnings through the Carolinas. Bottom line . . . We're screwed." A tightness in his throat betrayed the sense of failure that permeated his being.

"You didn't get to be a vice president because you lacked for ideas," Ginny countered.

"I'm out of ideas."

"No, honey, no, you aren't. I know you've got more. You made a name for yourself by always getting the job done, by overcoming the odds. That doesn't change now, just because the odds seem, well, insurmountable." Desperation echoed in her voice. "Get a snow plow, a Sno-Cat, a Humvee."

"Wait," he said. "Do you know anyone with a Humvee?"

A soft "no" shot down that possibility.

He considered his own car, an S550 Mercedes, and wondered if it would stand a chance in a snowstorm. Probably not. It was rear-wheel drive, not four-wheel, and lacked snow tires. He'd grown up in Massachusetts and knew what he was up against when it came to blizzards. A rear-wheel drive vehicle without snow treads would end up as nothing more than an interstate igloo. Then a spark of an idea ignited somewhere deep within his brain, a candle in an ocean of darkness.

"Let me call you back, Ginny. You're right. I'm not out of options yet."

Chapter Nine

G-Wagen

American-International Systems Solutions, Inc.
Wednesday afternoon, December 28

AFTER TALKING with Ginny, J.C., hoping for a miracle, called Hertz.

"Wonder if you might have any four-wheel drive vehicles available in Atlanta?" he asked when someone answered.

"Sir," a syrupy-voiced Southern belle announced, "we're fresh out of everything. The storm, ya know. People are rentin' anything they can to get out of the city. Headin' to Florida, I reckon. Sorry we can't be of service to y'all."

"Me, too." He hung up. *Humvee.* The thought lingered in his head. Not about a Humvee, but something close. Forget car rental companies.

On his cell phone, he punched in a number he knew by heart, the Mercedes dealer who'd sold him his S550 and his wife's E400.

"Carl Montoff, please," he said when the dealer's receptionist answered.

Carl came on the line after only a brief wait.

"Carl, J.C. Riggins here."

"Hey, Mr. Riggins. Great to hear from you, sir. Merry Christmas and Happy New Year. How're Ginny and Cole?"

Ginny and Cole? I haven't talked with this guy in six months, yet he remembers the names of my wife and kid; probably why he's the sales manager.

"They're fine. Thanks for asking." J.C. didn't wish to go into detail or engage in small talk; matters more urgent called. "Look, I've got a bit of a strange request. I've had my eye on one of your GL models for a while now. Its all-wheel drive capability really interests me. And I thought, well, with this snowstorm coming, it might be a great time for a test drive. You know, really put one through the wringer on slippery roads. I grew up in Massachusetts, so—"

"Right. I remember. You went to Boston . . . no, it was Northeastern University, wasn't it? Then to Virginia for graduate work?"

"How do you remember stuff like that?"

Carl laughed. "I've got what's known as an eidetic memory. Kind of like a photographic memory, but not quite the same. Anyhow, you want something that'll take on the snow?"

"Well, I'm not planning a long trip or anything," J.C. lied, "but I'd really like to see how your GL model does, let's say 'over the river and through the woods.'"

"To grandmother's house?"

"Something like that." *Is this guy onto me?* J.C.'s breathing accelerated ever so slightly.

"Well, if grandmother lives in the mountains, you might want something a bit more robust than a GL." J.C. could almost hear the "wink" in Carl's inflection.

"You mean something like a Humvee?"

"Mr. Riggins, shame on you. You dare use the word Humvee in a Mercedes environment. How plebeian." He chuckled. A lighthearted response.

"Sorry."

"Come on in, I think we can set you up with something."

"Something?"

"You ever hear of a G-Wagen?" He pronounced Wagen vah-gun.

"Don't think so."

"No matter. It's really not called that anymore, but it's something vaguely similar to a . . . Humvee." He whispered the word, as if it were something not uttered in polite company.

"Really?"

"Only vaguely. Let's just say you'll raise a stein to German ingenuity after you go off-roading. That is, assuming you go off-roading."

"No plans." True enough. He didn't have any *plans*, but . . .

"You never know." Carl finished his thought for him.

"I'll see you in half an hour," J.C. said.

RQB Mercedes Dealership
North Metro Atlanta
Wednesday afternoon, December 28

THE THICK, SLATE-colored overcast had all but swallowed the sun by the time J.C. arrived at the Mercedes dealership in midafternoon. Patches of ice dotted the lot in front of the showroom. The knife-edged breeze of earlier in the day had lapsed into a bitingly cold stillness. It reminded J.C. of winter days in Massachusetts, days when the atmosphere slid into a false calm, an ominous quiet prior to a big storm.

Carl, a sturdy man with a ruddy, avuncular face, met J.C. at the entrance. Glasses pushed back on his head, nesting in an unruly shock of white hair, the sales manager looked more like a kindly college professor than a businessman.

"Mr. Riggins, good to see you again. How about a cup of coffee? Feels like Alaska out there today."

J.C. declined as the queasiness from his emotional reaction to the events earlier in the day still dogged him.

Carl eyed J.C.'s bald head. "Mercedes sells a nice fleece cap, you know."

J.C. brushed a hand over his scalp. "It's to show solidarity with my son. He's undergoing chemo."

"Yeah, I remember. How's he doing?"

J.C. gave Carl a brief update.

"Tough stuff," Carl said. He touched J.C. on the shoulder, a compassionate gesture. "My prayers are with you, brother."

Though a regular church attender, mainly at Ginny's insistence, J.C. didn't consider himself particularly religious. Still, he appreciated Carl's expression of concern. "Thank you," he mumbled.

"Well, come on," Carl said. "Let's take a look at the G-Wagen."

J.C. followed him into a massive garage adjacent to the showroom. About a dozen automobiles and SUVs sat on lifts or stood with their hoods yawning as a cadre of mechanics worked on them.

Carl led J.C. to a far corner of the facility where a hulking black vehicle, appearing more like a boxy paddy wagon than a slick, modern SUV, lurked.

"It's a couple of years old," Carl said. "We just took it in on a trade."

J.C. studied it. "It looks like a Jeep on steroids."

Carl shrugged. "G-Wagen, although Mercedes doesn't call it that any longer, is short for *Geländewagen* or cross-country vehicle. And yes, it was originally designed for military applications, ironically, based on a suggestion from the Shah of Iran in the 1970s."

Carl patted the hood of the vehicle as though he were petting a family puppy. "These days, they're part of what's known as the G-series. This is a G-550—"

"I've seen them in movies," J.C. said. "Drug dealers and Russian bad guys drive them." *Probably the only people who can afford them.*

"True, but the counterpoint is that the Popemobile is based on a G-500. But let's say, for sake of argument, you're heading for Grandmother's house and not circumnavigating the Vatican, or pushing coke, and let's presume Grandmother lives on top of Grandfather Mountain with no paved roads."

"She's a bit of a hermit?"

"No. She just wants to see if this chunk of German steel with the mechanical grunt of a *Panzer* and creature comforts of a Rolls-Royce can get you there." He gestured at the clunky-looking SUV. "Just under four hundred horsepower, all-wheel drive, three locking differentials, eight inches of ground clearance." He opened the driver's door. "Seven-speed automatic, paddle shifters, Burl walnut, leather, blah, blah, blah. It'll knock Granny's support hose off."

"So it'll climb the Appalachians in a snowstorm?"

"Like a mountain goat."

Just what I need. J.C. considered asking what the driving range on a tank of gas was, what size snow tires the thing took, and, tongue-in-check, whether it came with a plow attachment, but decided he'd better not tip his hand, at least not any more than he might have already. Carl undoubtedly harbored suspicions, however minor they might be—J.C. was, after all, a good customer—about someone asking to borrow a demo in the face of a blizzard warning. *Bless you, Carl, for bringing up the idea of a trip to Grandmother's house.*

"Get in," Carl said and handed J.C. the key. "Crank it up."

The G-Wagen growled to life with a truck-like roar, all business.

It took less than twenty minutes for J.C. and Carl to handle the paperwork necessary for J.C. to keep the vehicle until the weekend. As he drove off, he glanced down at a note he'd hastily scribbled at the dealership: Ginny, bank, tire store, Home Depot, Kroger.

North Metro Atlanta
Wednesday afternoon/evening, December 28

DRIVING THE G-500 proved a completely different experience from that of his sedan. For one thing, the driving position offered a trucker's view of the road. J.C. looked *down* at most of the traffic around him, including even the XXL SUVs like Lincolns and Cadillacs. Due to its high center of gravity, the G-Wagen wallowed a bit in turns, not a lot, but enough to suggest it would never break any speed records at Road Atlanta. But what the big Mercedes might lack in finesse, it more than made up for in brute power. J.C. envisioned it busting through snow-drifts like Amtrak's Empire Builder knifing through a High Plains blizzard.

He pulled into a SunTrust bank parking lot, stopped, and called Ginny on his cell. He explained he'd be a bit late getting home, but wanted her to know he had a plan in mind and would explain everything after he arrived.

He entered the bank and, from his checking account, withdrew a substantial amount of cash, contingency funds for his planned journey. He didn't know if he would need the money, but having a stash of liquid currency on hand seemed like a good idea, even if the trip itself didn't.

Prior to leaving the dealership, J.C. had examined the SUV's tires. The all-terrain Yokohamas looked okay, but he wanted something better than "okay" for his "demo" drive. His next stop: John Flatt's Tire and Battery Center, a huge facility known by locals merely as "the flat tire place."

As he pulled into the center, he realized he might again be a Johnny-Come-Lately. He couldn't find an open parking spot. Apparently, everyone in North Metro Atlanta had decided they needed snow tires.

He gave up looking for a slot and parked in front of the main entrance. Inside, he found a standing-room-only crowd: men and women in eclectic Southern winter attire ranging from hoodies and flimsy windbreakers to down vests and bulky parkas. Headgear spanned the gamut from Atlanta Braves baseball hats (accompanied by red and blue earmuffs) to Russian ushankas.

J.C. stepped to the reception desk. A stout, harried-looking young man with weary eyes, greasy hands, and a name tag reading "Thumper" greeted him.

"If you're here for snow tires, sir, I'm afraid you're too late. We've pretty much been stripped clean." He expelled a long breath. It had obviously been a long day.

"I was hoping to find something for a G-Wagen."

The kid frowned. "A what?"

J.C. pointed out the front entrance. "A Mercedes G-550."

"Oh, cool! A Russian mafia staff car."

J.C. sighed. "Yeah. Whaddaya think?"

The kid shook his head. "Naw. I'll check, but we've only got one or two sets left, and they're for subcompacts. But even if we had some that fit your SUV, you'd be at the back of the line." He tapped in some information on his computer.

"Would this move me to the front of the line?" J.C. extracted his wallet, pulled out a hundred-dollar bill and, with his hand covering most of it, slid it across the counter to Thumper.

Thumper looked at it, back up at J.C., and shook his head again. "I'd love to do business with you, sir, but, like I said," he stared at the computer, "there's nothing available."

J.C. leaned across the counter. "Well then, do you think you might be able to call around to some other stores, find four snow tires for my bad-guy car, and earn yourself another Ben Franklin in the process?" He removed his hand from the bill on the counter.

Thumper glanced around the shop, apparently making sure no one was watching, and pocketed the bill. "I'll do my best," he said. "I can't guarantee anything, and it may take a few hours. Give me a telephone number where I can reach you. It looks like we're going to be open well into the evening."

J.C. agreed to the deal, got Thumper's cell number, and departed for his next stop, Home Depot.

Home Depot, not surprisingly, had been plundered of anything remotely applicable to combating the impending winter assault. The shelves stood naked of deicing materials, sand—even the type used in kids' play boxes—and snow shovels. J.C. marched through the aisles searching for targets of opportunity, things he thought might come in handy on his planned journey to Durham.

He issued a soft, self-deprecating snort. *Planned* wasn't quite the right word. More like a Hail Mary pass into the teeth of a blizzard.

He found one orphaned shovel, a short-handled spade, and placed it in his shopping cart. It wasn't designed to move snow, but would be better than nothing. He picked up an expensive high-intensity LED flashlight and added that to the cart. Other items included a first aid kit (even though the G-Wagen undoubtedly had one), several blankets used to protect furniture when moving (he might need them for warmth), a braided nylon tow rope with grab hooks (an item he hoped he wouldn't need), a sturdy-looking utility knife, a roll of duct tape, and some hanger wire. A friend who'd served in the Army once told him you could fix anything with duct tape and baling wire. J.C. figured hanger wire would be the next best thing.

His final stop: Kroger. The Huns had come and gone. Now early evening, the huge grocery store loomed like a brightly-lit but abandoned ship in a strip mall of otherwise darkened shops. Inside, soft pop music from overhead speakers wafted through the chilly, picked-bare structure as if offering a modicum of commiseration to the handful of tardy shoppers who wandered the aisles like lost souls in purgatory. They, like J.C., seized what few leftover canned goods they could find, mostly stuff he viewed as inedible, and that in normal circumstances would never have sold: gag-food like Brussels sprouts, lima beans, and creamed spinach.

He chanced upon a box of granola bars, the only one left, and found a ripped bag of kitty litter. Kitty litter, he knew from experience, could be used for traction on hard-packed snow or ice.

The checkout clerk, a wizened lady with thick glasses and a threadbare sweater, pointed out the tear in the bag.

"I've got some tape in my car," J.C. said. "I'll patch it up when I get there."

Outside, a haloed full moon hung in the sky smudged by the overcast. The wind had picked up again, its icy talons clutching at J.C.'s neck. He turned up the collar on his overcoat, then placed the kitty litter bag on the passenger seat of the G-Wagen and, within a matter of a minute or two, had it taped up. He metaphorically patted himself on the back for purchasing the duct tape and utility knife.

His cell phone rang.

"Hey, it's Thumper from Flatt's Tire," the caller said. "Is this Mr. Riggins?"

"It is. Thanks for getting back to me." J.C. cranked the engine to get some warmth into the vehicle.

"Well, Mr. Riggins, I've got some good news and some bad news."

J.C. sighed. "Lay it on me."

"Okay, the good news is I found you some tires. The bad news is they're in Macon."

"Crap."

"Ah, but more good news. I can get 'em here."

"Great." J.C. checked the time, almost seven; the tires could be here by nine. Time enough to get them mounted and reach AISSI by ten to pick up the proposal. He could launch immediately after that and maybe beat the worst of the snowstorm into the Carolinas.

"Wait. A little more bad news, I'm afraid."

J.C. squeezed his eyes shut and shook his head. Thumper must have been a cheerleader in college, one of those guys who lead the old yea-boo riffs.

"Just give me the bottom line," J.C. said.

Thumper cleared his throat. "See, the thing of it is, I can't get 'em here right away. I've got a bud with a pickup in Warner Robins who said he'd ferry 'em up here, but he's working a swing shift at the air base and won't get off until midnight. So it'd be like two or three in the morning before—"

"Too late," J.C. snapped. "It could be snowing by then."

"Sorry, Mr. Riggins, I did my best."

J.C. pondered his situation. He briefly considered driving to Macon and picking up the tires himself, but it would be after nine before he could get there. The store might be closed by then. Even if it remained open, he'd still have to get the tires mounted, haul ass back to Atlanta, go home to say goodbye to Ginny and Cole and grab a bite to eat, then finally pick up the proposal. It would be well after midnight by then, and he'd be exhausted before even launching his journey to Durham.

So it came down to this: He could press on without snow tires, get a jump on the weather, and try to beat the heaviest of the snowfall into the Carolinas. Or he could hope the worst of the storm would hold off, wait for the tires, get them mounted, then sally forth with the assurance of having Zamboni-like traction if the blizzard caught him. Either way was a gamble.

"I know you tried your hardest, Thumper," J.C. said. "Thanks. I'll get back to you before midnight and let you know one way or the other whether to get the tires up here."

He leaned his forehead against the steering wheel and sucked in a series of deep breaths. For the first time since committing to his Quixotic quest—the adjective lit up abruptly in his mind—a bear trap of doubt snapped shut around his chest.

Chapter Ten

Warning

Magnolia Heights Subdivision
North Metro Atlanta, Georgia
Wednesday evening, December 28

J.C. AND GINNY sat on a leather couch in the family room. The Christmas tree, from which needles had begun to shed, sparkled with tiny white lights while orange flames bobbed and weaved in the fireplace. In one corner of the room, a silent flat-screen television flickered in a kaleidoscope of color as NE-TV offered wall-to-wall coverage of the impending blizzard.

Cole darted into the room. "Can we play in the snow tomorrow, Dad?" he asked, his small face painted in hope.

"Sorry, Big Guy, I've got to go on a trip."

"Awww."

"When I get back, okay?"

"Okay," Cole said, his voice soft, dejected. He turned to leave.

"There'll still be lots of snow on the ground when I get back," J.C. said. "Besides, it'll probably be too stormy tomorrow to play outside."

Cole looked back at his father. "But not too stormy to travel?" He trudged off, obviously unhappy.

Ginny chimed in. "Kid has a point. You don't have to do this, you know."

"I do," J.C. said. "We've been over this. I screwed up. I have to unscrew it. For Cole's sake if nothing else."

"No, you don't," Ginny said, an undercurrent of sharpness embedded in her voice. "Even if the company gives you the bum's rush, there are still good cancer centers right here in Atlanta."

"Change horses in the middle of the stream? After all Cole's been through? Look, the Anderson Center is the best thing we've got going in our lives right now. If I lose my job, we lose Anderson, and Cole loses the medical anchor in his life. That's not going to happen." The words came out forcefully.

"People die in blizzards," Ginny said. She looked directly at J.C., a mixture of fear and concern lodged in her eyes.

"We aren't in North Dakota," J.C. answered, making certain he kept his voice low and even. "It's not like I'll be traveling lonely farm roads in the middle of nowhere where homes are twenty-five miles apart. I'll be on some of the busiest interstates in the country."

"Not if they're shut down, you won't be."

"Ginny, please. I'm not gonna die. I mean, what's the worst that can happen? I lose the race with the storm and get stuck in a snowdrift for a couple of days and have to live on bottled water and granola bars."

"You might get arrested for being someplace you're not supposed to be."

"Look on the bright side, honey. At least I won't get carjacked."

"I hate to point it out, but you thought you were on Easy Street with the proposal prep, too, and that kind of blew up."

"Yeah, it blew up," J.C. barked. "I know. That's how we got here." He stood and stalked into the kitchen.

"I'm sorry, honey," Ginny called after him. "I didn't mean to rub salt into a wound. It's just that I'm worried. I can't help it. You could crash or something."

"Jesus, Ginny, I'm driving a German *Panzer.*" J.C. re-entered the family room. "And I hesitate to remind you, you were the one who urged me not to give up on getting this proposal delivered."

"I know," she said, her voice subdued, "but I didn't really think things would be getting as bad as they seem to be."

He pointed at the TV. "Turn it up. Let's hear what they're saying about the storm."

A young female reporter, who didn't look more than a couple of months out of college, stood in front of the south terminal of Hartsfield-Jackson International Airport. She'd flipped back a fur-lined hood from her head, but swaddled in a three-quarter length down parka, ski gloves, and calf-length boots, she appeared to be leaning into a Siberian gale on the Russian Steppe.

"Oh, for heaven sakes," Ginny said, "it's not even snowing yet, and the wind must be blowing all of what, ten miles per hour?"

"It's for dramatic effect," J.C. said. "Shhh."

". . . and already Delta has canceled over eight hundred departures out of Hartsfield-Jackson tomorrow." The reporter waved her hand at the terminal behind her. It appeared virtually devoid of travelers. The young lady straightened—a sudden cessation of the wind perhaps?—and continued speaking. "So not only do hundreds of thousands of highway travelers face the prospect of becoming stranded in the Southeast tomorrow, but air travelers across the country, not to mention the globe, may find themselves marooned if Hartsfield shuts down. Now back to Charlene and Randy in the studio, the warm studio." The reporter pulled the hood back over her head as though facing a renewed assault of arctic wind.

"Stay warm, Julie," responded one of the studio anchors, obviously Charlene. "Let's see what Sam Rackley has to say about all this. Sam."

The station's meteorologist, putting on his best gloom-and-doom face, stepped in front of the camera. Superimposed behind him, a map of the Southeast, centered on Atlanta, highlighted the web of interstate highways radiating from the city. At the bottom of the TV screen, a red-lettered crawl: BLIZZARD WARNING NORTH GEORGIA, UPSTATE SOUTH CAROLINA, WESTERN NORTH CAROLINA.

Sam, middle-aged, tanned, and undeniably handsome with wavy blond hair, could have been a refugee from the Southern California surf scene. He shook his head slowly, as though he were about to deliver devastating news.

"Wow," Ginny whispered, "he should be on the cover of romance novels."

"Shhh," J.C. ordered again.

"Folks," Sam said, "we're facing a serious situation here in North Georgia. A rare, dare I say unprecedented, blizzard is about to wallop us." He pressed a handheld clicker, and a radar image of current precipitation appeared on the map to his rear. He turned and gestured at it. "There's no snow falling yet, but a cold rain is dousing the Florida Panhandle and South Georgia. As that precipitation sweeps northward, it will encounter much colder air entrenched over the Appalachian Piedmont. The temperature in Macon now is thirty-three degrees, while here in Atlanta, we're well below freezing at twenty-seven."

He pressed his clicker again. A new map came up. Sam pointed at a large, red "L" in the Gulf of Mexico. "A rapidly strengthening storm center located about one hundred fifty miles south of Apalachicola will churn northeastward, relatively slowly, I might add, along this front stalled over northern Florida." He indicated an alternating red and blue line strung from the "L", the low pressure center, to the offshore waters of the Carolinas.

"The expected slow movement of this low is what will make it different from most developing winter storms in the Gulf, allowing it to unload snowfall worthy of New England on the Southeast. Another key factor, of course, is the cold air trapped between the storm and the Appalachians."

Cole reappeared, his attention focused on the TV. "This is so cool, Dad," he piped up, already forgetting the journey his father faced. "We need to get a sled."

"We will. Let's watch the forecast now."

Another map came up on-screen. "Here's what we expect for snowfall amounts," Sam said. "From Middle Georgia to Central South Carolina, six to ten inches." He swept his arm along a swath from the lower left of the screen to the upper right. He moved his arm to point farther north. "From around Metro Atlanta into Upstate South Carolina, ten to fourteen inches. But remember, with winds forecast to gust as high as fifty miles per hour, drifting snow will become a real problem. We could have drifts as deep as four to five feet."

Someone off camera whistled softly.

"Yes," said Sam, looking in the direction of the whistler, "that's why the blizzard warning. Maybe this is run-of-the-mill for Boston, but not for Atlanta. This storm will be crippling."

J.C.'s stomach knotted, and a looseness he cared not to acknowledge crept through his bowels. Perhaps he'd been too cavalier in his attitude. His planned odyssey seemed on the precipice of becoming *Mission Impossible* without Tom Cruise. He doubted even a *Geländewagen* could batter its way through shoulder-high mounds of wind-driven snow. He also realized that to embark on his trip without snow tires, without every bit of help he could get, would be idiotic.

Sam continued speaking. "We expect the snowfall to develop over Atlanta between two and four tomorrow morning and increase rapidly in intensity. By 8 a.m., it should be snowing heavily all over the city. Just plan on staying home tomorrow, folks."

J.C. muted the TV and reached for his cell.

"What?" Ginny said.

"Calling a guy named Thumper," J.C. answered. He punched in Thumper's number. The young man answered.

"I'll take the tires," J.C. said. "How soon do you think we can meet?"

"Let's allow some extra time for my bud to get here from Macon," Thumper said. "Just in case the weather gets really nasty really fast. I can probably get the store open by four in the morning. Will that work?"

"I'll be there."

"You got a trip or something planned, Mr. Riggins? I hope you don't mind me asking."

"It's an emergency."

Thumper started to ask another question, then apparently thought better of it. "See you at four," he said.

J.C. disconnected the call. Ginny stared at him, her eyes misty, her face etched in concern. "You don't have to—"

He raised his finger to her lips, hushing her. "I do have to," he said, wishing he didn't.

Windy Hill Towers
Wednesday Evening, December 28

TOM PRIZ, A little melancholy and still nonplussed after his very personal tête-à-tête with Sophie, sat in a recliner in front of his plasma TV, sipping a Jack Daniel's on the rocks and watching Sam Rackley finish his weather segment. On the floor beside Tom, a half-eaten pepperoni, mushroom, and pineapple pizza rested in state in a Papa John's cardboard box.

Stormy Weather chimed on Tom's cell phone.

"Hey," Al Tillman said, "you didn't happen to catch that moron Rackley on TV just now, did you?" In the background, Tom heard strains of the Rolling Stones' *Jumping Jack Flash*.

"*Jumping Jack Flash*? I thought you were into the classics, old man." Tom muted his TV.

"What? The Stones aren't classic? Classic rock, junior. Definitive sounds for the late twentieth century. No different from Haydn, Mozart, and Sibelius in their times."

"Who?"

"Jean Sibelius. Finnish composer. He wrote *Finlandia*, the *Karelia Suite*—oh, never mind. Rackley the Moron, did you see him?"

"Where in the hell are you, Al?"

"In the office."

"Why aren't you at home?"

"Because I'm old and lonely. Because the Dragon Lady requested my presence. Because we're shorthanded. Most of our employees are hunkered down in their domestic storm bunkers. Oh, and a certain coworker of mine is under house arrest."

"Why is Sam Rackley a moron?" J.C. asked, ignoring Al's jibe.

"Because he's leading the good people of Atlanta to believe they aren't gonna see more than fourteen inches of snow."

Chapter Eleven

Doubts

Windy Hill Towers
Wednesday evening, December 28

TOM PICKED UP his glass and, with a vigorous twist of his wrist, created a micro-cyclone of whiskey and ice cubes. "So that makes Rackley a moron, because he didn't predict *more* snow, even though he's forecast a greater amount than has ever fallen here?"

Silence ensued on the other end of the call.

"Okay," Al finally said, "I recant my indictment. The guy's just inexperienced. He got the part about the slow movement of the storm right, but he didn't take it far enough. His missed the fact the upper-level system is going to cut off and stall for six to eight hours. That's when we'll get clocked. It'll be like Boston in '78 with an inch or two an hour."

"You're sure?"

"Of course not, but I've seen enough of these things to know the atmosphere doesn't give a damn whether it's doing something weird over Massachusetts or Georgia. Within limits, the results are the same."

Tom expelled a long breath. "So, the Gandalf Crystal Ball says?"

"Twenty inches, maybe two feet."

"That's insane."

"It's a Walmart crystal ball."

"Take it back."

"Can't. The roads will be impassable tomorrow. And probably for the better part of a week."

"So you're hunkering down at work?" Tom rescued a piece of droopy pizza from the Papa John's box. He sniffed at it, nibbled, made a face, and tossed it back. Cold.

"Yeah," Al said. "I doubt many people are going to make it in. I know the newspaper guy is supposed to show up again. And Sophie.

But they're strap hangars. They'll be more hindrance than help."

Tom stood and paced to the window of his condo. The distant lights of Atlanta cloaked the city in an electric mantle of shimmering colors: red, white, green, yellow, blue—an urban tribute to the season, though in reality the multi-toned spectacle was no different from any other night. "What time do you expect the worst?" he asked.

"Not until Friday, but it'll be bad enough tomorrow with the surface storm center crawling across South Georgia. I'm thinking a half-inch to occasionally an inch an hour. If I were you, I'd get back in here. You're within walking distance, right?"

"Listen to me, Al. If and when I return, it'll be because I got the request from my parole officer, not you."

Al muttered something Tom couldn't understand and hung up.

Tom flopped back into his recliner. A bachelor pad miasma of un-washed dishes, un-dusted furniture, and unlaundered clothes permeated the room. "Hey, Billy and Bonnie," he muttered, "I miss you guys."

On his cell, he punched in Billy's number. "Hey, kid, how about you, me, and Bonnie go sledding tomorrow? It's gonna snow, you know. There's a great hill on the golf course near your house."

"I know, Dad. But Mom already said if it doesn't get too bad she and Rick would take us."

Rick, the stepdad. "Yeah, well, okay. Maybe later in the week."

"Sure. That would be fun."

They made small talk for a few more minutes, then Billy put Bonnie on the line with a stern warning not to burn up all of his minutes. She whined that Rick didn't pay enough attention to her, that she wanted to come back to live with "her Daddy."

Tom told her it would take time, that she had to go through a period of adjustment, but that everything would smooth out and there would eventually be plenty of attention and love. She said goodbye through drama queen sobs.

Tom reached for the Jack Daniel's and drained the glass.

American-International Systems Solutions, Inc.
Wednesday evening, December 28

CYRUS BILLINGSLY, his tie loosened, eyes heavy with fatigue, and lips pressed together in a death clench looked up as J.C. entered his office. Containers of half-eaten Chinese takeout littered his desk. Odors of Mongolian beef and mu shu pork hung in the air.

"It's ready," Billingsly said, not bothering with a greeting. He swiveled in his chair and pointed at three securely-taped, sturdy-looking cardboard boxes sitting side by side on a credenza. Each container emblazoned with the AISSI corporate logo, a red lightning bolt backed by a blazing yellow supernova, appeared about the size of a five-ream paper box, the kind you'd pick up at Office Depot or Staples. An address label on each indicated its destination: Rampart Aerospace & Defense Corporation, Military Systems Division (RADC-MSD), Research Triangle Park, Durham, North Carolina.

"And *I'm* ready," J.C. said.

"I presume you have a plan." It seemed both a statement and a question.

J.C. briefed him, explaining about the *Geländewagen* he'd "borrowed" for a road test, his appointment to get snow tires mounted, and his plan to get out of Atlanta early in the morning in an effort to beat the worst of the snowfall.

Billingsly seemed unimpressed by the strategy, squinting at J.C., apparently in circumspection, as J.C. rattled on.

"A snipe hunt," Billingsly growled after J.C. had finished. "You don't have a prayer. This isn't New England, you know, where the interstates are clear of snow six hours after a storm. No. The roads around here will end up looking like the Greenland Ice Cap in January. They'll probably have to call in rotary plows from the Sierra Nevada to clear them. You're dead, man."

"Thanks for your support, sir." J.C. tried to keep the sarcasm out of his voice, but came up short.

"I didn't bring this on, Mr. Riggins. This was *your* doing. I'll give you credit for the 'old college try,' but you're off on a 'where-angels-fear-to-tread' mission." Billingsly leaned forward, rested his elbows on the desk, and steepled his hands in front of him. "What's your planned route?"

"North on I-85 through Upstate South Carolina and western North Carolina until it intersects with I-40 in Greensboro, then into Durham on I-40."

"The ol' bull rush, huh? Meet the enemy head on. Why not head east on I-20 through Columbia, South Carolina, then north on I-95 into North Carolina? Maybe stay south of the worst of the weather."

"I checked the forecast pretty damn closely, sir. Even that far south the forecast is for eight to twelve inches of snow, plus I'd be adding a hundred miles to the trip."

"Farther south then. Into Savannah, then north on I-95." Billingsly snapped out the words in his best flag-officer voice.

"Two hundred extra miles," J.C. responded. "Plus what do you think I-95 is going to look like? With all the other interstates blocked, every holiday traveler in the Southeast is going to try to squeeze onto it. You'll have a six hundred-mile-long parking lot from Jacksonville to Richmond."

Billingsly grunted. "Point taken. So, I guess that's it then. Off into the wild blue, or feral white, maybe." He shrugged.

"Look, once I get the snow tires on, I'm outta here. By four thirty I should be flyin'. I can outrun the storm. It isn't supposed to really start dumping here until around sunrise. I'll be well into South Carolina by then."

"Dumping or not, 85 will still be snow covered. You won't be doing the speed limit."

"I'll be in South Carolina." J.C. made the statement with a firmness disconnected from the uncertainty burning in his gut. His grandfather had always told him, "If you sing loudly enough, you'll scare away the monsters." Billingsly probably needed to plug his ears.

"This isn't a run-of-the-mill snowstorm, you know," Billingsly reminded him.

"There isn't any such thing in the South, sir."

Billingsly sighed, probably more out of exasperation than frustration. "You've got survival gear, I trust?" Even as a civilian, he remained ever the commanding officer, checking on the preparedness of his troops, or in this case, trooper.

J.C. nodded and gave him a brief rundown.

Billingsly stood. "I'll help you carry the boxes down to your— what did you call it?"

"G-Wagen."

"Yes. Oh, and one more thing." He pulled a business card from a holder on his desk, turned the card over, wrote something, and handed it to J.C. "My cell number. I'll be available twenty-four seven. Stay in touch." Almost as an afterthought he added, "Please."

They loaded the boxes into the rear of the Mercedes. In the glow of the high-pressure sodium lights in the parking lot, Billingsly glanced at his wristwatch. "Well, who knows? Maybe you've got a chance. Over forty hours to go. Ya know, nobody thought the Doolittle Raiders would make it either." He proffered his hand to J.C.

J.C. accepted it. He tried to recall the Doolittle Raid, the bombing of Tokyo by B-25s flying off an aircraft carrier as a "show-the-flag" attack on the Japanese in the wake of Pearl Harbor. As he remembered it, well, remembered reading about it, the planes reached Tokyo, but most crash-landed in China after dropping their bombs. A mixed bag in terms of success. He hoped he and his hundred thousand dollar demonstrator, the G-Wagen, would fare better, but the doubts had begun to swarm, like winged termites on a warm spring afternoon.

He cranked the vehicle. A gust of wind sent an empty Styrofoam food container cartwheeling through the parking lot. It careened off a patch of ice, tumbled into a chain link fence, and came to rest, pinioned by the elements. J.C. stared at it, wondering if he weren't seeing his own fate.

He slipped the Mercedes into gear and drove off. In his rearview mirror, he watched Billingsly, suit jacket clutched around his neck to ward off the icy wind, trudge back toward the AISSI building, shaking his head in slow motion. Not exactly a vote of confidence.

Magnolia Heights Subdivision
Wednesday night, December 28

J.C. SET HIS ALARM for 3:30 a.m. and crawled into bed. Four or five hours of sleep—assuming he could actually fall asleep—wouldn't be enough to fully restore his mind and body, not after the kind of day he'd had, but it would be better than nothing. The alternative would be remaining awake, or trying to do so, and watching the hours and minutes slink by until it was time for his departure. If he did that, he knew he'd do nothing but dwell on the boogeymen, both real and imagined, that lurked in his future.

Exhausted, he tumbled into a dream world of winter whiteness almost as soon as he'd pulled the sheet and blanket up to his nose. . . .

"And he whistled, and shouted, and called them by name:
Now, Dasher! Now, Dancer! Now Prancer and Vixen!
On, Comet! On, Cupid! On, Donner and Blitzen!"

BUT THE REINDEER hadn't flown to the top of a porch or the top of a wall. Surrounded by wolves on a snowbound road, they lay in deep drifts, their almost-skeletal bodies barely visible. St. Nicholas, a German Army "coal scuttle" helmet perched on his head, stood in his trapped sleigh firing a 12-gauge Mossberg at the encircling predators.

Unseen by St. Nick, a wolf the color of obsidian stalked through the chest-deep snow directly to the rear of the sleigh. The animal stopped and crouched, then sprang forward in a rush, preparing to leap at the tubby, white-haired man with the shotgun. . . .

J.C. screamed a warning that awakened not only him, but Ginny as well.

"Jesus, honey," Ginny said, "don't do that. You scared me to death. A dream?"

He nodded. "What time is it?"

"Not quite three."

"So much for my midwinter's nap."

"Tell you what," Ginny said, swinging her legs over the side of the bed, "I'll fix you some eggs and toast while you get dressed."

"Yeah, okay," he mumbled. He sat up and rubbed his eyes. "Sorry I woke you."

"I would have killed you if you hadn't. Cole wants to say goodbye, too. I'll roust him after I fix breakfast."

A short while later, they sat at the table in the family room. Outside, snow, illuminated in the deck lights, sifted down in snow globe laziness, white veils sweeping back and forth at the whim of the wind.

"It started early," Ginny said.

"Not what I wanted to see," J.C. responded. He shoveled in a mouthful of scrambled eggs followed by a large bite of multi-grain toast.

Cole, as animated as he'd been since returning home, darted to and fro in front of the sliders leading to the deck. "Will you be home by this afternoon, Dad? We could go sledding, or build a snowman, or have a snowball fight, or make snow angels. Will you, Dad?" He came to where J.C. sat and leaned his head against his arm.

J.C. pulled him close. "I don't think so, Big Guy. But I won't be gone long, and the snow will be around for days. We'll have plenty of time for some fun."

"Okay, I guess." Cole's voice echoed his disappointment.

"I think your mom can probably handle the snowball fight bit this afternoon. Right, honey?"

Ginny glared at J.C. "Mom can probably handle the build-a-snow-man-and-knock him-down bit."

J.C. smiled, took a swig of his coffee, and turned on the TV. Radar images showed the snow had already spread over most of North Georgia and adjacent parts of South Carolina.

A voiceover indicated the snowfall rate was forecast to pick up throughout the morning with many roads becoming impassable by noon. Only essential travel was advised.

A man appeared on-screen, a grizzled-looking, middle-aged weathercaster. "A blizzard warning remains in effect," he said. "Winds will increase steadily today, and by this afternoon blowing and drifting snow will exacerbate travel problems, which should be bad enough from the snowfall alone." The camera closed in on him. "Friends, this is going to be a real taste of New England, believe me. Forget this is the South. Please stay home today. Don't go out unless it's an absolute emergency. It's already dicey out there. It'll be downright dangerous within a few hours."

J.C. switched off the TV.

Ginny reached out and gripped his arm. He read the fear in her eyes; it had elevated well beyond mere concern. She started to speak.

"I smell gingerbread," he said, cutting her off at the pass.

She relaxed her grip but held her gaze on him. "I'm frightened. I can't help it."

"Gingerbread," he said.

She sighed, stood, and walked to the kitchen. "I baked some cookies for your trip."

Cole danced after her. "Can I have one?"

"After lunch. They aren't breakfast snacks." She turned to J.C. "I made some sandwiches, too. Ham and cheese. Roast beef with a little horseradish mustard."

He pecked her on the cheek. "I need to hit the road. The kid will be at the tire store shortly."

Ginny stuffed the sandwiches and cookies into a picnic cooler and filled a thermos with coffee. "This should keep you going for a bit."

"As backup, Waffle Houses are always open—no matter how bad the weather." J.C. wrapped Ginny in a bear hug and pulled her to him. "I'll be fine." He imbued his voice with more confidence than he felt.

"Call me," she said. "Every hour. I want to know where you are and how you are."

"I'll be fine," he repeated.

"Call."

"I will, I will." He kissed her and released his embrace.

Cole, who had briefly disappeared, rejoined them. "Teddy's going with you," he announced. He handed J.C. a one-eyed, cut-foot, brown and white teddy bear almost three feet tall. "He'll be like your guardian angel."

J.C. knelt. "Wouldn't you rather have Teddy stay with you and Mom?" Teddy had been Cole's constant companion since J.C. had won him by knocking down stacked "milk bottles" at a county fair when Cole was three. Teddy had endured as many hospital and doctor visits as Cole.

Cole, his face wrinkled into a mask of childhood contemplation, examined Teddy. "No. I think he's part polar bear. He needs to go with you."

"Thanks, Big Guy." J.C. tucked Teddy under his arm and stood. "Time to beat feet."

Ginny picked up the cooler and thermos and followed J.C. and Cole into the garage. "Got everything?" She ran through a verbal checklist. "Parka. Gloves. Phone charger. Flashlight. Shov—"

"I'm ready to roll," he assured her.

"Okay." She ran her gaze over him, a drill sergeant scrutinizing a recruit.

He at least *felt* prepared. Pendleton shirt. Insulated pants. Gaiters (refugees from New England). Timberland hiking boots. Wool watch cap.

"Do I pass inspection?" He patted the cap perched on his head. "You know, I really need this now that I'm bald."

He placed the thermos on the front passenger seat and the cooler on the rear seat along with Teddy.

"Buckle him up," Cole commanded.

"He'll be fine, son."

"No, you have to fasten his seat belt."

A glare from Ginny underscored Cole's request. J.C. buckled the teddy bear into the seat.

"Ready, I guess," J.C. said. He embraced Ginny.

"I don't like this," she whispered. Moistness clouded her eyes. She squeezed them shut. A single tear slid down her cheek, slow-motion proof of the emotions roiling within her.

"You worry too much." He didn't mention the disturbing, snow-bound, shotgun-toting Santa Claus nightmare he'd had. Its specter hung over him like a snow squall about to swallow the landscape.

He kissed Ginny and hugged Cole. "Take care of Mommy."

Cole nodded, then stood on his tiptoes to peer through the G-Wagen's rear side window. "Do you have your gun, Daddy?"

J.C. stared at Cole. *A strange question. Why would he think of that?* "No. No need. I'll be battling bad weather, not bad guys."

"Oh."

J.C. punched the garage door opener, climbed into the vehicle, which he'd backed into the garage, and started the engine. The G-Wagen's headlights shot into the dark, reflecting off a swirling crystalline ballet on a stage of black velvet.

Mantles of white shrouded the ground on either side of the driveway, but the drive itself had been swept clean of snow by the wind. Tendrils of tiny flakes slithered across the bare concrete like Sahara sand driven by desert gusts.

J.C. eased the Mercedes into the storm. An old saying from New England crept into his consciousness: Big flakes, little storm; little flakes, big storm.

Chapter Twelve

Into the Storm

North Metro Atlanta, Georgia
Early Thursday morning, December 29

THE SNOW, FINE and powdery, fell in thick, whirling sheets as J.C. steered the G-Wagen onto a deserted, snow-covered boulevard and headed toward the tire store. No plows in sight. Not that he would have expected them in Atlanta.

The radio, tuned to an all-news station, broadcast a string of advisories that sounded like those from an Old Testament prophet warning of dire consequences for those who failed to heed the counsel of officialdom: Stay off the roads.

The all-wheel drive SUV felt solid and surefooted on the slick road, but J.C. knew as the snow continued to accumulate, he'd need something other than the all-terrain tires currently on the vehicle. He no longer pictured himself driving in the South, but mentally transplanted himself into a January nor'easter in Massachusetts.

He arrived at the tire store shortly after four. The building sat cloaked in darkness with no signs of anyone around. The parking lot, frosted over with several inches of snow, supported that notion. The only tire tracks visible belonged to J.C.'s vehicle.

He pulled up to the garage doors and let the G-Wagen idle while he fished out his cell phone. Normally patient, he knew each minute counted in his race against the storm. He punched in Thumper's number. No answer. He slammed the phone onto the passenger seat.

Ten past four. Fifteen past. Twenty past. *How long do I wait?*

His cell phone rang. He yanked it off the seat.

"Thumper?"

"Yeah, man. I'm sorry. I'm late, I know. But the roads are really greasy. I'm not used to this shit."

"Okay, okay. Take it easy and be careful. Have you heard from your friend in Macon?"

"He's on his way, but he says I-75 was like a skating rink. Once he got north of the Fall Line, things slowed to a crawl. He fell in behind a salt truck and followed it to I-675."

"Where is he now?" *Glad I didn't try to make it to Macon.*

"On the Perimeter, east side, coming north. He says there's one lane that's pretty clear—you know, ruts down to the pavement—but traffic's only moving about forty miles per hour."

J.C. drew in a deep breath and expelled it silently through his mouth. He ran a quick calculation in his head. It could be another forty or forty-five minutes before Thumper's friend arrived with the tires. By the time they were mounted, it would be five thirty. He'd be over an hour behind his planned schedule right out of the starting blocks.

Yet given the storm had already begun, it seemed foolish to try "save" time and press on without snow tires.

"All right," J.C. said, "tell your bud to keep coming. I'll be here."

He killed the engine and watched the snowfall dance in the wind. Thick curtains of white slanted one way and then another, emulating flocks of birds in tightly-knit formations, darting across the sky in seemingly random choreography.

J.C. JERKED HIS head up, startled by a rapping on his window.

"Hey, man. You okay in there?"

J.C. looked around, grappling for his bearings. He found them quickly. Tire store. Snowstorm. He'd dozed off. He turned and stared into the face of whoever had knocked. A face half-hidden in a hoodie. He squinted at it. Thumper.

J.C. opened the window. "Sorry," he said, "guess I nodded off."

"Come on," Thumper said, "let's get inside, get warm. I'll brew some coffee." In his bulky hoodie, a red University of Georgia version likely pulled on over several shirts, he looked like a dancing bear as he trudged through the falling snow.

"Are the tires here yet?" J.C. checked his watch. Almost five. He stepped out of the G-Wagen and followed Thumper.

"They're about ten or fifteen minutes away," Thumper answered. "My bud, Eddie's his name, called a few minutes ago. He's on Jimmy Carter Boulevard headed this way."

Twenty minutes elapsed before Eddie arrived, fishtailing through the deserted parking lot in his pickup, partly because he could, mostly because he likely lacked winter driving skills.

Thumper and Eddie, working together, had the Yokohamas off and four Michelin ice and snow tires mounted on the SUV in a matter of minutes.

"Whaddya want I should do with the Yokohamas?" Thumper said.

"Is it okay if I leave them here and come back in a few days and get them remounted?" J.C. asked.

"Not a problem, Mr. Riggins." Thumper paused. "You sure you want to set off into this storm, snow tires or no? It's supposed to be a really bad one, ya know."

J.C. handed Thumper a credit card. "It's not that I want to, it's that I have to."

"Well, be careful, sir." Thumper entered the sale in the store's computer.

Nine hundred dollars lighter and eight ounces of coffee heavier, J.C. pulled onto Holcomb Bridge Road and headed toward I-85. He had debated whether to use secondary roads or stay on main routes while working his way toward the interstate. He decided his chances of getting through would be better on primary roads. On a two-lane street, if a car spun out or wrecked, it could easily block both lanes. On multi-lane boulevards there would be more room to navigate around any impediments.

Also, he knew primary roads would get priority over others for plowing and salting. Well, priority after the interstates, at least.

The snow fell even more heavily as he crawled east on Holcomb Bridge, then Jimmy Carter. Traffic remained sparse, non-existent over many stretches, and the G-Wagen churned through the thickening white blanket like a Sno-Cat.

The landscape, typically an unattractive tangle of strip malls, fast food eateries, and gas stations, seemed to morph into something from a quieter, simpler time, whitewashed of the commercial sins begat by urban sprawl and greed, something, perhaps, from a nineteenth century Currier and Ives winterscape.

J.C. reached the diverging diamond intersection at Jimmy Carter and I-85 and eased the Mercedes across the overpass, preparing to turn left onto the interstate. Ahead, a police car, blue lights strobing through the snowfall, blocked the entrance ramp to the highway. An officer stepped from the car as J.C. approached.

J.C. brought the SUV to a stop and cracked open the window.

"Good morning, sir," the officer said. "Out early in bad weather, huh?"

"Earlier than I'd like, officer." *Don't tell me the interstate is closed already.*

Snow quickly coated the police officer's blue watch cap and flight jacket topped by a reflective safety vest. Embroidered on the cap in gold letters: GWINNETT COUNTY POLICE. The officer ran his gaze over the G-Wagen, and J.C. wondered if he were being sized up as a Russian Mafioso driving a vehicle stuffed with illicit drugs.

"Where are you headed?" the officer asked. Snowflakes clung to his eyebrows like tiny ornaments. Clouds of condensate puffed from his mouth with each word.

J.C. considered the question and decided to keep his destination close-hold until he understood why the ramp was blocked. "Just up 85 a little way."

The officer stepped closer to the SUV and lowered his head toward the window and out of the biting breeze. "Well, DOT's going to close the interstate to the South Carolina border in about thirty minutes. How far are you planning on going?"

"Only as far as Sugarloaf Parkway," J.C. lied. He had no idea how far that was, but guessed it was close enough to fall safely within a thirty-minute travel time.

"Okay," the officer said. "That's only about ten miles up the road. Even at a creepy-crawly speed you should make it before we close shop. And it looks like you're well equipped to handle winter driving. Nice wheels." He gave the G-Wagen an admiring nod.

"Thanks."

The officer gave the Mercedes a pat on the roof. "Be careful. You and Mr. Bear have a good day now. I'll move my cruiser."

J.C. nodded. *Mr. Bear?* He glanced at Teddy strapped into the rear seat and smiled. He waved to the officer as he steered the G-Wagen down the ramp, chunks of snow flying from the winter tires like clods of dirt from a John Deere at a tractor pull.

He assumed nobody would monitor whether he actually exited at Sugarloaf and also assumed no one would expend resources chasing him down on a "closed" interstate once he got rolling. He'd probably end up in the pokey if he got stuck someplace, but he had no intention of letting that happen. For all intents and purposes, he was on a Cannonball Run to South Carolina.

On the interstate, he maintained a steady speed, beginning at thirty miles per hour, then increasing to forty miles per hour as he became more comfortable with the Mercedes' ability to track unerringly through the snow. The snow itself seemed deep enough to be plowable, but he saw no signs of any such activity. He surmised the plows and salters were biding their time until the interstate was officially closed before launching their counterattack on the winter assault.

The twelve-lane interstate, normally clogged with morning-rush traffic, appeared more like a snow-encrusted ghost town in the predawn darkness. Only a handful of cars and a scattering of eighteen-wheelers pushed through the intensifying storm. Wind-driven snow slanted through J.C.'s field of vision, and tiny drifts, a product of increasingly strong gusts, begin building on the shoulders. Occasionally, tiny haboobs of snow swirled across the highway, creating near-white-out conditions.

South of Steve Reynolds Boulevard, an overhead DOT electronic message sign advised: BLIZZARD WARNING I-85 CLOSED TO S.C. BORDER 7 A.M.

J.C. pressed on, crawling through the tangled I-85 interchange with Highway 316, the route leading to Athens and the University of Georgia. Several cars had spun out, their noses stuck in roadside drifts like a fox after a rabbit gone down its hole. A Highway Emergency Response Operator, a HERO unit, its orange and red warning flashers challenging the storm, stood guard over one of the stranded vehicles, but there wasn't much assistance that could be rendered until a tow truck showed up.

As J.C. approached the Sugarloaf Parkway exit, he slowed even more. He momentarily considered "playing by the rules," getting off the highway where he said he would, but quickly discarded the notion. He couldn't gamble on the interstate being reopened anytime soon. He had to get to Durham. Besides—a readymade excuse—a pickup truck had lost traction and become stuck on the looping, climbing exit ramp, blocking the way. In the tried and true Southern tradition, the driver gunned the engine, certain additional speed would spring him or her from the snowy trap. The effort served only to dig the stalled truck deeper into its gulag.

J.C. continued north on the interstate, maintaining a slow but steady pace. The traffic, what little there was, thinned even more as he passed the I-85/I-985 split. Shortly, he found himself virtually alone on the road, knifing directly into the wind. Despite its nearly three-ton bulk, the G-Wagen shuddered in the powerful gusts.

The highway lane stripes had disappeared, buried by what J.C. guessed was close to a half-foot of snow. Along some stretches of the road, the pavement had been swept almost bare by the wind, but in other spots, the big SUV pounded through drifts already over a foot high.

J.C. couldn't remember how many lanes this part of I-85 had, but guessed it was only two in each direction. He struggled to locate the right edge of the road, but visual cues had disappeared, buried under a white blanket. In an effort to stay on the highway, he slowed even more. At this rate, he fretted, he might not reach Durham until after New Year's.

By late morning, near Commerce, he spotted the first phalanx of plows in the southbound lanes of I-85. He glanced in his rearview mirror. Still nothing on the northbound side. He continued to push ahead, the lone vehicle on the road. Perhaps it was best he didn't encounter any snow removal equipment. The drivers might report him to police, and that could spell the end of his journey. He judged now he had only a few more miles to the South Carolina border. Of course, he had no idea if I-85 in that state would be open, legally.

But his luck seemed destined to run out before he reached the state line. Ahead, looming out of the gray-white bleakness of the snow, now flying almost horizontally, appeared the flashing lights of a police cruiser parked on an entrance lane to a weigh station. An officer, wearing a Smokey Bear hat tilted low over his eyes, emerged from the car and motioned for J.C. to pull over.

He did, his gut feeling as though a rat were gnawing at it from inside out. As he neared the cruiser he could see GEORGIA STATE PATROL emblazoned in large orange letters on its doors. Several inches of snow caked its roof. It had been here a while. As J.C. pulled to a stop, the outline of another vehicle, a small civilian model of some sort, materialized out of the gloom in front of the cruiser.

He focused on the trooper as the man waded through the snow toward the G-Wagen. J.C. slid the window down and swallowed hard.

The trooper, rough-looking, unshaven, and red-eyed—a long night perhaps—gave J.C. a withering stare. "Road's closed, partner. What are you doing out here?" He leaned against the side of the Mercedes as though seeking support.

"Emergency," J.C. said. "I have to get some medical supplies to South Carolina." Another little lie—okay, maybe not so little.

"Yeah. Well, the interstate's closed in South Carolina, too. Could I see your driver's license, please?"

J.C. retrieved the license from his wallet and handed it to the trooper.

The officer studied it, then handed it back. "You're out here illegally, Mr. Riggins." He paused. "We need to rectify that."

With those words, all hope of saving AISSI's future, his job, and Cole's finely-tuned medical status quo, seemed to evaporate.

A puff of icy wind flung a tiny tornado of snowflakes into the SUV.

Chapter Thirteen

Second Chances

Windy Hill Towers
Thursday morning, December 29

TOM PRIZ, SIPPING a cup of lukewarm coffee, stared out his condo window into a dull, white void. Through the fog and snow that whipped around the building, only amorphous forms could be made out seventeen stories below, creeping across a colorless tundra. It seemed more like a scene of a Siberian winter rather than one in the American South.

Single lines of traffic snaked over the snow-covered and normally clogged lanes of the I-285/I-75 interchange. Most people, it seemed, had heeded the warnings not to venture out.

In the background, Tom's TV broadcast an endless string of headlines and advisories. Hartsfield-Jackson was closed until further notice. Delta Air Lines alone had canceled over 1,000 flights, both departures and arrivals. Air travel over most of the country, but the Eastern Seaboard in particular, was spiraling toward chaos. Despite an early warning of the airport's closure, hundreds of travelers, maybe over a thousand, still found themselves "prisoners" in a facility that likely would run short of food before the end of the day.

People were urged to remain wherever they were. Every effort, a breathless newscaster announced, was being expended to keep at least one lane open each way on the Perimeter. Ditto for I-20, I-75, and I-85 through the city and Georgia 400, the expressway north. But, one DOT official conceded, it might be a losing battle. Even though the metro area had beefed up its snow and ice removal strike force in the wake of a crippling 2011 snowstorm, the fury of a full-blown blizzard might be too much to overcome.

The litany of challenges continued: Outside the metro area, the unprecedented act of closing I-85 northeast to South Carolina, I-75 north to Tennessee, and I-20 west to Alabama had been undertaken. In the face of a blizzard of historic proportions, the plan was to take preemptive action in an attempt to keep plows moving on the interstates in hope of quickly reopening them once the storm slackened.

Tom turned from the window and walked to the kitchen. The faint odor of yesterday's deceased pizza assaulted his sense of smell. Also hanging the air were vapors from the watery detritus of last night's Jack Daniel's stagnating at the bottom of a rocks glass. Tom found his appetite for breakfast abruptly DOA.

He peered into his refrigerator, hoping to find some orange juice. The only liquids in residence proved to be a carton of spoiled milk—adding to his olfactory miasma—a six-pack of Coors, and a half-empty bottle of Columbia Valley Riesling.

"Shit," he muttered and slammed the door.

Stormy Weather chimed. He tracked the source to his bedroom and pulled his cell phone from beneath a stack of dirty clothes.

"Tom Priz," he said.

"Hey, junior. Where in the hell are you? We're about to turn into Buffalo, New York, and you're sleeping in?"

"We already had this conversation, Al. I was *given* the week off, remember?"

"Well, the Dragon Lady wishes you to be draggin' your ass in here now. Only two people and our Fearless Female Führer have managed to get into work this morning. We're desperate for slave labor."

Tom sat on his bed. "You're her mouthpiece now? Let her tell me."

Al expelled a long breath. "Sure, hold on. I'll find her." Heavy, labored breathing followed as Al began his search. "Hey," he said between deep inhalations, "I got an idea. I'll tell her she doesn't even have to order you back on the job. All you want is tit for tat." He broke into a wheezing, hacking laugh that sounded on the edge of strangulation.

"Al, have you ever seen a psychiatrist?" Tom said. "I think you're some kind of sexual deviant with repressed desires." He rose from the bed and strode back to the living room.

"At my age, sonny, there's nothing left to repress," Al rasped. "Oops, hold on, my infrared sensor has detected her Highness in the immediate vicinity."

There came a muffled exchange of voices, then Sophie. "Tom, we could use your help in here."

"I thought I was on a leave of absence." He struggled to keep his frustration in check, to keep his voice on an even keel.

"It seemed like a good idea at the time. We can still do it later if you'd like."

"No, I wouldn't like."

"Good. Come on in."

"So, you agree our differences were more a matter of semantics than anything?"

"No, damn it, I don't," Sophie shot back. "Don't you friggin' get it? Sometimes your scientifically-based conservatism or circumspection or whatever in the hell it is just doesn't cut it. You gotta tell the people what's gonna happen without being all wishy-washy about it, and maybe blow trumpets and beat drums to get their attention."

Tom drew a deep, measured breath and remained silent. In truth, he wanted to be at work, dealing with what would undoubtedly go down as one of the great storms of the twenty-first century, but he didn't need the *Sturm und Drang* of dealing with Sophie. Still, ironically, he did want to see her again, curious to discover if their pseudo-sexual encounter in her office was a one-off flirtation or an invitation to be her lover. Uncertainty raged within him.

"Tom?"

"I'm on my way."

After the call, Tom stared out into the wintry fury whipping the city. He had to admit, he'd been summoned by a Lorelei, the mythical siren on a rock in the Rhine who lured sailors to their destruction. But—and he hated to cop a plea to this—deep down, he savored it.

HE SLOGGED A quarter-mile through ankle-deep snow to NE-TV headquarters, the wind hurling phalanx after phalanx of stinging crystals into his face. He caught a glimpse of his reflection in the glass doors of the facility as he entered. His nose and cheeks looked as though they had suffered the consequence of falling asleep in bright sunshine on the shimmering sands of Panama City Beach, Florida.

"Wow, Mr. Priz," the security officer at the front desk said, "you look like Santa might have if his sleigh had broken down in Siberia."

"Feew 'at way, too," Tom mumbled through numbed lips. He brushed snow off his ski hat and parka and swiped his ID card through the reader. He took the elevator to the fifth floor operations center where he found Sophie and Al waiting for him.

"Thank you, Tom," Sophie said, but nothing more. In those few words, he sensed an electric charge, a strong current running both ways.

Al remained quiet, his gaze drifting from Sophie to Tom and back again. He appeared to sense something between the two, but perhaps couldn't quite decipher it.

"Come on, Al, let's get busy," Tom said.

They walked together toward the forecast center.

"Hey, what's with you two?" Al asked. "Something's going on, isn't it? Maybe a little afternoon delight?" He nudged Tom with his elbow. "How about it, junior?"

"You really do need to visit a counselor," Tom muttered.

When they reached the forecast center, they found Don Hemphill, the *Atlanta-Journal Constitution* reporter, seated at a table writing on his iPad. Only two forecasters, half the usual complement, busied themselves at workstations.

"Well, I can see why I was recalled to active duty," Tom said. He turned to Al. "How about bringing me up to speed on the situation, if you can drag your thoughts away from your Harlequin novel for a few minutes."

Al grunted, issued a muted hack, and motioned for Tom to follow him to a wall of large-screen computer monitors.

"The primary surface low," he said, pointing, "is sliding northeastward from the Gulf of Mexico toward the Jacksonville-St. Simons Island area. The rain-snow line extends from extreme southeast Alabama to near Columbia, South Carolina. Just south of that, there's a narrow band of freezing rain. Nasty."

"Snowfall rates?" Tom asked.

"The isentropic lift is near its maximum now over northern Georgia and Upstate South Carolina, so they're picking up on the order of an inch an hour."

Hemphill moved to where Tom and Al stood. "Excuse me," he said, "isentropic lift?"

Tom smiled. "Weatherman talk for lift created by a warm front. In this case, there's a lot of lift." He gestured at the map on the monitor. "We've got warm, juicy air from the Gulf of Mexico and off the Atlantic being sucked in by our strengthening storm. That air is being hurled up and over a rock-solid mound of very cold air parked over the Piedmont. Bingo. Heavy snow. Something we don't often see in the Southeast."

Hemphill drew diagrams and typed notes on his iPad, trying to keep up with Tom's explanations. "So," he said as he continued to draw and type, "the heaviest snow is occurring right now?"

Tom looked at Al, flashing him a tacit sign to take over the briefing.

"Sort of," Al said. "At least for the immediate future."

"Meaning?" Hemphill asked.

"Meaning the snowfall rates should taper off this afternoon as the storm continues to press northeastward. But I'm thinking that later tonight and early tomorrow, we'll be underneath a comma head here in North Georgia."

"What?" Hemphill asked, clearly puzzled.

"Comma-head cloud. It's a feature that, on satellite imagery, looks like a big ol' comma. It occurs near the upper-level storm center where the air can be very unstable and the precipitation quite heavy. Sometimes you get 'thunder snow' in a comma head."

"So what you're telling me," Hemphill said, "is that the storm center aloft lags behind the storm center at the surface?"

"You should have been an atmospheric scientist," Al said. "Yes, you're right."

"And you said the snowfall will taper off later today and pick up again tonight?" Hemphill asked.

"The snow might even end for a while," Al answered. "Often there's what we call a 'dry slot,' a tongue of dry air that develops between the warm frontal snow and the comma head."

"So you wanna summarize the sequence of events you foresee for Atlanta?" Tom asked.

Al rubbed his chin and cleared his throat before answering. "I think we'll see the snow taper off this afternoon, maybe just to occasional light stuff, then pick up again late tonight or early tomorrow morning."

"Amounts?" Tom said. This had always been the thorny issue between him and Al.

"Well, we've already got six or seven inches on the ground, so probably another four or five before it peters out this afternoon."

"And after that?"

"Wham, bam, thank you, ma'am with the comma head."

Hemphill typed rapidly on his iPad.

Tom touched him on the arm. "You don't need to quote that verbatim," he suggested.

"So how much wham-bam?" Hemphill asked, a slight smile on his lips.

"Probably another eight to ten inches."

Hemphill whistled softly.

"And don't forget the winds," Al said. "The worst is yet to come with the storm still deepening."

"Drifts?" Hemphill asked.

"Big time," Al answered.

"How big?"

"You don't need to quote me directly on this, either. But how about, 'Ass-hole deep to a giraffe'?"

Tom rolled his eyes. "He isn't one of us," he said, inclining his head toward Al.

Hemphill laughed. "So noted."

"Let me put it this way then," Al responded. "A lot of folks in Atlanta will get up tomorrow morning and won't be able to see out their sliding glass doors onto their decks."

Near Lavonia, Georgia
Thursday Midday, December 29

"WE CAN'T HAVE non-emergency vehicles out here on the interstate hindering snow removal crews during a storm," the trooper said.

To J.C. the statement seemed disingenuous. "I haven't seen a plow—"

The officer held his forefinger to his lips. "Let me do the talking, sir."

J.C. nodded.

"Maybe we can help each other out."

"Sir?"

"The transmission on my cruiser seized up. I'm stuck. I radioed for help, but every single one of our troopers is on a call right now—accidents galore on secondary roads—and it might be hours before a tow truck could be dispatched." The officer's eyes flickered, and he issued a barely audible gasp.

"You okay, sir?"

"Fine. Just cold from waiting out here. Look, here's the deal. You give me a lift back to post headquarters in Toccoa, and we'll call it even."

"Call it even?"

"You drop me off, then go your way . . . just not on the interstate."

"No ticket?"

"No citation, no warning. Just you being a helpful citizen. How about it?"

"How far is Toccoa?"

"About ten miles north on Route 17—maybe twenty-five, thirty minutes in this weather."

J.C. pondered the trooper's offer, though there really wasn't much to consider. It was, in fact, a no-brainer. He'd been caught driving illegally on the interstate but had just been thrown a lifeline—strange but welcomed. "Let's go," he said.

"Good. I appreciate your help. Hold on a second."

The officer trudged to the cruiser, opened the back door, and pulled out what looked like an aluminum attaché case. He returned to the SUV and yanked open the passenger-side door. A mini-snowslide cascaded from his hat as he lowered himself, gingerly it seemed, onto the seat beside J.C.

"Oops," he said. He rolled slightly to one side and reached underneath himself. He pulled out the thermos of coffee J.C. had placed on the seat before leaving Atlanta.

"Fuel for the trip?" the trooper asked.

"Hot coffee."

The cop set the thermos in the floor well and tossed the attaché case into the rear of the G-Wagen. He appeared to do a double take, then suppressed a chuckle. "You've got a teddy bear riding shotgun?"

J.C. shrugged. "Never know when you might run into a bad guy."

The officer flashed J.C. an easy smile. "No, you never know."

"Don't you need to lock up the cruiser or anything?" J.C. asked.

"Like who's gonna bother it in the middle of a snowstorm?" The trooper removed his hat and set it on the dash. "Just pull straight ahead through the weigh station back onto the interstate." He leaned his head against the headrest and closed his eyes.

"Where do I exit?"

"About a mile up the road," the trooper said without opening his eyes.

J.C. eased the G-Wagen forward through the storm, the snow almost blinding now, hurtling through the air parallel to the ground. He passed the cruiser, then the car parked in front of it. He glanced at it as he went by.

"Hey," he said, "what happened to that car? It looks like its back window is blown out."

"It's a derelict," the officer said. "Been there for some time."

What? You just let a car sit abandoned on an entrance ramp to a weigh station?

Chapter Fourteen

Trooper McCracken

On the road to Toccoa, Georgia
Thursday midday, December 29

THE G-WAGEN lost traction, but only briefly, coming up the un-plowed exit ramp from I-85 to State Route 17, the road to Toccoa. J.C. turned left on 17 and crawled northward, maintaining a steady speed of about thirty miles per hour. Occasionally, a vehicle, an SUV or pickup, passed him going the opposite direction.

The shoulder of the highway had disappeared beneath an ever-thickening quilt of snow, but J.C. managed to follow old tracks, filling with snow but still vaguely discernible, in the northbound lane. The surrounding countryside, dichromatic and indistinct in fuzzy tones of gray and white, appeared to be gently rolling farmland. The Deep South, yes, but now encrusted in a frozen mantle it could have passed for a bleak winter landscape in New England or the Upper Midwest.

"How much farther?" J.C. asked, glancing at his semi-slumbering passenger.

"Just keep going." The trooper didn't bother to open his eyes.

Not much of a conversationalist.

J.C. tried to spot a road sign with the mileage to Toccoa on it, but most of the signs were plastered with snow and unreadable. He gripped the steering wheel and plowed on, an achy numbness working its way across his shoulders—manifest tension from driving on snow-packed roads.

He decided to try again to initiate a conversation with the patrol-man. "I'm Jonathan Riggins, Officer." But he felt foolish as soon as the words came out of his mouth. The cop, of course, already knew that.

"Trooper. I'm a trooper, not an officer." The man opened his eyes. "Trooper McCracken. I appreciate your help, Mr. Riggins." He checked his wristwatch and peered into the storm, perhaps trying to spot a familiar landmark. He shook his head. "Hard to tell where we are. But I'm guessing maybe another twenty minutes."

He shifted in his seat, a slight movement, and grunted in apparent discomfort. "Been a tough morning. You know, with the cruiser crapping out and all." He surveyed the interior of the G-Wagen. "Nice wheels. New?"

"A loaner." *How do I explain that?* "Mine's in the shop for a few days. The dealership thought I should have something that would get me through the snow."

McCracken eased himself into a more upright position. "Well, it does a good job. Maybe the state patrol should invest in a few of these things."

Hardly in the state's budget, J.C. thought, but didn't verbalize it. He glanced at McCracken. The man certainly didn't appear to be the archetype of a state trooper. Sporting shoulder-length hair, thick eyebrows, and a prominent forehead, he had an almost Neanderthal look. Yet his voice belied that. He spoke without an accent and came across as educated and assured. At least those characteristics would seem to fit the profile of what the state might like in a patrolman.

J.C. attempted to come to grips with why the trooper had been at the weigh station in the storm. It just seemed so strange, but no ready answer came to mind. He gave up trying to analyze the situation and instead focused on driving, in and of itself a demanding challenge.

They rode in silence for several minutes, then, in the middle distance, through the thin, dim light of the falling and drifting snow, flashing blue lights loomed—a Georgia State Patrol vehicle approaching from the north.

"Look," J.C. said, nodding his head at the windshield. "You want to flag 'em down?"

"No. Keep going." McCracken reached inside his parka as if to retrieve something, but didn't bring his hand back out. "They're on a call. Besides, we're almost to the post."

Less than a minute later, a second police car, SHERIFF STEPHENS COUNTY emblazoned on its side, raced by, heading south.

"Busy morning," J.C. said. He glanced at his passenger.

"Lotta accidents." McCracken twisted in his seat to watch the sheriff's car disappear into the falling snow.

J.C. reached an intersection where a divided highway T'd into Route 17 from the left.

"Take a left here," McCracken said.

J.C. looked at him.

"It's the Toccoa Bypass."

"I thought the post was *in* Toccoa."

"It is. On the west side of town. This is a shortcut." McCracken's right hand remained inside his parka.

A ripple of unease shot through J.C. Things weren't fitting together. A state trooper in distress with no help from his compatriots, a guy who instead calls on a civilian for assistance, and an abandoned car sitting on a ramp of a commercial weigh station. Surely there'd been ample time to move it before the snowstorm hit.

Another thought sprang into J.C.'s head. *Why hadn't the trooper radioed that he was returning to the post with the help of a Good Samaritan? Something he could have done either from the cruiser or by using one of those ubiquitous shoulder mics.* Despite the warmth from the G-Wagen's heater blasting through the vehicle, a cold sweat seeped over J.C.'s skin.

J.C. fumbled for his cell phone.

"What are you doing?" McCracken asked, an icy edge to his words.

J.C. sucked in a lungful of air and steadied his voice. "Thought I'd call 911 and let them know I'm bringing a state trooper into Toccoa."

"That's not a good idea." The phrase came out hard and biting, as though from a teacher disciplining an unruly child.

J.C. paused with his thumb hovering over the keys. He looked at McCracken—if that's what his name really was—and saw something dark in the man's eyes, not exactly evil, but certainly foreboding. He placed the phone on the center console.

"Good," McCracken said. "I know you're just trying to be helpful, Mr. Riggins, but what I said earlier still applies. The guys are tied up with emergency calls. Real emergencies. We don't need to clutter the switchboard with Dudley Do-Good stuff. Okay?"

J.C. nodded. "Well, we must be almost there anyway."

"Yeah, we're almost there." McCracken peered out the windshield into the flannel morning streaked with thick, wind-whipped snow. "You handle this stuff like a pro. Where'd you grow up? Snow country, I'll bet."

"New England. Massachusetts." J.C. paused, suddenly not wanting to engage his passenger in conversation. On the other hand, he decided it might be better to find out as much as he could about him. Whoever he was. "And you?"

"Eastern Kentucky, the coal fields. I was born in a town called

Louisa." He winced, an almost imperceptible reaction, as he wriggled himself into a more upright position on the seat. "Where over thirty percent of the population lives below the poverty line."

"Good reason to leave. When did you join the state patrol?" *If you did.*

"A few years ago."

Vague.

The G-Wagen shook as a blast of wind smacked it broadside. Snow swirled around the SUV, encasing it in a bleak embrace. For a moment, it was as if nothing else existed save for the two men, the vehicle, and the storm. J.C. imagined them trapped in their own little snow globe universe. He glanced at the speedometer. Around twenty miles per hour. Barely moving.

"So you left Kentucky and came to Georgia?"

"Not directly. I spent a couple of years in college at Appalachian State. But . . . oh, I don't know." He voice trailed off.

"But what?" J.C. wanted to keep McCracken talking. It didn't matter if the guy was spouting bullshit. All he wanted to do was establish a connection with him, just in case.

"I never felt I fit in there. Even though I aced most of my courses, I always sensed I was viewed as being lower caste, maybe because of where I came from. Besides that, I didn't know what I wanted to be, what I wanted to do with my life. So eventually, I just bailed out and bummed around for about a year. Florida. Mississippi. Texas. Got into some minor trouble. Then decided to clean up my act. That's when I put in an application with the state patrol."

"Paid off, huh?" J.C. noticed that McCracken still hadn't removed his hand from inside his parka.

"Yeah, I guess."

I guess?

J.C. checked the time. They'd been driving for about fifteen minutes. He calculated they must have traveled five miles. Surely they'd reached the western edge of Toccoa. It wasn't exactly a sprawling metropolis.

"It must be about time to turn," he said.

McCracken rocked forward in his seat. "Jesus," he said, the word threaded with pain.

"What?"

"I'm hurt."

He pulled his hand from his parka, smearing blood across the garment as he did.

"Oh, man. Oh, man. You need a doctor. How far are we from a hospital?"

"No. No hospital. Keep driving."

"Keep driving? What the hell do you mean? Aren't we going to Toccoa?" Even before J.C. asked the question, he knew the answer. Knew his passenger wasn't a cop. Knew they weren't going to Toccoa. He'd harbored the suspicion earlier, but didn't want to nurture it. Lightheadedness swarmed over him; fear, he supposed. He tipped his head down to keep from fainting, but just as abruptly as the feeling had surged through him, it passed—or maybe he willed it to pass. He snapped his head up and forced himself to focus on his dilemma, to analyze where he stood.

He had a wounded man as a passenger. The guy wasn't in good shape. He, J.C., remained in control of the situation. He had the vehicle. He would determine where they went. He would not be deterred from his broader mission, to reach Durham, North Carolina, for his son's sake if nothing else.

What looked to be a major intersection loomed out of the swirling snow. J.C. slowed the G-Wagen and prepared to turn right, the direction in which Toccoa should lie.

"What are you doing?" McCracken asked, his words razor-edged with an undertone of malice.

"Going to Toccoa," J.C. answered, new resolve in his voice. He ignored McCracken's, or whoever he was, implicit threat.

"No. You're not."

McCracken reached beneath his parka with his bloody right hand. He withdrew it, this time holding a black, large-caliber automatic pistol. Something a police officer would carry. Something that put McCracken, not J.C., in control.

Chapter Fifteen

Intimidation

The Natural Environment Television Network
Thursday midday, December 29

SOPHIE STROLLED into the forecast center shortly after noon and seated herself at an empty work space next to Tom. Tom, busy examining the latest numerical model outputs, didn't acknowledge her.

She sat in silence for a minute, then said, her voice low, "I suppose you've got your knickers in a twist about the other day in my office?"

"I don't wear knickers."

"It's a metaphor."

"Yes, Sophie, I know."

She leaned closer to him, not violating any amorphous personal boundaries, but near enough that he caught the freshness of her breath. Her demeanor exuded a coolness that seemed to match the weather. "It wasn't an accident," she said.

He nodded.

"But it won't happen again, at least at work."

He nodded once more, at a loss for an intelligent response. He always felt as if he were tiptoeing along a tightrope whenever he dealt with Sophie. For the moment, he decided to let her take the lead and march off in whatever direction she wished.

"So here's what I'm wondering," Sophie said, "now that our focus has returned to business: Why can't you just admit, at least in this instance, I was right?" She leaned back, gestured at the window, and sang softly: "Let it snow, let it snow, let it snow." She ended her little serenade with a smile.

Tom grimaced, at least inwardly. He forced himself to analyze the situation—what had taken place over the last week—and decided it might be wise to at least partially capitulate. "In this particular situation," he said, choosing his words carefully, "your decision to headline the threat of a major snowstorm was correct. I salute you for that."

"But?" she said. "I know there's a 'but' coming."

He sucked in a silent breath. "But given similar circumstances in the future, I'd stand by my 'conservative' guns."

"Again." She made a declarative statement sound like an interrogative.

"I think we got lucky on this storm. In the long run, and admittedly it might be quite a long run, given we have so few winter storm threats here, my approach would prove the wisest."

Sophie clenched her lips, the pipe-sucking expression Tom had seen so often. He knew he'd best be ready to duck and cover.

"Jesus, you're hardheaded," she said. Her words rang with contemptuousness.

"And you're not?" he snapped.

"I deal with the reality of situations."

"So do I."

"Not *my* reality, you don't."

He massaged his temples with his thumb and forefinger. As often in the past, their conversation had deteriorated into open hostility. His partial concession obviously hadn't been enough for his boss. Without thinking, a gut reaction, he allowed his lips to form the word "bitch," though he checked himself from verbalizing it.

Sophie, a red tide of anger rising in her face, sprang from her chair. "That, my friend, is how you lose your job."

"What the hell do you mean?" He stood to face her.

"You think I can't read lips?" she shouted.

"What you can't read is my mind." He paused a beat. "I didn't *say* anything."

She attempted to stare him down, but he refused to kowtow to her icy gaze. After several moments she wheeled and stalked from the room.

Tom felt a hand on his shoulder. Al stood by his side, shaking his head. "Well, they say faint heart never won fair lady, but you may have gone overboard there."

Tom pulled away from Al. "Fair lady? Bullshit. And what in the hell makes you think I'm trying to win anything?"

"I'm old, junior, not senile or unobservant. Just because the last erection I had was building a treehouse for my grandson doesn't mean I can't sense sexual chemistry."

"For God's sake, Al, will you drop it," Tom said, raising his voice.

"Once and for all."

Hemphill appeared. "Is there a subtext I'm missing here?"

"No," Tom growled.

Al grinned, an elderly elf. "Yes, but not one you'd be wise to write about."

Northeast Georgia
Thursday midday, December 29

J.C., HIS HEART thumping like a hydraulic jackhammer, stared at the pistol held by his passenger.

"Best keep your eyes on the road," McCracken said.

J.C. flicked the steering wheel to the left as the G-Wagen veered off-course, chewing through thick snow along the right edge of the road. The "edge" seemed only nominal, buried as it was under a mantle of solid white.

J.C., his chest heaving, drew in a series of deep breaths. He found himself unable to think, unable to articulate some sort of response to the abrupt shift in his situation. He flinched when his cell phone rang. He glanced at the caller I. D. Ginny. He'd forgotten he'd promised to call her once an hour.

"It's my wife," he said.

McCracken nodded. "Play it straight." He rested the gun in his lap.

J.C. answered the call. "Hi, honey. I'm sorry. I know I said I'd call, but once I got going I just got totally focused on pushing through the storm. I apologize. *Mea culpa.*"

"But you're okay? You had me worried." A tone of admonishment colored her words.

"I'm fine. I'm somewhere near . . . I'm almost to the South Carolina border."

McCracken bobbed his head in approval.

"The roads are bad?" Ginny asked.

"Very bad. I'm not even supposed to be out here."

"But you're moving?"

"Slowly."

"Okay. Good. But please, please, please stay in touch. I know it's tough out there, but I'm stressed, too."

If only you knew. "I'll call, Ginny, but it might be another couple of hours before I can get back to you. Everything's fine. Love you. Give my love to Cole, too."

They disconnected the call, and J.C. placed his cell back on the console.

"Who's Cole?" McCracken asked.

"My son."

"Nice to have a family."

"It is. Do you?"

"Let's not get too buddy-buddy, Mr. Riggins." McCracken waggled the pistol at the windshield. "Let's just press on. That's what would make me happiest at the moment. And you, too."

"Why me?"

"Let me put it another way. That's what will keep you alive."

Oh.

The snow-blown landscape grew indistinct and wavy, and J.C. sensed himself beginning to levitate or float, as though some sort of out-of-body experience were coming on. A push on his shoulder snapped him back to the moment, back to reality.

"Hey, hey, hey. I didn't mean to cause you to lose it, buddy." McCracken tucked the gun back inside his parka and raised his hands. "Look, ma. No Glock."

The blood pumped back into J.C.'s head, and he settled down, refocused. "Who are you? Really? And where are we going?"

"McCracken's my real name, but I'm not a cop."

Duh.

J.C. held a steady pace, albeit a plodding one, through the storm. The road had grown virtually indistinguishable from the surrounding landscape. The only thing that marked the highway now was a pair of old tire tracks in the outside lane, rapidly disappearing beneath the blowing and drifting snow.

"Where are we headed?"

"I like that, Mr. Riggins, your use of the first person plural, *we*. You're on board then?"

"On board?"

"With the program."

"What program?"

"Jesus, is that all you can do, answer a question with a question?" He grunted softly and blinked.

J.C. looked over. "How bad?"

"I'll live."

J.C. recalled the abandoned car, the blown out back window. *Had there been a shootout?*

"You're shot?"

"Yes, I'm shot."

"You were in a gunfight with a cop?"

"Man, the questions just keep on comin'."

"Why shouldn't I have questions? I'm the one being carjacked here."

"Carjacked? You volunteered to help."

"Okay, I volunteered. My volunteerism has a limited tenure."

"Ya think?" McCracken's words rang with intimidation.

A plow, the first one J.C. had seen since leaving the interstate, approached from the north. He considered swerving in front of it, a desperate measure to end his predicament, but decided against it. It wouldn't be a wise move when he had no idea what lay beneath the snow in the median, when his passenger possessed a gun, and when the plow—even if the Mercedes could make it across the divide—might be unable to stop in time.

"Look, just tell me where we're going. I'll get you there, then be on my way. Not to try to one-up you, but I'm on the clock to get to where I'm going."

"A matter of life and death, no doubt?" Sarcasm.

"Yes, as a matter of fact."

"Try me."

J.C. did, telling him about Cole. The leukemia. The trips to MD Anderson. The possibility of a stem cell transplant. His screw-up with the proposal. His determination to get the document to Durham.

After he'd finished, McCracken stared at him, as if trying to evaluate the veracity of the narrative. "Assuming you aren't jerking me around, that's a gut-wrenching story."

"It's true," J.C. mumbled.

"We all live pretty fucked-up lives, don't we?"

"Do we? So what's your story?" J.C. decided to continue trying to develop a rapport with McCracken. After all, he was the guy with the firepower, the guy in control.

"You really wanna know?"

"Sure. I mean, it's either that or listen to Rush Limbaugh."

"Is that a joke? I mean, I like Rush." He looked out the window, perhaps trying to gauge where they were. "Just keep driving. Forget the conversation."

"And if I don't?" J.C. said, feeling suddenly emboldened for no rational reason.

"Don't what?" The words came out accompanied by a slight grunt of discomfort.

"Don't keep driving. Just stop the vehicle."

McCracken pulled out the Glock again. "Wanna try it?"

J.C. swallowed hard and slowed the G-Wagen. Despite every conscious thought in his head telling him not to, there remained one little voice saying, *Call this guy's bluff.*

McCracken smiled, a wolfish grin, lifted the gun, pointed it toward the back seat, and pulled the trigger.

An explosive percussion deadened J.C.'s hearing. A fog of cloth, cotton and dust swirled through the vehicle's interior.

J.C. swiveled his head and looked at the rear seat. "Jesus! You shot Teddy!"

McCracken shifted his aim, pointed the Glock at J.C.

Chapter Sixteen

Cave Man

**Northeast Georgia
Thursday afternoon, December 29**

TEDDY, HIS HEAD slumped forward, seemed to be gazing with his single button-eye at his now half-missing chest and wondering what had happened.

McCracken prodded J.C. on the shoulder with the pistol. "Get my point?"

In response, J.C. increased his speed slightly and kept the G-Wagen moving.

"Good," McCracken said. "Ya know, stuffed animals are a hell of a lot less messy than humans. Can you just imagine the blood splatter you would have—"

"I get your point," J.C. snapped. He gripped the steering wheel with a fierceness born of fear.

"Anyhow," McCracken continued, "sorry about your buddy Teddy—"

"He's my son's buddy. Cole sent him along as a guardian angel."

"Hmmm." McCracken made a show of studying Teddy, at least what was left of him. "Kinda fucked up that job, didn't he?"

"Like I said, you made your point, Mr. McCracken."

"You can call me Butch." He moved the gun back to his lap. "I'm 'Cave Man' to my friends, but we can keep it at Butch."

J.C. peered straight ahead, into the flying snow, a blurry world of gray-white streakiness. He could see only a matter of yards down the road; he may as well have been on the Mass Pike as on a road in rural Georgia. Yet here he was, somewhere in the Deep South, mushing through a blizzard with a trigger-happy, wounded nutcase nicknamed Cave Man, who actually bore some resemblance to a Neanderthal.

"What do you want from me?" J.C. asked, forcing his voice not to quaver.

"Compliance."

"Could you be more specific?"

McCracken drew a long, slow breath and stared out into the storm. "I want just what you're doing. Driving me to safety."

"Where? How far? Look, the story I told you wasn't bullshit. I have to get to Durham. If you don't believe me, the document I have to deliver is in boxes in the back." He inclined his head toward the rear of the SUV. "You're welcome to take a look at it."

"It's not that I doubt you, Mr. Riggins. It's that I just don't care. Your priorities aren't mine. We're going where I want to go. What happens after that . . . we'll see."

We'll see? J.C.'s heart raced. His chest tightened. *We'll see?* Not exactly reassuring words from a guy with a gun who may have shot a Georgia State Trooper. If that *was* the case, there was no way McCracken was just going to let him go, even if he delivered McCracken to wherever he was headed.

J.C. hadn't wanted to admit it earlier, but realized now how dire his situation had become, morphing into something he might not survive. Images of Cole and Ginny flashed through his mind. *Focus on them. Let them be my reason for being, my reason for acting.* He willed himself out of the equation, removed his self-centered fear, and replaced it with concern for his family.

He concentrated on steadying his breathing. After several moments, his heart rate settled, and his chest muscles relaxed. He'd do what he had to. Whatever it took to get him and the proposal to Durham. For Cole. For Ginny. That seemed a purpose worth living for. A purpose worth dying for, too. Damn McCracken. Damn the blizzard.

The Natural Environment Television Network
Late Thursday afternoon, December 29

TOM, AL, HEMPHILL, and a couple of other employees gathered in front of a TV monitor in the forecast center as a special news bulletin came on.

A local reporter, a middle-aged veteran whom Tom had seen before, but whose name escaped him, stood in the storm on the shoulder of an interstate highway. Behind him, a long line of eighteen-wheelers idled in the right-hand lane, their exhaust streams flattening in the wind, mixing with the blinding snow.

"I'm standing on the edge of I-285 north on the east side of Atlanta," the reporter said, using one hand to hold his hat in place against the wind. "As you can see, traffic is basically stopped. Interstate truckers, along with a few cars, have been unable to move because of the closures of I-75 and I-85 north out of Atlanta. All of the vehicles you see stuck here came into the city from the south on I-75 or-85, or from the west or east on I-20. Now they're unable to continue their journeys north."

The camera panned to a shot of a plow pushing through the snow in the lane adjacent to the stymied vehicles, mostly semis and tankers.

"As you can see," the reporter continued, "the DOT is working hard in an attempt to keep at least one lane of I-285 passable for emergency vehicles. Which, by the way, is the only traffic allowed out here now.

"There is mounting concern for the drivers of these stalled vehicles, and the governor is considering activating the National Guard in an effort to ferry those trapped to nearby motels or shelters."

The camera zoomed in on the reporter. "But the highways," he said, "aren't the only places where we have travelers in trouble. Let's go to Willie Edgerton at Hartsfield-Jackson Airport."

The shot switched to a reporter standing outside the South Terminal of the airport.

"Thanks, Ron," Willie said. "Yes, there's trouble at the airport, too, where all arrivals and departures, over twenty-five hundred of them, have been canceled today. Needless to say, with this being the busiest airport in the world in terms of travelers, the cancellations have disrupted air traffic globally. And with the shutdown expected to continue into tomorrow, a mess that could take a week or two to untangle will grow worse.

"Normally during the holiday season, over a quarter of a million passengers stream through Hartsfield-Jackson daily. Today, the usually bustling ramps give the airport, at least from the outside, the appearance of a snow-covered ghost town somewhere in Siberia." Willie smiled, a set of alabaster teeth showing against a flawless ebony complexion.

"Despite all the advance warnings, however," Willie went on, "there are people—travelers—stuck here. Airport officials estimate about two thousand folks are going to be long-term, and probably somewhat unhappy, guests of Hartfield-Jackson for at least another day if not longer.

"My colleague Ron mentioned a few moments ago that the governor is considering activating certain elements of the National Guard. Another reason that contingency is being evaluated is to provide a means to get some of the necessities of life—food, water, cots, blankets—to those trapped at the airport.

"In the meantime, blizzard-like conditions are expected to persist—"

"Arrghh," Al shouted, drowning out Willie the reporter. "He didn't really say that, did he?"

One of the forecasters muted the TV.

"Didn't say what?" Hemphill asked.

"Blizzard-like," Al answered. The words came out raspy, like a semi-snort. A drop of something squirted from his nose; he wiped it with the back of his hand.

"What's wrong with blizzard-like?" Hemphill said. He held his iPad at the ready.

"There is no such thing."

"What do you mean?"

Tom inserted himself into the conversation. "Blizzard, at least in the meteorological world, has a strict definition. So you either have blizzard conditions or you don't. 'Near-blizzard' is fine, but phrases like 'blizzard-like' or 'blizzardy' are crap. They could mean anything."

"To a weather guy," Al said, "hearing 'blizzard-like' is akin to listening to fingernails screeching across a blackboard or greenboard or whatever they use these days."

"So a blizzard technically is what?" Hemphill asked.

"I don't recall the exact wording," Al responded, "but a true blizzard requires winds of thirty-five miles per hour or more with falling or blowing snow reducing visibilities to a quarter-mile or less for at least three hours."

Hemphill typed on his iPad. "So the amount of snowfall has nothing to do with whether a storm is a blizzard or not?"

"Strictly speaking, that's correct," Tom said. "You can have blizzard conditions, what most folks would call a 'ground blizzard,' without any snowfall at all. As long as the winds are howling and the visibility is shot to hell, it's a blizzard."

"Temperatures don't have any bearing?"

"They used to, but no longer. Way back when—you can ask Al *when*—there used to be criteria for a 'severe blizzard' that included temperatures of ten degrees or lower."

"*Don't* ask me when," Al said. "Half the time I can't even remember whether I'm coming or going." He squinted his eyes in an apparent thoughtful pose. "No, strike that. I haven't come in years, and these days, I seem to be *going* all the time."

"You poor man," Sophie said. She had appeared silently at the edge of the group.

Al's face turned the color of an inflamed beet. "Sorry, I thought—"

"You were among men?" Sophie said. "That's all right. Just consider me one of the guys." She gave Tom a pointed look, as if to say, *I know* you *don't.*

Tom smiled at her. His earlier ire had semi-evaporated but still hovered. *You ain't one of the guys.* He meant it on several levels.

"I just came by for a last check before I head home," Sophie said. She turned to Al, addressing, Tom noted, a consultant and ignoring him, the company's chief of meteorology.

"Are we still looking for the snow to taper off shortly, then crank up again in earnest late tonight or early tomorrow?" she asked.

Al, his countenance still the shade of a ripe persimmon, nodded. "We are."

"Good. Then I should be able to make it home before the nastiness returns. Can't guarantee I'll get back here in the morning, though." She looked again at Tom.

Tom maintained a stone-faced expression. *Given the mess the roads are in, why would you even* consider *driving?* But this was Sophie. Not a run-of-the-mill mortal.

He pictured her Lexus buried up to its windows in a deep drift on Cobb Parkway. He smiled a goodbye to her as she walked out the door.

Chapter Seventeen

Revelations

Northeast Georgia
Late Thursday afternoon, December 29

J.C. DECIDED TO attempt to reengage McCracken—Butch, Cave Man, whatever—in conversation. To try to run from or overpower a guy brandishing a Glock would be foolhardy. He knew he still needed some sort of connection with McCracken. It might save his, J.C.'s, life.

"So, the story you told me earlier," J.C. said, "about Kentucky, Appalachian State, kicking around after you left school, total fabrication?"

McCracken looked at him through lidded eyes and seemed to wince. "No."

"But you never joined the Georgia State Patrol?"

"No." McCracken turned his head and stared out the windshield, gazing into the whirling snowfall, seeming to search for something.

An overhead highway sign loomed out of the storm.

"There," McCracken said.

The sign, half-plastered with snow, indicated, as near as J.C. could discern, the towns of Clarksville and Clayton to the right. Highway 441. J.C. knew it. He and Ginny had traveled it several times, heading to a pleasant little boutiquey town in the North Carolina mountains, Highlands.

"Take a right here," McCracken said, "then another right in a few hundred yards."

The G-Wagen churned through the snow, now probably eight or ten inches deep, without missing a beat, and J.C. made the consecutive turns onto 441 north. The road, another divided four-lane route, looked to have one lane in each direction that had been plowed within the last couple of hours. But already, fresh snow coated whatever had been cleared. In some spots, deepening drifts made even the plowed lanes difficult to navigate. Traffic remained sparse to non-existent with only an occasional pickup or van easing through the storm.

"If you want some coffee, Butch, there's some in the thermos there." J.C. pointed at the foot well where McCracken sat. "And there are some sandwiches my wife made in back."

"Maybe some coffee." McCracken retrieved the thermos and awkwardly unscrewed the top with his left hand. He kept his right inside his parka, presumably on the Glock. Instead of trying to pour the coffee into the thermos's cup, he drank directly from the bottle. The aroma of vanilla-hazelnut filled the SUV.

"Look, we need to pull over someplace so I can call Ginny, my wife," J.C. said. "It's been over an hour since we talked. If I don't call, she'll worry that something's wrong."

"Something *is* wrong." McCracken chortled and half-choked as he took another swig from the thermos.

"I still need to call her."

"Sure. You know the ground rules. No stupid shit. Right?"

"I'll play by the rules."

"I'll bet all the teachers loved you."

J.C. pulled the Mercedes onto the shoulder of the highway and let the engine idle. Occasional gusts of wind rocked the vehicle as windwhipped snow swirled around it in a disorienting jitterbug.

Ginny answered J.C.'s call almost immediately. "Are you okay?" Apprehension and concern resonated in her voice like a plucked violin string.

"I'm fine, honey. I'm making good time."

"Where are you?"

In trouble. He looked around, searching for the lie. "On I-85 in South Carolina."

"They say the snow might let up this evening."

"That's good."

"But I don't know if that means in the Carolinas, too."

That's okay. I'm not in the Carolinas. "So it's about over in Atlanta?"

Ginny paused. "N-o-o-o." She drew the word out. "It's supposed to get worse tomorrow."

He gripped his phone with the fierceness of a vise. What Ginny was telling him, without really knowing it, was that he'd better be out of here—wherever *here* ended up being—tonight. Of course, worrying about the time frame of his exodus might be academic. What he probably ought to be centered on was getting out of here, period.

McCracken leaned close to J.C. "You're about to strangle your cell," he whispered.

J.C. nodded and relaxed his grasp. "Okay then. Be safe, Ginny. Just hunker down in the house tomorrow. I'll keep calling."

"Wait," she said. "Where are you planning on staying tonight?"

I don't have a clue. "I may just press on, especially if the snow lets up. Love you, honey. I'll call again. Soon." He gave McCracken a pointed glance.

"Love you, too, hon'."

After they hung up, McCracken asked, "What did your wife say that triggered the death grip on your phone? Your knuckles turned white."

The question caught J.C. unprepared. "What? Oh, that. She heard . . . she told me that . . . Cole was having a bad day. He . . . he probably misses me. Yeah, that."

McCracken studied J.C.'s face. He seemed to contemplate the answer, then said, "Come on, back on the road."

J.C. nosed the Mercedes back onto 441, into the teeth of the storm.

"Anyhow," J.C. said, still attempting to forge a rapport with McCracken, "after you left school and beat around for a while, what then? Where did you end up?"

McCracken leaned back against the headrest. "Here," he said, his voice strained. "In the middle of a blizzard with a guy driving a Mercedes G-Wagen."

"Before that."

"Not sure you want to know."

"Will it make a difference one way or the other?"

"Questions, questions."

"You know a hell of a lot more about me than I know about you."

McCracken remained silent for some time, staring into the flannel bleakness of the fading afternoon. He shifted in his seat and grunted softly in apparent discomfort. "Like you," he said, "I've managed to step on my schlong." He paused. "Well, maybe not like you. You've never been arrested, have you?"

J.C. let the question pass.

"I've been picked up half a dozen times," McCracken said. "Misdemeanors."

"Misdemeanors?" J.C. said. "That's how you got shot, committing a misdemeanor?"

"I guess I took my game to the next level."

"What happened?"

McCracken didn't answer. Instead, he leaned his head back and closed his eyes, letting J.C.'s question hang in abeyance. Finally he said, "Traffic stop." He opened his eyes and looked straight ahead.

"You were speeding?"

"In a snowstorm? Not hardly."

"What then?"

"The cop was interested in the car I was driving."

"Stolen?"

"I like to think of it as 'requisitioned.'"

"For?" J.C. prompted.

"A group I work with."

"What group might that be?"

"They're called the Appalachian Devils."

Great. Probably not a Doctors-Without-Borders type of organization. "Care to elaborate?"

"It's a motorcycle club."

"That needed a car?" J.C. said, his tone flat.

"Tough to get around in the snow on a bike."

J.C. held the G-Wagen at a steady, sure-footed speed, continuing to guide it through the accumulating snow. He squinted into the gloaming. It seemed the snowfall had begun to slacken, though he had to admit, it could be just wishful thinking.

"So," J.C. continued, "you took exception to being pulled over?"

"It wasn't convenient for me."

"I'll bet."

"Like you, I was carrying something that needed to be delivered." He inclined his head toward the rear seat, toward the attaché case.

"Something other than a business proposal, I'd guess."

McCracken didn't respond.

J.C. decided to cut to the chase. "What happened to the trooper who shot you?"

"He's taking a nap."

"Dead?" *Might as well be blunt.* J.C. swallowed, fighting through a constriction in his throat. His respiration turned short and shallow.

McCracken shrugged. "I'm here. The cop isn't."

J.C.'s stomach roiled. He realized, assuming he had a cop killer as a passenger, his chances of surviving the day were damn near close to zero. McCracken wasn't just going to let him go after he got to wherever it was they were headed.

J.C. slowed the SUV as it pushed over packed snow and ice on a bridge crossing Tallulah Falls Lake just south of the visitor's center for Tallulah Gorge. He glanced at McCracken who remained impassive. At the moment, he looked non-threatening. But J.C. knew once McCracken no longer needed his assistance—no longer needed transportation—he, J.C., would be expendable.

An almost palpable thrumming surged through J.C.'s head as he analyzed his situation. He knew he'd have to make a move soon to save himself. He had to assume they weren't going to remain on 441, a main road, much longer. Although given the sparse traffic on the highway due to the storm, the term "main" didn't really apply.

He tried to remember if there were any towns of consequence coming up. Only one came to mind, Clayton. He guessed—and that's all it was, a guess—they were perhaps ten miles from Clayton. *Would they stay on 441 until they reached it? Maybe not.*

He had to act now. *But how? With what?* A Glock can do a lot of damage to a man.

Chapter Eighteen

Twilight

The Natural Environment Television Network
Late Thursday afternoon, December 29

PULLING ON HIS gloves, Tom stood just inside the main entrance of NE-TV. He gazed into the slate twilight. A furious wind continued to hurl the snow into acrobatic swirls and curls, but the snowfall rate itself had dwindled. Now, only squadrons of tiny crystalline flakes flew through the air. But the damage had been done. A heavy blanket of white, perhaps eight or ten inches thick, cloaked the ground. In spots, drifts several feet deep accentuated the polar look of the landscape.

The roads appeared devoid of traffic, as if over five and a half million people had gone into hibernation. On an interstate in the middle distance, a line of snow-covered semis, like wooly mammoths from the Ice Age, hunkered silently on the shoulder, their journeys at a temporary end. Occasionally, blue or red lights strobed off the low-hanging overcast as emergency vehicles plied their trade. Slowly. Carefully.

Tom pulled his parka tight around his neck and stepped into the storm. He wondered how long it would take to reach his condo. The slog into work, through ankle-deep snow, had taken fifteen minutes. He moved forward, kicking through snow now up to his shins, in drifts, over his thighs. It would take a hell of a lot longer than fifteen minutes to beat his way home.

He lowered his head into the wind and walked/slid through the parking lot toward where a sidewalk intersected the exit drive. *Used to intersect*, he corrected himself. The sidewalk had disappeared beneath the undulations of the snowscape.

Halfway down the drive, the snow up to his knees, he pulled up abruptly. Twenty yards ahead of him, a black Lexus LS460 sat at right angles to the drive, its rear end snugged deep into a drift. Sophie.

Tom broke into what he imagined might be the biggest shit-eating grin ever. *There is a God after all.*

He waited for a moment, wanting to see how Sophie would handle her predicament. He had a pretty good idea and was not disappointed. She gunned the engine, the rear tires buzzing against the ice and snow, clawing deeper into their icy prison, the rear of the Lexus sinking into the drift like the *Titanic* into the frigid depths of the iceberg-laden North Atlantic.

Tom moved to the car and rapped on the passenger-side window. The window slid down.

"Stuck?" he asked.

Sophie glared at him, her eyes narrowed to fiery slits.

"Well?" he said.

"Jesus, what's it look like? No, I'm sitting here having a bowel movement."

Tom lifted his head from the window and stared over the roof of the Lexus so she couldn't see him laugh.

"Go back into the building," Sophie commanded. "Tell the guard to call a tow truck or something."

Tom forced the smile from his face and bent to respond to Sophie. "You don't really think you're going to get somebody out here until tomorrow, do you?"

"Well, have the guard call a cab then."

"Sophie, for crying out loud, have you seen any vehicles at all on the street since you've been out here? Just one?"

Sophie ignored the question, or more to the point, the fact Tom wished to illuminate: The streets had become impassable.

"Have him call," she snapped. She seemed to think a cab with a plow attachment must be idling on hot standby somewhere, just waiting for her imperial summons.

"Call yourself," Tom said. "I'm heading home." He stepped back from the window and started down the drive again.

"Hey!" Sophie called. "What the hell am I supposed to do?"

"You're the boss. You figure it out. I'm not your indentured servant." He pushed on through the powdery snow.

Sophie attempted to open the Lexus' door, but the drift that imprisoned the car had blocked the door, too.

"Tom," she said, almost pleading. "I can't get out."

Tom stopped, cursed under his breath. *I'm such a friggin' dufus when it comes to Sophie.* He waded through the snow back to the car.

"I can't get out," she said again. Somehow, she managed a lost little girl look.

Tom folded his arms in front of him and pretended to study the situation. "Keep the engine on idle, the heater on high, and crack the window so you won't die of carbon monoxide poisoning, and you'll be fine."

"Tom—"

He began digging with his hands at the snow that blocked the door. "They probably have some cots set up in the building for folks who can't make it home tonight," he said as he worked.

"I'd like a hot shower," she muttered.

"You'll probably have to settle for a sponge bath."

"Isn't there a hotel or motel or something nearby? How far away is that Marriott Courtyard?"

"Too far to walk to in these conditions."

"You're really enjoying this, aren't you?" she said, her voice subdued. "Her Highness the Lyoness trapped in her car, up to her ass in a snowdrift."

"I'd be lying if I said I wasn't." He continued to claw at the snow. He found it difficult work with no shovel; his undershirt began to dampen with sweat; his chest heaved as he drew in cavernous breaths.

"Well, at least you aren't condescending about it," Sophie said. Then a bit louder: "Hey, you're a little out of shape, aren't you?"

"Thanks for pointing that out," he gasped. He stopped digging. "Try the door now."

She pushed. The door swung open. She stepped out into the snow, up to her knees. Tom extended his hand to her. She reached for it, but lost her balance and toppled forward, landing in a heap at Tom's feet. He pulled her up.

"Well, that was graceful," she said. She brushed the snow off her coat. The snowfall had ceased, but the wind continued to whip snow from the surface and twist it into tiny white tornadoes that whirled like dancing ghosts through the parking lot.

"Come on," Tom said. "I'll help you back to the building."

"Sponge bath?" Sophie grumbled and held her ground.

"Look, what do you want me to do?"

The eerie wail of a siren filled the dusk, an emergency vehicle slogging to a call. Or maybe a Valkyrie riding the wind.

Sophie stared at Tom, as though expecting him to answer his own question.

I'm not going there, Sophie. I'm not going to take the bait. Yes, I'm tempted, but—

"Your place is only a few blocks from here, isn't it?" she said. "Look, I just want a warm shower and soft place to sleep overnight. If you've got a couch, I'm fine with that. I'm not in the mood to play footsies, or anything else, tonight."

Tom expelled a long breath, the condensation from his exhalation stringing into the frigid air like gossamer smoke. "I've got an extra bedroom." He wondered if his voice reflected the exasperation he felt. "You can shove a dresser against the door."

She smiled. "I'm not worried about that, Tom. We may have our differences, and scream and shout at each other at times, and make snarky comments, but you've always been a gentleman, and I respect that. You've never come-on to me, and I respect that, too. Yeah, yeah, I know, I made a move on you, but let's kind of shove that off to the side for now. Just think of this as an overnight business trip, okay?"

"I wouldn't have it any other way." *Wow, how damn disingenuous can I be?* "Look, my place is a mess. We may have to dine on beer and ramen, but you're welcome—"

"It's gotta be better than shacking up in the corporate lunchroom."

"Follow me, then. I'll break trail. Careful, it's icy underneath the snow. This is gonna take a while."

Northeast Georgia
Late Thursday afternoon, December 29

WAVES OF BLOWING and drifting snow, like fugitives from an arctic steppe, continued to sift over the highway, but the snowfall had ended. J.C. recalled that Ginny had told him the snow had been expected to let up late in the day, then return in earnest tomorrow. Another reason for acting now, not later.

J.C. weighed his options, none of them good. A physical assault, while heroic, seemed foolhardy. He didn't have a weapon. McCracken had a pistol. In fact, J.C. concluded, he might have two. If the Glock had been taken from the trooper after the shoot-out, that meant McCracken probably had a gun of his own.

So, where does that leave me? Besides in deep shit? Maybe I can outwit him. Maybe.

J.C. tensed and glanced at his passenger.

"What?" McCracken said, irritation threading his voice.

"I need to phone my wife."

"Again? You just called—"

"I promised her once an hour, okay?"

"It hasn't been an hour since you last talked to her."

Think fast. Why so soon again? "She's taking Cole to a doctor's appointment in about twenty minutes."

"Kind of late in the day for that."

"It's the only time the doctor could squeeze him in. It's important Cole be monitored closely. You know, with his leukemia and all."

McCracken sat up straight and looked around. "Okay, there's a turnoff to a campground coming up on the right. Pull over and call, but make it quick." He waggled the Glock.

J.C. steered the Mercedes into the turnoff and stopped. He grabbed his phone and punched in Ginny's number.

When she answered, J.C. said, "Hi, honey. I just wanted to touch base with you before you took Cole to his doctor's appointment." He pressed the phone hard against his ear so McCracken couldn't hear Ginny's response.

"What? What doctor's appointment?"

"I know. Just be careful. The roads are awful." J.C. hoped McCracken didn't deduce that the roads in Atlanta were likely as bad as they were here, and that nobody was driving, or that everything, including doctors' offices, was probably shut down.

"What are you talking about?" Ginny said. "Cole doesn't have an appointment." Pause. "Are you okay?"

"Nope. Just getting ready to pull in for the night. Wishing I was back in Atlanta and sitting down to another one of your prime rib dinners. You know, like the one we had just before Christmas."

"That was . . . a . . . pork roast. What in the hell is going on, hon'? Something's wrong."

"Yes, that's true. Look, I gotta get going. I'll call again after you get back with Cole. Love ya, Gin. Bye." She hated being called Gin; he never used that name.

"No, wait. Tell me what—"

He removed the cell from his ear and simultaneously pressed the button that reduced its volume. He pressed it repeatedly, making certain no sound would be emitted. But he didn't disconnect the call. He hoped Ginny had caught on. She obviously had realized something was wrong. He could only hope she remained on the line, listening.

As McCracken watched, J.C. reached beneath his sweater and slipped the phone into his shirt pocket. His pulse rate quickened. A band of perspiration ringed his head.

"So," he said, dipping his chin slightly, wanting to make sure Ginny heard his words if she'd remained on the line, "how much farther? Where the hell are we going? Isn't Clayton just up the road?"

"Let's go," McCracken said, gesturing him back onto the highway. He continued to stare at J.C. with the intensity of a bird of prey. It was as if he sensed something amiss.

"Look, can't you even give me a clue about our destination?" J.C. pleaded. "I'd like to—"

McCracken raised the pistol and pointed it at J.C. "Put the phone on the console."

"What?"

"You aren't hard of hearing. You've got three seconds."

J.C. fumbled for the phone, yanked it from his pocket, hit the disconnect button, and placed it on the center console.

McCracken looked at it. He shook his head in a slow, almost sad motion.

He pulled the trigger on the Glock. The explosion rang through the SUV with deafening resonance. The vehicle swerved, plowed through a drift, and nosed to a stop in a snow-filled culvert at the edge of the road.

Chapter Nineteen

End Of The Road

Northeast Georgia
Thursday evening, December 29

J.C. SLUMPED OVER the steering wheel, his ears ringing from the reverberation of the gunshot. McCracken yelled something at him, but J.C. couldn't hear the words, only saw the guy's mouth moving. J.C. sat back in his seat, thankful the airbag hadn't deployed. Thankful he remained alive. Frigid air swept in through the shattered driver's-side window, the one McCracken had shot out. *Better the window than me.* His heart hammered in a wild staccato beat; his chest heaved as he gulped great lungfuls of air.

McCracken, given over to a visage of fury, continued to yell. After he expended his anger, he leaned down to retrieve the cell phone from the foot well where it had tumbled when the SUV careened off the road. He placed the phone on the center console and, with the butt of the Glock, hammered it into a tiny heap of glass, plastic, and metal debris. Finished, and using his forearm, he swept the mess into the rear of the SUV.

The effort seemed to exhaust him. He grimaced, clamped his hand back inside his parka, and sank into his seat.

The ringing in J.C.'s ears subsided, at least partially. He noted McCracken's breathing had become labored. "There's a first aid kit in back," J.C. said. A gust of freezing wind flung a stray flurry of snow into the G-Wagen.

McCracken glowered at him. "What, you're going to make nice now?" he said, his voice a low rumble. "After that asshole move you tried with the phone? How fucking dumb do you think I am?"

"I don't think you're—"

"Shut up. Let's get out of here. We'll worry about first aid later."

J.C. put the Mercedes into reverse and, with a feathery touch, pressed the accelerator. The SUV found purchase in the snow, wallowed slightly, and backed out of the culvert, slabs of snow sliding forward off the hood like downhill skiers.

The highway remained virtually deserted as J.C. again pushed northward, climbing now in deepening dusk. In the G-Wagen's headlight beams, the windswept snowscape shimmered like the white metallic finish of a high-end automobile.

J.C. wondered if Ginny had remained on the line after he'd said goodbye. She knew something was wrong. But had she picked up on the reference to Clayton? Heard McCracken's command to put the phone on the console? Called the police? Or had she become so rattled, so upset by their conservation that she'd plunged into some sort of catatonic state and become immobilized? Unlikely. She'd always been able to perform in a crisis, but he realized he could have shoved her close to the edge on this one. Her ongoing concern over Cole put her under tremendous stress to begin with, but then to get a confusing call from her husband from somewhere in the middle of a blizzard, well . . .

Perhaps all that was of no consequence now anyhow, since McCracken would have to assume he'd been busted and would get off 441 as quickly as possible, distancing himself and J.C. from Clayton. So, even if Ginny were able to alert the authorities, and assuming resources were available to check out her report—probably a poor assumption given the storm—McCracken would make certain they ended up far from Clayton.

A scattering of vehicles—pickups, farm trucks, vans—appeared on the road, crawling over the hard-packed snow. On the right, J. C spotted a high school, a short distance later, a Walmart. A plow passed by heading south. J.C. gathered they must be almost to Clayton. The road narrowed. Still four lanes, but no longer separated by a median strip. Now just turn lanes, or so J.C. guessed. The snow cover obliterated any traffic arrows that might have been on the road.

Even with his stocking cap pulled over his ears and the collar on his parka turned up, J.C. shivered as polar gusts licked at his face through the blown-out window. He turned the heater on high.

He slowed the SUV to just over walking speed as they eased through Clayton, a typical small town with one- and two-story buildings—banks, shopping centers, restaurants, gas stations, motels—crowding the sides of the highway. All of them, save for one or two service stations and a small restaurant, appeared closed.

A city police car approached from the north. For a fleeting moment, J.C. allowed himself to hope. Hope that an alert had been sounded and disseminated. Hope that law enforcement might be on the lookout for a Mercedes *Geländewagen* with Georgia dealer plates. Hope that his deliverance was imminent. But the cruiser passed by without reducing speed. No interest in an expensive SUV with a missing window.

McCracken, pistol on his lap, watched the patrol vehicle pull away, continuing southward. No U-turn. "Tough break, Mr. Riggins. Well, you didn't want to become a hostage anyhow, did you?" He leaned forward, staring intently out the windshield. "Up here, take a right."

J.C. turned on a road between a Days Inn and an off-brand gas station. Signs on either side of the road advertised a Wendy's and a Burger King. He tried to catch the name of the road, but snow plastered over part of the sign. Maybe Brickman or Dickman or Rickman.

The road proved to be unplowed with only faded, snow-filled tire ruts marking single lanes in each direction. A pair of headlights turned behind the Mercedes and followed. A frisson of renewed hope exploded in J.C. as he tracked the lights in the rearview mirror. Police? The beams alternately faded and brightened as waves of blowing snow tumbled through the darkness, challenging the lights. Then, as quickly as the beams had materialized, they vanished. Into a driveway. His expectations suddenly roadkill, J.C's. gut churned. He found McCracken watching him, grinning like a Cheshire Cat.

A minute or two later, they reached an intersection. "Right," McCracken ordered. Warwoman Road. In short order, they left behind Clayton's small town environment. Now just occasional farmhouses and scattered crossroads appeared. Then nothing. Only winter woods in deep snow.

The G-Wagen downshifted and began to climb. McCracken peered ahead intently, calling out turns, left and right, right and left, until J.C. had no idea of his direction of travel. He might as well have been lost in Germany's Black Forest. Twice, they overshot a turnoff, McCracken apparently failing to recognize a landmark camouflaged by the snow. They would then backtrack, turn, and continue. Navigating switchbacks. Climbing hogbacks. Dipping into hollows. Once fording an ice-encrusted creek. Overall, they gained altitude, scaling the terminus of the Southern Appalachians.

It was in these mountains, or at least in their North Carolina cousins—for all J.C. knew, they might well have crossed into North

Carolina—where the Atlanta Olympics bomber, Eric Rudolph, had gone to ground for over five years before he'd been captured.

J.C. understood he could well disappear forever up here; this could be his abandoned-warehouse-in-the-South-Bronx moment. A bullet in the back of his head. A shallow grave deep in the forest. Gone for good. Strangely, he found himself at peace with that notion, accepted his fate. It wasn't that he'd given up. No, no way. It's just that he understood and acknowledged the cost of whatever action he'd need to take.

What gnawed at him with almost palpable intensity was the realization he might be unable to deliver for Cole. To fight for him. To help defeat his leukemia. To rejoice in victory. And once that battle was won, to fish, play ball, and joke with his son. To hug him. To watch him mature into a young man. To see him off to college. J.C. sensed his dreams shattering, falling in shards around his feet to be shoveled up like nothing more than roadkill.

And Ginny, as much a part of him as Cole. While J.C. could acquiesce to his own demise, he understood it would be crushing for his wife. An amputation of her heart and soul. Not right. Tears welled in his eyes, clouding his vision, but not his resolve.

A small herd of deer, probably a family, broke from the woods and bounded across the road. They appeared oblivious to the headlight beams and wind-blown snow curling around them, intent on their mission, whatever that was. Survival, perhaps. *The same as mine*, J.C. thought.

"You ever loved anyone?" J.C. said.

"What?" McCracken responded, as though he hadn't heard the question.

"Have you ever loved anyone?" An eddy of snow, scooped off the ground by the wind, scurried through the G-Wagen's shattered window. The vehicle's engine continued to rumble, pushing the SUV ever deeper into the mountains. Steadily and slowly toward J.C.'s fate.

McCracken shrugged. "What's your point?"

"No point. I asked a question."

McCracken grunted. "You aren't gonna preach to me about Christianity or some silly shit, are you? Love your neighbor? The greatest of these is love? I've read the Bible."

"Do you believe it?"

"What part?"

J.C. thought for a moment. "Greater love has no one—"

"Oh, ho. Is that what you plan to do? Lay down your life for someone? Your kid? Your wife, maybe? Motivated by love? That's where you're wrong, my friend."

"Wrong about what?"

"Being motivated by love." McCracken, the Glock still on his lap, removed his hand from it and massaged his temples. J.C. glanced at the gun. McCracken moved his hand back to it. "You'd be dead before you could touch it," he warned in a matter-of-fact tone.

"I wasn't going to try," J.C. said. "Why am I wrong about love?"

It had begun snowing again, but only lightly. A gust of wind rocked the Mercedes and hurled another mini-blizzard of snow into the vehicle. J.C. tugged on the hood of his parka so that it covered his left cheek, the one most exposed to the elements.

"Why are you in this SUV driving a guy you don't even know to God-knows-where?" McCracken asked, not directly answering J.C.'s question.

"Because the guy has a gun," J.C. snapped. *Stupid question.*

"Precisely. That's my point. People are motivated by fear, not love."

"That's bullshit."

"Is it? You told me you were out here, possibly in the worst snow-storm in the history of the South, because of your son. Well, at least he's one of the factors. And you're gonna tell me that's because you love your son, right?"

"Of course."

"But what *motivated* you wasn't love, it was fear."

"Fear? Come on, Butch, that's just goofy. Fear of what?"

McCracken smiled, his face, like a cheap Halloween mask, glowing blue and white in the interior lighting of the G-Wagen. "In your son's case, fear of him dying. I'm sure you love your son, but what spurred you to action was fear. Look around you, man. Every endeavor you undertake is triggered by fear. Fear of failure, fear of rejection, fear of consequences, fear of death, of dying, of disease."

J.C. stared into the darkness and flying snow. *Maybe McCracken has a point. Maybe not.* "I take care of my family because I love them."

McCracken chuckled. "You take care of your family because if you didn't, they'd leave you. You fear being alone, having to fend for yourself. We're all alone, my friend. We all live in fear."

"I love God."

"You love God because you've read the Old Testament. You know what happened to people who didn't love God, or at least didn't obey

Him. ZAP! And it's burnt offerings for supper.

"Or church. Why do you attend church? Here's why, because your friends do, and you're afraid of being ostracized if you don't. Or maybe you're just afraid of going to hell if you don't show up every Sunday to worship, or Saturday if you're Jewish or Muslim. Love God? Get off it. You're terrified of Him. You see, even love is driven by fear."

"People do good all the time. Kind gestures aren't driven by fear."

"No? What would happen if you didn't perform, as you call them, 'kind gestures'? What would people think of you? A paper tiger, or more to the point, a paper Christian. You're afraid you wouldn't measure up. That you'd be a fraud in the eyes of God, the eyes of your friends."

"Come on, Butch—"

"Oh, call me Cave Man. We're friends now."

"Really?" J.C. said, the word riddled with skepticism. "You're gonna kill me."

"Yeah, probably. But who knows? Maybe I'll grow to love you." He smiled a crooked smile, then leaned forward, groaned, and clutched at his side. He sat up, still smiling. "Or maybe, if you're lucky, I'll bleed out before I have to kill you."

The snow depth now reached to the bumper of the Mercedes with deeper drifts to headlight-level. Progress had become laborious, the vehicle creeping, at times struggling, along an ever-narrowing, ever-steeper track.

McCracken leaned forward in his seat, staring at the road ahead, as though in expectation. "There," he said. He pointed at a tight passageway into the forest on their left. "Go past it. Then back into it."

"I won't be able to see it."

"You've got backup lights."

He passed where McCracken had pointed, stopped, slipped the Mercedes into reverse, and backed up. He stuck his head out the fractured window and, in the glow of the backup lights, attempted to gauge his turn. Though the track into the trees appeared barely wide enough for the G-Wagen, he hit it almost perfectly. The SUV, engine growling, churned backward. Geysers of snow flew forward from underneath the fenders, but the vehicle eventually lost traction and stalled.

McCracken studied the dashboard. "Try locking the rear differential," he said. He nodded at three buttons on the dash in front of the gearshift lever.

J.C. punched the button on the right. The G-Wagen dug in, found traction, and clawed its way up the narrow path. Not for long, however. In short order, the snow became too deep and the track too steep for even fine German engineering to overcome.

"I guess that's it," McCracken said, resignation in his voice. "Get out."

J.C. pushed open the door of the G-Wagen and stepped out into calf-deep snow. McCracken did the same on the opposite side of the SUV. The vehicle's headlight beams, pointing down toward the road, reflected off the snow and cast a diffused light back up the slope.

J.C. wondered if anyone would ever find his body up here, in the wilderness of . . . wherever they were. *My body? All that will be left will be bones. Picked clean by scavengers. By time. By eternity.* He closed his eyes, leaned into the wind, and said a silent prayer asking God to care for his wife and son; asking for forgiveness for his failures as a man, as a husband, as a father; asking why his destiny couldn't have been different; why his life had to end in a cold, snow-covered forest so far from those he loved.

He paused, arrested his emotions, then closed his petition to God with renewed resolve, asking for strength, wisdom, and courage; courage to avoid going gently, to avoid being a passive victim; courage to go down fighting, taking his enemy with him.

Strange, he mused, that he felt no apprehension, no fear, no sense of terror. Only disappointment mixed with determination. He opened his eyes and found McCracken standing beside him, the Glock dangling from his left hand. His eyes appeared unfocused, his stance unsteady. J.C. gauged the distance from himself to McCracken. *Better to go out with violence than kneeling in the snow.*

"Don't," McCracken said. He raised the pistol. "Don't."

"Why not?"

McCracken, his arm fully extended, pointed the weapon at J.C.'s head. "Back there, on the road after we left Clayton, when you asked me if I had ever loved anyone, you were going to make an appeal to my humanity, assuming I have any, weren't you? You know, 'Let me live, I love my kid. Let me live, I love my wife.' But admit it, I'm right. You're driven by fear, not love. Fear of leaving your family alone. Fear of failing them. Fear of the guy with the gun, standing here, a finger's twitch from blowing your brains into the next county."

"Okay, you're right." *What difference does it make?*

A strong gust of wind ripped through the tops of the trees and blew a cascade of snow, like a white waterfall, from the higher branches of a copse of loblolly pines. J.C. tilted his head back as the swirling crystals settled around him. He opened his mouth and caught dozens of the tiny, tumbling flakes on his tongue. He thought of Cole.

And wondered if people ever heard the gunshot that killed them.

Chapter Twenty

Sophie and Tom

Windy Hill Towers
Thursday evening, December 29

SOPHIE STEPPED into Tom's condo and looked around. "You need a maid."

"Maybe I need a raise so I can afford a maid."

"Maybe you need to worry less about a raise and more about holding onto your job."

"Maybe I need a boss who likes me."

Sophie turned to look at Tom. Her intense blue eyes held him in a gaze that seemed simultaneously icy and fiery, simultaneously put-of-fish and come hither. "Your boss likes you just fine," she said. "Maybe a little too much, as you damn well know. Look, I've been trying to get a message through to you. Please, please, please, climb down off your high horse and understand there are practical ramifications to the business we work in."

She shed her coat and handed it to Tom. She bent and slipped off her Uggs. "Tell you what, Tom, let's declare a cease-fire for the next twelve hours and see if we can't get through the night without any further skirmishes. Deal?" She extended her hand.

"Sure." They shook hands, which Tom decided was about as much sexual contact as they were going to have, at least tonight. How, he wondered, could a woman be so damn infuriating and at the same time so damn alluring? *It's gotta be something she practices.*

He pointed down the hall. "If you'd like to take a shower now, I'll see if I can't find some food that hasn't turned into a Petri dish yet."

"Don't worry about it. I can whip up something for us."

"You can cook?" The words came out before Tom could stop them. He could have shot himself.

She checked her wristwatch. "Well, the truce lasted all of seventeen seconds. That's gotta be some kind of record."

"I didn't mean it like I thought you couldn't be domestic," Tom responded, a firm determination in his voice. "It's just that I only know you as a business executive."

Sophie moved her hand to her chin and struck a thoughtful pose. "Maybe you need to get to know me in other frames of reference."

Tom studied her, absolutely stumped as to how he should take that. He'd thought they were operating under a sexual white flag tonight. Was it a come-on? A case of "no" meaning "yes"? He had to admit, he was clueless when it came to male-female relationships. *Which is probably why I'm divorced.*

"Look," Sophie said, "I want to earn my keep here. Why don't you grab a drink, relax, and I'll see what I can find in the kitchen. I promise I won't make any snarky comments, and I promise you I can cook."

"You might end up having to just warm up something in a Papa John's box."

"Well, I can do beer and pizza as well as the next gal."

I'll bet you can. "Have at it. I gotta call my kids. I'll be in my study if you feel the need to loose a snarky comment."

She smiled, and in it Tom could see what made her so maddeningly irresistible at times.

AFTER DINNER, such as it was—barbecue sandwiches on kaiser rolls verging on extinction, macaroni salad, and baked beans Sophie had somehow managed to make delicious (brown sugar, perhaps?)—she and Tom stood by the window overlooking the city. Since the snow had stopped, Atlanta's skyline gleamed vividly to the south. Seventeen stories below, streamers of snow snaked along the ground, whipped by a furious wind. On the interstates, only the isolated flashing lights of plows, sanders, and emergency vehicles cut through the night.

"So," Sophie said, "the worst is yet to come?"

"Maybe you should ask Al, he's—"

She reached up and gently placed her fingers on Tom's lips. "Cease-fire, remember?"

Her touch felt almost electric, sexual, and Tom hoped Sophie hadn't sensed his reaction to it. He raised his arms in supplication. "Sorry," he said. "Yes, when the comma head, the center of the upper-air storm comes over us, all hell is gonna break loose."

"When?"

"Later tonight, early tomorrow."

"Well, if we get trapped here, I'm afraid the next round, as you suggested earlier, will be ramen and beer. I didn't see any more barbecue in the fridge."

"It probably curdled."

"I didn't know barbecue did that."

"It can in my care," Tom said. "Anyhow, if the larder is empty, we'd better plan on mushing into work tomorrow."

"And if the boss lady and her chief of meteorology stroll in together?"

"Tongues will wag."

She nodded. "Well, let's consider the more immediate future. What's your bar stocked with?"

"What's your pleasure?"

"A hot shower, actually."

"Tell you what. Grab your shower. I'll make some Irish coffee."

"Decaf, of course."

"Of course. And we'll sit and watch the news on TV."

"Well, whoever said you weren't romantic?" A smile, that maddeningly irresistible one, blossomed across her face again.

When she came back into the room after her shower, she strolled to the window and looked out at the city slumbering under a deep blanket of wind-knit snow. "It's ironic," she said.

"What's that?" Tom moved to her side and inhaled her fragrance, nothing perfumed, just a vibrant, soapy freshness.

"Remember a few years ago when an inch or two of snow was forecast, and everybody went to work, kids went to school?"

"Yeah, and then it started snowing, and everybody boogied for home at the same time?"

"The city went into gridlock for over twenty-four hours. Couldn't handle two inches. So now we get a biggie, and everybody stays home, and the plows and sanders are able to do their thing."

"And are overwhelmed," Tom said. "Poor Atlanta, can't win for losin'. We just don't do winter storms well, despite what the governor promised."

"So, Irish coffee?" she said.

"Yes, but I didn't have any fresh cream." He pointed at two steaming mugs atop a glass and wrought iron coffee table in front of a leather sofa.

"Why doesn't that surprise me?" she said. She walked to the couch and seated herself. Tom handed her a mug.

"Thanks," she said. "Let's see what's going on at work."

Tom flipped on the television and brought up the NE-TV channel, then sat on the opposite end of the sofa from Sophie.

An on-camera meteorologist, a bubbly blonde who looked barely out of high school, stood in front of a high-def image giving a summary of the "Great Dixie Blizzard," as it had come to be known.

"Sally Blalock," Sophie said softly. "Nabbed her right out of the University of Washington when she was just a pup. Sharp beyond her years."

"So here's what's happening," Sally said. "A rapidly strengthening surface low is crawling across extreme southeastern Georgia now and is expected to continue deepening as it swirls northeastward just off the Carolina coast." She drew an electronically-generated arrow showing the storm's projected track.

"Northwest of the low's path, heavy snow and high winds will continue to lace the western Carolinas. But here's the real bugaboo, an upper-air low lagging behind the surface system." On a different graphic, a satellite water vapor image, she pointed at a swirl of gray over Alabama. "This is the comma head cloud, a pool of very cold aloft that's producing heavy snow and, yes, even thunder and lightning. So don't be fooled because the snow has temporarily tapered off in Georgia. The worst is yet to come.

"Our forecasters believe there's another ten or twelve inches—yes, perhaps as much as another foot of snow, believe it or not—lurking for North Georgia, the Southern Appalachians, and western portions of North and South Carolina. Couple that with fifty miles per hour winds, and you've got something rarely experienced in the Deep South."

"Love her," muttered Sophie. "Hey, switch to one of the local channels. Let's see how the city is handling this."

Tom changed channels and caught the tail end of a wrap-up on the status of the metro area. A montage of videos showed the long lines of stranded tractor-trailers on the Perimeter; haggard and frustrated travelers encamped at Hartsfield-Jackson; downtown Atlanta looking like a city shuttered for the winter in the Yukon; plows struggling to keep a single lane open each way on the interstates.

The shot cut to a striking but somewhat exhausted-looking—probably from too many hours on duty—black woman at the anchor desk as she read from a teleprompter. "With blizzard warnings continuing into tomorrow, there is now talk of canceling New Year's Eve activities around the city including the Chick-fil-A Peach Bowl and the Peach Drop at Underground. This, of course, would be unprecedented." She paused and looked down at a computer monitor on her desk.

She looked back into the camera and resumed speaking. "Some breaking news just in from the State Patrol. Earlier today, a Georgia state trooper was found in his cruiser, shot, on Interstate 85 near the South Carolina border. The officer is in critical condition, but is expected to survive.

"A dash camera showed he had stopped a stolen car when a brief gun battle ensued. The camera was damaged during the exchange of gunfire, so no further imagery was available. Police have mounted a manhunt for the suspect, but authorities say it will be an extremely difficult and slow search due to the blizzard and the demands it is making on their ranks."

The anchor paused and again looked at her desktop monitor.

She raised her head and began speaking again. "Meanwhile, in what could be a related development, a north metro woman reported that her husband, driving a Mercedes SUV with Georgia dealer plates on I-85, may have been taken captive and forced to drive in the direction of Clayton, Georgia. Police are investigating, but at the moment are uncertain if this alleged incident is related to the shooting of the trooper."

The anchor lady sighed and sat back. "Well, that's even more drama in what already has been a very dramatic day here in—"

Tom, using the remote, clicked off the TV. "As though a once-in-a-millennium snowstorm wasn't enough," he said. "I thought the interstates were closed. Why do you suppose someone was out there?"

Sophie polished off her Irish coffee. "I don't know, but my news sense tells me there's probably a good story behind it."

Tom recalled that Sophie had been an executive producer for NBC Nightly News before coming to NE-TV. He stood, wobbled a bit, the long day and after-dinner whiskey catching up with him. "I'm beat," he said. "My turn to shower, then I'm gonna hit the sack. Could be another exhausting day tomorrow. The guest bedroom is down the hall, past the bathroom, on the left."

Sophie rose from the couch, gazed at Tom for a fleeting moment, took a step toward him, then stopped. "I appreciate your hospitality," she said. "Sleep well."

"Good night," he responded.

"I'm not gonna push a dresser in front of the door," she said as she walked away.

Tom watched her. *And I'm supposed to know what that means.*

He showered, laid out fresh clothes for the following day, flopped into bed, watched TV briefly, then stared at the ceiling and thought about Sophie, his kids, his ex-wife . . .

His divorce from Maggie had not been contentious, but it hurt that he hadn't been able to make a go of it as a husband and father. Maggie and he remained good friends, and he knew she certainly had more to offer the children, time-wise, than he. At least he saw Billie and Bonnie on a regular basis. Thank goodness Maggie didn't live far away. She and her new husband, Rick, "the bank president," had an east Cobb mansion.

Sure, bank president. Regular hours, big money. Nothing I could compete with. But he wondered if he had wanted to.

And Sophie. It seemed *strange*—he couldn't think of a better word—that the only woman who ever spent a night in his condo was turning out to be someone with whom he frequently locked horns, not lips. He snorted a soft laugh and fell into a dream-riddled sleep.

He found himself on the streets of a snowbound city he didn't recognize. He slogged through hip-high drifts, people he didn't know trailing him, apparently chasing him. Angry people, shouting, shaking their fists. He tried to push through the deep snow even more rapidly, but the harder he struggled, the more bogged down he became, as though mired in quicksand.

Then suddenly, he broke free. He discovered a path, a mini-canyon, carved through a wasteland of snow that towered above him on either side of the passage. He sprinted along the path. At its end stood a brightly lit cabin with long icicles dangling from the eves, something out of a Thomas Kincaid painting.

A large bear wearing a straw boater and a red collar with jingling bells stood guard in front of the structure. The bear reared on its hind legs, motioned for Tom to come forward, and pushed the door open for him.

Tom hesitated, then darted into the cabin, slamming the door behind him. A woman decked out in royal robes, furry boots, and a bejeweled crown pivoted from where she'd been standing in front of a wood-burning fireplace. She unrolled a scroll and read from it.

"Tomasz Przybyszewski," she announced in a Polish accent, "a warrant has been issued for your arrest for gross negligence in your failure to warn the people of this kingdom."

"No, no. I did warn them," Tom pleaded.

"Not soon enough." She furled the scroll. "If your warning had been timelier, we could have evacuated the kingdom. Starvation would not be the great threat it has now become."

"No one is starving."

"Thousands!" the woman screamed. "The penalty for your failure is death. The people will mete out the punishment." A furious pounding sounded from the exterior of the door.

Tom stared.

"The people," the woman announced and disappeared.

A dream. I know it's a dream. A nightmare. Tom willed himself awake. He sat up, disoriented, groggy. The pounding morphed into a soft rap. It stopped. Then it came again. From his bedroom door.

"Tom, it's Sophie." The words seemed coated in soft non-urgency.

"Sophie?"

The door cracked open. Sophie leaned in. "May I?" She paused. "I'm dressed."

Story of my life. "Sure." He pulled the sheet and a down comforter up over his hips.

Sophie, clad in her tight jeans and clingy sweater, seated herself on the foot of the bed.

Tom bunched the comforter over his groin. *How in the hell do you hide a boner in bed?*

Chapter Twenty-one

The Forest

Northeast Georgia
Thursday evening, December 29

"COME ON," MCCRACKEN said. "Let's get going. Quit catching damn snowflakes with your tongue. You're weirding me out."

J.C. closed his mouth and stared at McCracken. "*I'm* weirding *you* out?"

McCracken gestured with the gun, up the slope, deeper into the woods.

"For Christ's sake, man, we're in the middle of nowhere," J.C. snapped. "Why not just do it here?"

"Do what?"

"Shoot me!" The words, propelled by frustration, leaped from J.C.'s mouth. "Why do we have to play fucking games?" His voice rose to a shout, challenging the howl of the wind.

"Don't be impatient for the end of life, my friend. Right now I need you."

"Need me?" J.C. stood his ground, not moving.

"I'm shot. I'm hurting. I'm bleeding. I need some help getting where I'm going."

J.C., focused on his own fate until now, hadn't noticed his captor's posture: hunched over in obvious pain, his right hand inside his parka, perhaps attempting to stanch the bleeding.

McCracken again motioned with the Glock.

J.C. took a labored step through the snow and began pushing up-hill.

"Wait, hold it," McCracken commanded. "The case. Get my case out of the backseat. You carry it. I'll tell you which way to go. Oh, and grab a couple of flashlights, too."

"I've only got one."

"Get it."

J.C. returned to the G-Wagen, shut off the ignition, and placed the key in the pocket of his parka. He retrieved the LED flashlight he'd purchased at Home Depot and the aluminum attaché case McCracken had tossed into the vehicle at the weigh station.

"Shine the light up the hill," McCracken said.

J.C. did, moving the beam from side to side. The track they stood on appeared to narrow even more as it climbed into the snow-covered forest.

"Go," McCracken ordered.

J.C. did, plowing through the snow like a human icebreaker. But not for long. After about ten minutes he pulled up, leaned over, set the case in the snow, and placed his hands on his knees. His breath came in deep, audible pants.

"You're out of shape, man," McCracken said.

"No shit. Why don't you break trail some?"

"Because I'm wounded. Because I don't want you behind me. Slow down if you have to. You aren't gonna do me any good if you do a permanent face-plant in the snow."

"Thanks for your concern," J.C. gasped.

"Only a few hundred yards to go."

"Then what?"

"Then, if I can spot the marker in this frigging snow, we turn left and follow a path through the woods."

"We *are* following a path through the woods," J.C. said, his breathing slowly returning to normal. "Where in the hell are we going?"

"Onward and upward, my friend. Take it easy." McCracken pointed the way with the gun, as though he were a Civil War army officer directing a charge into enemy positions.

They moved on, J.C. carrying the attaché case in one hand, the flashlight in the other. The snow had ceased falling, but the serrated wind continued to blow and drift what already covered the ground. Although he couldn't see behind them in the darkness, J.C. imagined that their tracks filled with snow within moments of being made. He realized he would never find a way out of here on his own.

He also knew that probably was of academic concern. Once he was no longer of use to McCracken, he wasn't just going to be released with a thanks and a handshake. Not by someone who'd shot a cop, maybe even killed a cop. J.C. understood he knew way too much about what McCracken had done and where he had gone, and thus had become an expendable commodity.

Lost in his thoughts and fears—fears; McCracken would love that—J.C. continued to press forward, sometimes taking giant steps like a moose in deep snow, at other times just shoving through the stuff like a winter bison in Yellowstone. He stopped frequently to catch his breath. McCracken didn't seem to mind, for even *his* breathing had become labored.

After another fifteen minutes, McCracken called out, "Hold it. Shine the light on that rhododendron up there, the one by the sweet gum."

J.C. moved the beam. The light reflected off the snow-encrusted, cold-curled leaves of a huge rhododendron.

McCracken moved to J.C.'s side and studied the bush. "Damn. I can't tell. All this snow. Everything's buried." Like a dog exhuming a bone, he dug at the snow surrounding the base of the bush with his foot. He hit something, bent to examine it. It looked like a large stone with a red *X* painted on it.

He stood. "This is where we turn."

J.C. moved the light around. "Where? There's nothing here but trees."

"Between those two big pines." He pointed. "There's a path there."

"There's nothing but snow."

"Trust me. There's a path."

"Sure there is," J.C. muttered and stepped into the woods. He sank to his thighs in a drift. If the going had been difficult before, it now became virtually impossible. Every step required maximum effort. Every ten feet of travel seemed like a total cardiovascular workout. Despite a windchill he figured must be close to zero, J.C. began to sweat.

After ten or fifteen lung-busting minutes, the path, such as it was, leveled slightly. The forest pressed in on either side of the track that in spots seemed no wider than a man. But if nothing else, the density of the trees cut the wind. Still, it moaned through the crown of the pines like a lost lover seeking her partner.

Once, J.C. thought he sniffed wood smoke, but knew that couldn't be.

Then, something else. He held up his hand, signaling McCracken to stop.

"Yeah, I could use a break," McCracken said.

"No, I heard something. Thought I did anyhow."

"There's nothing up here to hear. Except the wind. You aren't starting to go mental on me, are you? Come on, man. Pull it together." McCracken coughed, winced, and suddenly sat heavily in the snow. "Oh, shit. That hurts." He slumped forward, right hand inside his parka, the left pointing the Glock into the snow.

J.C. looked on, calculating his chances.

McCracken lifted his head. "Bad idea," he said through clenched teeth. "I can get off a shot faster than you can get—"

"I wasn't going to try anything."

"Maybe not. But you were thinking about it. Help me up."

J.C. set down the case, extended his hand, and pulled McCracken to his feet.

The sound drifted in again. "Listen," J.C. said, "hear that?"

"The wind, whining through rocks someplace. Let's move."

"No, it wasn't the wind. Listen, damn it. Don't talk."

Both men stood still, their heads cocked, as though that might help them filter the rush of the wind from other sounds.

Then it was there, a long, low howl.

"Wind," McCracken said, firmness in his voice.

A second howl, slightly different in tenor from the first, penetrated the night.

J.C. stopped sweating. Now a chill, the sort that doesn't come from the cold, permeated his body. He stared at McCracken, McCracken at him.

"Okay, not the wind," McCracken said. "Coyotes."

"I've heard coyotes before. Coyotes bark and yip, they don't howl."

"So what howls?"

"Wolves."

"Wolves? You've gone completely batshit crazy on me, dude. There aren't any wolves within a thousand miles of here. I've heard there are some in Minnesota, and in the Rocky Mountains, but not around here. Might be a couple of wild dogs."

McCracken had barely finished speaking when a chorus of howls, closer than those previous, speared through the darkness. The pitch of the cries rose and fell smoothly, a primitive call to arms.

"More than a couple," J.C. said, his voice shaky.

McCracken looked around. For the first time, J.C. thought he spotted something akin to fear in the man's eyes. But maybe it was just the way the flashlight beam angled in on his face. "Don't mean to freak you out, but I just remembered something."

J.C. stared. "Yeah?"

"There's a guy around here who's been raising some wolves illegally. He's nursed maybe a half-dozen sick and injured gray wolves—you know, the big ones from out West—back to health."

"And he lets them run wild?"

"No. Of course not. He's got about a hundred acres of fenced land up near the North Carolina border."

"A lousy hundred acres? That's gotta make wolves really happy." J.C. laced his words with sarcasm. "So if the wolves are fenced in—"

"Snowstorm, man. Drifts up to the fence top. Something you don't plan on around here, like a tree falling on the fence. I'm guessing the buggers aren't in prison any longer; there's an eastern pack of western wolves out there."

"Are you shitting me? A *pack* of wolves, and I'm standing here with a guy who's bleeding. Good God, you might as well be wearing a suicide vest made of raw hamburger."

The chorus came again. Stronger. Closer. Then silence.

"Give me the flashlight," McCracken ordered. J.C. handed it over, and McCracken placed it in his left hand, brought the Glock up in his bloodied right hand, rested it on his left wrist, and swept the surrounding darkness with the gun and flashlight moving in tandem.

Nothing. Only the wind.

Snow had begun sifting down again, perhaps a harbinger of the onslaught to follow.

McCracken pointed the beam through a gap in the trees. "That way," he said. "I'll hang onto the flashlight. . . . just in case."

J.C. moved off, clutching the case, tracking the bobbing beam of light. "Hey," he said, "hold the damn thing steady. I can barely see where I'm going as it is."

"And I can barely stand up, dickhead, so shut up and keep truckin'." McCracken, behind J.C., sounded weak and unsteady.

They hadn't gone far when the howling came again, different now, more urgent, higher pitched. Predators on a mission.

"How far away, you think?" J.C. asked. He assumed his captor had more experience in the wild than he had had, but maybe not.

"Damned if I know. Stop. Kneel down."

Both men knelt in the snow. McCracken swept the pistol and light from side to side again. Searching.

J.C. shivered, not quite believing his situation: crouched in an Appalachian forest, in the dark, in the snow, with a guy who'd popped a cop, and waiting for what? A pack of wolves to materialize out of the blackness? No. That just doesn't happen. He should be at home, comforted by warmth, surrounded by those he loved. He imagined himself sitting in front of the fireplace: pirouetting flames, a soft roar, Ginny nestled beside him, Cole curled up on his lap. Again, he thought he caught a whiff of wood smoke, but recognized it for what it was: an olfactory hallucination.

Then, in the woods, the flashlight beam reflected off a pair of yellow-green dots. McCracken fired. The gunshot echoed through the trees. The dots disappeared.

"Run," McCracken yelled.

"Where?" J.C. stood, adrenaline surging through his body.

McCracken swung the beam. "That way."

Chapter Twenty-two

The Pack

Northeast Georgia
Thursday evening, December 29

HIS CHEST HEAVING, his inhalations coming in great, gasping gulps, J.C. surged through the snow. McCracken, grunting and cursing, followed.

The baying, a mixture of howls and short, menacing barks, seemed to surround them.

J.C. burst into a clearing.

"Up the hill, to the left," McCracken gasped.

J.C. turned. Above him, on the crest of a rise about a pitching-wedge distant, sat a large, two-story stone structure. A residence of some sort, apparently—as incongruent as it seemed—with large pine-tar torches, their flames flattened in the wind, glowing on either side of a heavy wooden door. Smoke, laying out horizontally, poured from a rock-layered chimney.

It seemed like something out of medieval times. A castle on a snowy mountain in feudal Germany. Torches flickering in winter darkness. Peasants pursued by wolves.

"Go!" McCracken screamed.

J.C., his legs churning like a fullback's, launched himself up the hill. A gray form, head high, ears forward, moving fast, crossed through the snow in front of him. Big. Not a coyote. Not a dog. Not even close.

A second shape followed. Coming for J.C. He swung at it wildly with the aluminum case and actually made contact. The animal veered off.

J.C. jerked his head around to look for McCracken. He'd fallen, attempted to rise, but tumbled back. Two huge wolves, maybe a hundred pounds each and seemingly unafraid, stalked toward him. J.C. dropped the case, dashed to McCracken, yanked him erect.

Somehow, McCracken had maintained his grip on the Glock and the flashlight. He pointed both at the nearest wolf, squeezed off two rounds. The shots echoed through the woods but hit nothing other than snow. The wolves retreated.

J.C. and McCracken plunged through the drifts toward the massive wooden door of the stone house. Rumbling growls trailed them, filling the night, but the wolves held their distance. McCracken hammered on the door. Pain laced his face. He turned toward J.C. "The case," he said. "Where's the fucking case?"

"In the snow."

"Damn it." McCracken aimed the flashlight beam in the direction from which they'd come. "Go get it."

"No. I'm not going back out there."

"Yes, you are." He pointed the gun at J.C.

"Remind me not to save your ass again."

"What's in that case is more important. Go get it. I've got you covered."

McCracken moved the light over the snow. J.C. saw no movement, no wolves. Which, of course, didn't mean they weren't lurking just inside the tree line on the perimeter of the clearing.

J.C. dashed to the case, snatched it, and darted back to where McCracken stood. Once again, McCracken beat on the door. The door had no windows, but in a small, four-paned window about three feet to the right of the entrance, a bearded face appeared, then disappeared. The door swung open. Heavy metal rock music fled into the darkness.

The bearded face belonged to a bear of a man, squat, powerful, and hairy. He wore a fur-lined vest over a sleeveless "muscle shirt," all the better, J.C. deduced, to display arms so heavily tattooed they looked like the sleeves of a purple sweater. Jeans and motorcycle boots completed his attire.

"Where the hell you been, Cave?" the bearded man barked. "And who the hell is this?" He stared at J.C.

"Had a little trouble," McCracken said, his words slurred. "J.C. here helped me out." With the Glock in his bloodied hand, he motioned J.C. into the house. "J.C., meet Grizzly."

J.C. nodded at Grizzly. The man didn't seem the hand-shaking type.

Grizzly stared at McCracken's hand, yanked open his parka. "Shit. You're shot."

McCracken, pale and unsteady, mumbled something J.C. didn't understand.

Behind Grizzly, J.C. made out other people, both men and women, maybe thirty or so, in the interior of the house, an area illuminated only by flickering candles, a variety of hurricane lanterns, and a roaring blaze in a huge, river-rock fireplace. The music, loud and jarring, pulsed from a dimly-lit corner.

Grizzly called for a couple of the people to assist McCracken.

J.C. studied the inhabitants of the strange residence. Most of the men, rough and unshaven, sported motorcycle boots and leather jackets. A few wore raggedy sweatshirts emblazoned with death heads or red devils. The women looked equally as rough. Several, decked out in leather vests, hadn't bothered with bras. J.C. didn't have a difficult time figuring out he'd stepped into some sort of biker gathering.

The smell of wood smoke, cigarette fumes, and something J.C. remembered from his college days—the odor of pot—filled the house. At least a third of the bikers seemed in some sort of alcohol-induced stupor; others appeared well on their way. Few, except for Grizzly, paid any attention to J.C.

His piggy eyes glared at J.C. "Who the fuck are you?" The words came out wrapped in a growl.

"Your bud's prisoner."

"Yeah?"

"Yeah."

"Well, he looks a little worse for wear than you do. You bust a cap on him?"

"A cop shot him."

"What happened to the cop?"

"Cave Man shot him."

Grizzly shrugged. "Good." He turned to check on McCracken, then brought his attention back to J.C. "So how do you fit into this picture?"

"I showed up after the fact. At a weigh station on I-85. McCracken, Cave Man, flagged me down. I thought he was a state trooper."

Grizzly grunted, belched a truncated laugh. "What's in the case?"

"It's Cave Man's."

"I didn't ask that. I asked what's in it?"

"Cave Man thinks it's something important."

"I'll bet." Grizzly extended his hand toward it.

J.C. handed it to him. He decided whatever it contained, it was something he didn't wish to be associated with. He looked for McCracken, spotted him sitting on the floor, his back against a paneled wall, stripped to his waist with several bikers attending to him. A remarkably good-looking redhead, dressed much more sensibly and warmly than most of the other women, stood apart from the group watching the proceedings. Concern etched her face.

Grizzly, carrying the case, went to McCracken and knelt in front of him. They exchanged words, but J.C. couldn't hear them. Grizzly stood and returned to J.C. "Sit at the table over there." He pointed. "Don't do anything. Just sit." J.C. noticed he had McCracken's Glock stuffed in the front of his jeans.

J.C. seated himself on a long bench at a table hewed from pine. At the far end of the table, a group of bikers, their arms draped over each other's shoulders, swayed and sang an off-color and out-of-tune drinking song. One of them, a blond kid with long, stringy hair and hollow eyes, flashed J.C. a boozy, semi-toothless grin. He started to get up, but one of his buddies popped him on the back of his head and told him to stay put.

J.C. turned away, his stomach churning—from fear, from hunger, from defeat. If anything, his situation had gone from bad to worse. At least when he'd been alone with McCracken, it had been one-against-one, but now? He closed his eyes and thought of Cole, of Ginny. Images of the three of them together flashed through his memory and speared him in the heart: playing in the white sand on a sunny, humid afternoon on the Gulf Coast; hiking a winding trail through mountain laurel and Fraser firs on a brisk autumn day high in the Smokies; chasing butterflies on a warm spring morning in Calloway Gardens. Once upon a time, when all was right with the world.

A wave of nausea surged through him. He knew with increasing certainty that those memories, those days, were likely gone; it would be a miracle if he got out of this mess alive. The people in this room weren't just a bunch of weekend warriors out riding motorcycles for the fun of it and socializing over a beer or two. These were real-deal bad asses who were into things in which someone's life, especially an outsider's, didn't rank high on their priority list. *Don't*, he urged himself, *don't think like that. I can still beat these bozos.*

A tap on his shoulder. He opened his eyes and turned. The redhead stood next to him.

"I'm Lynne," she said.

She smelled of Obsession and beer and salami, an odd combination.

"You're a friend of Cave Man's?" J.C. asked, recalling her concerned look earlier.

She seemed confused, but quickly answered, "No." She shook her head. "No."

McCracken, his midsection swathed in a dressing that looked as though it had been professionally applied, arose from where he'd been sitting and strode toward the table.

Lynne's eyes narrowed. She bent close to J.C. "What's your name?" she asked in a hurried whisper.

"J.C."

"Funny name." She wheeled and moved away as McCracken approached.

McCracken seated himself beside J.C. He inclined his head toward Lynne. "Trouble," he said. A statement and a warning.

"Is she?"

"She's a bitch. Meaner than a mama hound with a stick up her ass. Watch yourself."

J.C. nodded at McCracken's bandage. "Looks like a good job."

"Psycho fixed me up. He was a medic in the army. Afghanistan. Said the bullet passed through cleanly. Didn't hit anything vital. Just sprung a leak in me." McCracken studied J.C. for a moment, then spoke again. "So, out there in the snow, when I fell. You stopped, pulled me up. Got me away from those things, the wolves."

"Yes?" *Where is McCracken going with this?*

"Why?"

J.C. looked away. *Good question. Why?* He'd wondered himself. Why rescue someone who'd threatened to turn your brains into Glock goulash?

"I don't know," J.C. said.

McCracken sat down beside J.C. "Love of fellow man?"

"Hardly." He studied McCracken's Neanderthal countenance. "I'll bet you're going to tell me I was driven by fear."

"Could be. Fear of me being eaten alive and you being left alone. Dessert for the pack."

A gust of wind punched down the chimney. Sparks and embers flew from the fireplace in a mini-pyrotechnics display. A billow of smoke followed, crawling over the exposed wooden beams of the ceiling like an inverted layer of ground fog.

"It wasn't fear. It wasn't love. I didn't think about it. There wasn't time. I just . . . reacted. A fellow human in trouble. Help him."

"Our innate goodness." McCracken snorted, a sardonic chortle. "Well, one thing," he continued, "with a bunch of wolves prowling the perimeter out there, I don't have to worry about you bugging out tonight."

"Yeah, maybe, but at least I wouldn't be oozing blood like chum in a shark tank." He looked again at McCracken's bandage. A faint, dark stain had appeared. J.C. decided not to disabuse his captor of the notion the wolves were really going to attack. He'd had time to think about it. Wolves, especially ones raised in captivity, don't hunt humans. If anything, they may have caught the scent of McCracken's blood and assumed the two men were bearing food for them, something they would have learned in captivity.

No, J.C. thought, *wolves are the least of my worries.* The pack in here, in this house, presented a much bigger threat. They were the real wolves, the predators, the killers. But his greatest concern was even if he could escape, he had virtually no hope of finding his way back to the G-Wagen, especially if what Ginny had told him about the storm proved to be correct, that the worst still loomed.

The music continued to throb, and the dim lantern light alternately dimmed and brightened through the diaphanous waves of smoke that drifted through the house. In a shadowy corner of the room, a couple, likely stoned *and* drunk, copulated in front of a small but enthusiastic cheering section, both men and women.

J.C. sensed he had stepped back in time to something not just Gothic in setting, but to a morality out of the Dark Ages.

McCracken, seemingly bored with their conversation, stood. "I'll see if I can find you a beer."

"Maybe something to eat, too?"

"Do I look like a fucking waiter?" McCracken marched away.

J.C. rested his arms on the table and lowered his head into them.

Slight pressure against his hip brought him upright. Lynne. She seated herself beside J.C. and moved her head close to his.

"I don't know who you are," she said, a syrupy Southern lilt coating her words, "but you're in a bad situation."

"You think I don't know that?"

"No, really, Mr. J.C." She bit her words off and looked around the room, a furtive glance. "These people, these animals, aren't going to let you leave here alive. And worse, no one will ever find out what happened to you."

Chapter Twenty-three

Closed Doors

Windy Hill Towers
Thursday night, December 29

SOPHIE, SITTING at the end of Tom's bed, rested her hand on his foot, covered as it was by a sheet and thick comforter. It seemed an oddly familiar, if not intimate, gesture. In the muted light leaking through the now-open bedroom door, Sophie appeared relaxed and— Tom hated to admit it—desirable. On the other hand, if Sophie hadn't struck him that way, as being desirable, he probably would have worried that he was traveling rapidly down Al's "a-good-dump-is-better-than" path. He *knew* he wasn't heading down that path as he struggled to keep his "maleness" under wraps.

"I come in peace," Sophie said.

"Non-aggression pact?"

"Do I need to worry?"

"Well, it's not often that a lady, other than my ex, creeps into my bedroom at night."

"I didn't creep. I knocked. Oh, and so your ex is still in the picture?" Sophie removed her hand from Tom's foot.

"I meant *before* she was my ex."

"But there have been others?"

Tom switched on his nightstand lamp, careful to keep the camouflaging covers in place. Attempting to figure out Sophie seemed an exercise in futility. Was her questioning some sort of effort to delve into his character? Or was she attempting to get the lay of the land, to discover if she might face any "competition."

"Why are you grilling me?"

Sophie drew a deep breath. "I didn't mean to. I overstepped my bounds. Once was enough. I'm sorry. It's none of my business." She sounded genuinely apologetic.

"But you came in here for a reason." *Probably not the one I'm fantasizing over, but I am curious.* A flurry of sleet ticked against the bedroom window.

"Sounds like it's starting up again," Sophie said, avoiding the question implicit in Tom's statement.

"It is." He waited.

Sophie shifted slightly, looked at the ceiling. "At work, I've been a little hard on you. I guess that bothers me more than I thought it might. I know you've got certain standards that you believe in, that frame your attitudes, and I probably haven't been as accommodating as I might to those viewpoints, but, God knows, you are hard-headed about them."

"Do you think I'm wrong?"

"Of course not. What I think is we need to find some sort of middle ground. And yes, I know that means I'll have to surrender some territory, too. Look, we're on the same team. Although I get a bit bellicose at times about defending my turf, I do value your input. The bottom line is, I don't want us working at loggerheads any longer."

"Why are you telling me this now? Here? You know, instead of calling me into your office or something?"

"Calling you into my office hasn't always yielded expected results."

They both smiled.

"You could have just walked on by me this evening," she continued, "smug in your revenge, when I was up to my ass in that damn snowdrift. Instead, you were a gentleman and stopped. You put aside any notions of 'poetic justice' or whatever and bailed me out. I actually appreciated that."

So, Her Highness has a soft side.

She stood. "Once again, I apologize. I know it's probably inappropriate to barge—creep—into a man's bedroom at night, but . . ." She shrugged.

But you did it anyhow, and I still don't know why.

She took a couple of steps toward him, glanced at the comforter gathered over his hips, gazed at him directly, and smiled. Not an enticing smile, nor one suggesting something nefarious, just a smile. He hoped.

"What have you got to read?" she asked.

"You mean books?"

"I'm kind of wound up. Reading helps me relax."

I can think of other things that might help. He didn't verbalize it. "Who are your favorite authors?" A pointless question. His "library" consisted of John Grisham and James Patterson paperbacks.

"Dickens, Steinbeck, Vonnegut, Hemingway. And Cormac McCarthy, though he's a bit more contemporary."

"Don't know him."

"You might. He wrote *All the Pretty Horses* and *No Country for Old Men*."

"I saw the movies."

"You should read more."

"I've got two kids and a job with a demanding boss."

"Touché," she said softly.

"Anyhow, the last book I read was about chasing tornadoes. *Supercell*. A novel. I don't remember who wrote it; it wasn't Cormac McCarthy."

"*Supercell*. That might work. Do you still have it?"

"It's in the bookcase by the TV." *Sorry, right now it would be a bit awkward for me to show you where it is.*

Sophie bent slightly, switched off the lamp on the nightstand, and touched Tom on the cheek, a gesture she seemed to let linger just slightly longer than the bounds of a platonic relationship might have suggested. Not surprising, their relationship had obviously crept beyond that.

"I'll find it," she said. "Good night." She smiled at him as she shut the door.

Tom lay in the darkness, listening to the soft moan of the wind through the high-rise.

Now how in the hell am I supposed to get to sleep?

Northeast Georgia
Thursday night, December 29

THE SOUNDS, SMELLS, and sights filling the room washed over J.C. like a breaking wave, sweeping him into a dark, alternate universe, a place he knew nothing about, couldn't relate to, didn't understand—a place that could well be the death of him. A rush of queasiness surged through him, whether from hunger, dehydration, or fear, he didn't know. Probably all three.

Lynne scooted closer to him. "I can help."

He stared at her.

"Honestly." She touched him on the hand, a quick, light caress. "I want out of here, too. This"—she nodded at the debauchery surrounding them—"isn't what I expected."

"Expected?"

"When I hooked up with Cave Man, I thought he was just a cool dude with a bike, a bit of a rebel. I thought it might be a trip to hang out with him."

"Yeah, this is a trip all right."

"This shit? No, this isn't what I was looking for. Cave told me that after Christmas he was going on a little winter retreat up in the mountains. Him, a few friends, some beer, a big fireplace. He wanted me to come along. It sounded like fun. I didn't expect a frigging outlaw biker orgy."

"How long have you been here?"

"A few days. And I feel like a prisoner now. Cave disappeared yesterday, told Grizzly to keep an eye on me, didn't tell me where he was going, only that he had to do something for 'his brothers.' Then he showed up with you, him looking like a loser from the Gunfight at the O. K. Corral."

She took another quick glance around her and spotted McCracken approaching. She stood. "Gotta go. Just remember what I said."

"What?"

"I can help."

Sure you can.

McCracken arrived, slammed a bottle of beer down on the table next to J.C. "Been talkin' to the bitch?"

"More like she was talking to me." J.C. took a long swallow of beer, didn't thank McCracken.

McCracken smiled, a pernicious grin. "Probably told you she could get you out of here."

J.C. didn't respond.

McCracken tipped his head back and guffawed, but it was laughter without hilarity.

"The song of a Siren," he said after he stopped cackling. "You think she gives a damn about you? All she cares about is herself. She'll get you killed, my friend."

"And this changes my circumstance, how?" J.C. asked, venom in his voice. He took another swig of beer.

McCracken shrugged. "I'll see if I can find you something to eat." He wheeled and walked away from the table.

"Don't do me any favors," J.C. snapped.

"Wouldn't think of it," McCracken said, raising his voice to be heard over the din filling the room.

J.C. DOZED OFF sometime after midnight, exhaustion finally overwhelming him. He awoke, still at the table, his head resting on his forearms, to a strange semi-silence punctuated only by scattered snorts and snores. He lifted his head and took stock of his surroundings. The bikers and their women, strewn about the room in various states of stupor, had collapsed into chairs and couches, or lay on the floor using folded-up leather jackets as pillows.

The flames in the fireplace had disappeared, leaving just occasional orphaned sprites leaping from blackened logs on a bed of glowing embers. The candles had guttered, and what little light remained came from half a dozen flickering hurricane lanterns.

J.C. looked around for McCracken and found him spread-eagled in an easy chair, his head tilted back, his mouth agape, sawing logs in a torpor likely the result of both booze and painkillers.

Grizzly, his craggy face framed in an explosion of whiskers, sat in an Adirondack chair near the main door, a shotgun draped across his lap. He'd likely taken on the task of guarding the exit, but with his head drooped forward and his chest rising and falling in a slow, steady rhythm, even he appeared to have nodded off. These guys, J.C. could see, were a bit short on military discipline.

J.C. eased into a standing position and surveyed the room. No one stirred in response to his movement. *Now or never*, he decided. He wasn't going to just sit here while a bunch of cretins who rode motorcycles decided his fate. Blizzard or not, he still had a chance. Probably not much of one, but he knew he had an absolute zero probability of surviving if he stayed put.

He stepped over the bench he'd been sitting on, zipped up his parka, and crept toward the door in slow, measured steps. A noise from a darkened corner of the house stopped him. Grunts, moans, a muffled cry, soft panting, a sigh. J.C. halted, holding his breath. Apparently the code of the bikers put a higher priority on sex than alertness.

The sounds ceased, but J.C. remained motionless for another two or three minutes. He estimated another ten feet to the door. He'd have to pass about five feet in front of Grizzly and his shotgun to reach the door. He squatted, fixed his gaze on Grizzly, and watched him. The biker, his chin dipped against his vest and his eyes closed, continued to inhale and exhale in a steady, even manner, his snores reverberating like coarse sandpaper scraping over pumice. Confident Grizzly had fallen asleep at his post, J.C. stood and took a step toward the door.

Movement behind Grizzly caught J.C.'s attention. Lynne. She smiled at J.C., then tapped Grizzly on the shoulder. Grizzly jerked awake, looked around, semi-bewildered, spotted J.C.

J.C. froze, stared at Lynne. *Meaner than a mama hound with a stick up her ass*—McCracken's words. *I can help*—Lynne's words. Obviously, McCracken had her pegged.

Grizzly, his face contorted like an old silvertip whose territory had been invaded, staggered from his chair, stumbled toward J.C., flipped the shotgun around, and drove the butt toward J.C.'s head.

J.C. attempted to duck and spin away, but too late. The blow caught the side of his head, and he spiraled into blackness.

Chapter Twenty-four

Fox and Geese

Northeast Georgia
Early Friday morning, December 30

HIS HEAD THROBBING like subwoofers in a lowrider, J.C. cracked one eye open. He had no idea how long he'd been unconscious, but guessed it hadn't been long; the same quasi-silent and quasi-dark environment that had prevailed before Grizzly hammered him with the shotgun butt lingered.

J.C. struggled to a sitting position on the floor where he'd fallen. He opened his other eye. Images failed to come into focus and seemed to swim and weave as if caught in the current of a mountain stream.

Several feet from him, Lynne knelt by Grizzly who sipped from a mug of steaming coffee, a votive offering, perhaps, from Lynne. She whispered something to Grizzly, then rose and moved toward J.C. She stopped in front of him.

She drew back her foot as if to kick him, then seemed to think better of it. Instead, she merely used her foot to push J.C. back to a prone position on the floor. "You asshole," she hissed. "Did you really think you were just going to stroll out the door?"

J.C. squeezed his eyes shut and didn't respond. Waves of pain rippled through his head. Dampness—blood?—slicked the right side of his face.

"Come on, you S.O.B., stand up," Lynne said.

J.C. felt her hands slip beneath his armpits. With her help, he wobbled to his feet. In a less than gentle manner, she steered him back to the table he'd been at earlier and plopped him down on the bench seat. "Stay," she ordered, as if he were a dog.

A gust of wind burst down the chimney, stirred the embers to life, and shot a shower of sparks onto the hearth.

Lynne glided away, through the semi-darkness, back to Grizzly who held his coffee mug aloft, a signal, J.C. guessed, for a refill. She leaned over Grizzly to retrieve the mug, edging her ample assets close to his face in an apparent attempt to raise his awareness . . . and perhaps something else.

His hand freed of the cup, Grizzly made a brush pass across her chest, but she stepped back and swatted his paw away. Like a bristly hog in rut, he started after her, but Lynne set a hand against his chest, said something, and he sank back into his Adirondack chair with an audible grunt.

Lynne returned shortly from a darkened recess of the house with his refill, placed it on an arm of the chair, said something, patted his head, and returned to where J.C. sat.

"You and Griz are pretty tight, huh?" J.C. said. "No wonder you get spooked every time Cave Man shows up. Looks to me like you're playing both ends against the middle. Bet you just can't get enough, right?" His anger bubbled over—anger at being duped by someone who told him *I can help*, who told him *I feel like a prisoner*, who told him *I want out of here, too*.

She slapped him, hard. With the pain-o-meter in his head already pegged, it felt as if she'd slammed a two-by-four into his skull. The coppery taste of blood pooled in his mouth.

Meaner than a mama hound . . .

He slid toward unconsciousness again.

"Listen, you dork," Lynne said, her mouth close to his ear. "Where in the hell did you think you were going when you were tippy-toeing toward the door? You didn't even have a flashlight, let alone a clue about which direction to head once you got outside. What a moron." She lowered her voice. "I said I could help."

J.C. spit blood, tried to speak, but couldn't form words.

Lynne wiped his mouth with a napkin. "What were you trying to say?"

"I said, that worked out really well for me." He slurred his words.

"It would have worked out a hell of a lot better if you'd given me a chance."

"A chance?"

"I had a plan."

"Sure you did. That's why I got coldcocked with a shotgun."

"You were dead if you went out that door. I had to stop you. Either Griz, the storm, or the wolves would have got you."

Not the wolves.

"Look," Lynne continued, "you aren't any good to me as a corpse."

"But okay as a punching bag, right?"

"I had to improvise. Sorry about that."

I'll bet.

J.C.'s head continued to hammer. He felt empathy for those who suffered migraines.

"I'm going to get Mr. Piggy another cup of coffee," Lynne said. "Hold on. Keep your eyes on me, and get ready to boogie."

"You gotta be kidding."

"Why would I be kidding?"

Then J.C. got it. "What's in the coffee?"

"Nothing. What do you think is in the coffee?"

"A Mickey?"

"You watch too many movies." She strode away.

She delivered a third mug to Grizzly and then sat on the floor beside him. J.C. noticed she'd slipped on a parka. She wrapped her arms around herself and tucked her head into the faux-fur collar of the heavy jacket as if she were cold. Grizzly, now wide awake, ran his sausage fingers through her hair with one hand and held the coffee in the other. The shotgun remained in his lap. Occasionally, they traded words, but J.C. couldn't hear what they said.

After fifteen or twenty minutes, Grizzly stood, handed Lynne the shotgun, and waddled off toward the back of the house.

Now J.C. understood. *Loads of caffeine and loads of beer. A guy's gotta piss. And Lynne had won his trust. Obviously, she was something other than an unwilling guest here. She knew these people. What the hell is going on?*

Lynne shot J.C. a heads-up glance. *Get ready to move.*

Head thumping, vision fuzzy, he stood, zipped his parka, and got ready for something—he wasn't sure what. But if it meant getting out of here, the something didn't matter.

Lynne turned to watch Grizzly. When he disappeared into the shadows, she motioned J.C. toward the door.

J.C. hesitated, wanting to flee, but still uncertain, still trying to make sense of the unfolding events.

"Now!" Lynne mouthed and again waved J.C. toward the door.

This time he moved, no longer attempting to analyze things. Lynne joined him at the door, flung it open, and pushed him through it. She followed. "Go, go, go," she yelled and pulled the door shut behind them, trying not to slam it.

They plunged into a dark world of swirling, wind-whipped snow.

She held the shotgun in her left hand, yanked a flashlight from her parka with her right, handed it to J.C., then pulled out a second light for herself.

Their beams revealed nothing but the white blur of airborne snow. J.C., disoriented, head thundering, flicked his light around in a semi-panic, searching for a reference point. They couldn't have been more than ten yards from the house, but he could no longer see it. He'd heard of whiteout conditions but never actually experienced them . . . until now, a really bad time to start.

Lynne directed her beam down at the snow cover. She moved it slowly back and forth.

"There," she said. Her light illuminated a faint depression in the snow, a sort of shallow culvert. "Follow that. It's the remnant of the trail you and Cave made when you came here. It'll lead us back to your vehicle."

J.C. wondered what good that would do, since they'd likely find the G-Wagen buried in snow, but anything seemed better than hanging around the biker castle. He plunged ahead, sinking to his thighs in snow. At least the terrain favored his efforts—downhill.

The snowfall, streaking horizontally, mounted a furious attack on his face. Despite keeping his head down following the ill-defined path, the seething flakes managed to sting his cheeks like tiny shards of glass.

Behind him, Lynne began to pant audibly, her heavy intakes of breath overriding the roar of the wind. She stumbled, fell into J.C.'s back, but righted herself and yelled at him to keep moving.

In spots, the relentless wind had whipped the snow into drifts that covered the quickly-disappearing depression in a sort of white scree several feet deep. Two or three times, J.C. had to claw his way forward, using his hands to clear a path.

"Hold up," J.C. said. He stopped, turned his back to the wind-driven snow, and listened. "I thought I heard something."

"Wolves?"

"No. Like someone shouting."

Lynne, too, turned and listened.

Fighting the wind, it came. "Lynne, you bitch! You're dead! Both of you!"

"Cave," she exclaimed, her eyes wide, her gaze darting. "He's coming."

J.C. knew all McCracken had to do was follow the trail they'd already broken. It wouldn't be like the Fox and Geese game he'd played as a kid in New England. Fox and Geese involved a circular maze in the snow. The geese had a chance. There was no maze out here, just a straight line. The geese would be dead meat.

"Better rack a shell into that thing." J.C. nodded at the shotgun.

She did. "Go," she commanded.

He plowed ahead, an elk in deep snow.

Lynne stumbled again. "Shit," she cried. This time, on a steep incline, she went down, rolled twice, lost her grip on the gun. It disappeared beneath the snow. She recovered, then scrambled frantically on her hands and knees, searching for the Remington. J.C. joined in the effort, plunging his gloved hand repeatedly into the snow, but neither he nor Lynne came up with the weapon.

"Forget it," J.C. finally said. They couldn't waste any more time. "We gotta move." He pulled Lynne to her feet. At least she still had her flashlight.

They pushed on, J.C. again leading the way. His legs, despite the downhill incline, felt as if they had sandbags tied around them. He knew his pace had slowed. Even wounded, McCracken had to be gaining on them.

Though J.C.'s head continued to throb, the adrenaline rush of his escape had dulled the sharp edge of the pain. He attempted to do a quick and dirty calculation on how much of a lead he and Lynne had on McCracken.

He guessed maybe it took a couple of minutes for Grizzly to take a leak, return to his post, and discover that Lynne and her detainee had got the hell out of Dodge. Then maybe another two or three minutes to sound the alarm, roust McCracken out of his stupor, and launch a pursuit. It *would* be McCracken, of course. Lynne was his "girl," J.C. his prisoner. Regardless of his condition, McCracken would be a motivated, one-man posse. J.C. figured they had five minutes on him, at best. Less, now that they'd wasted time searching for the buried Remington. Which also meant they had no weapon.

He pressed on, though he understood the futility of it. Human nature. Fight to the end.

"I see a light," Lynne yelled, challenging the wind.

J.C. looked behind him. A faint pinprick of light winked on and off through the heavy snowfall. McCracken had closed the gap more rapidly than expected. For a flashlight beam to be visible through the storm, it had to be only a matter of yards behind them.

McCracken must have seen their beams, too. The sharp crack of a large-caliber pistol split the wind, then rode away on a strong gust. The shot didn't come close, but it served notice the game was almost over.

Lynne, strangely composed, fell against J.C., wrapping her arms around him. "Well," she said, "we tried. At least the wolves didn't get us."

McCracken emerged from the white gloom, following the semi-cleared trail. "Hi, babe," he said to Lynne and raised the Glock.

Chapter Twenty-five

Flight

Northeast Georgia
Early Friday morning, December 30

J.C. STEPPED IN front of Lynne and faced McCracken. The absurd notion that his action would have looked good on the cover of a romance novel darted through his mind. "Come on, McCracken—"

"Cave Man," McCracken reminded him. "We're friends now."

"Cave Man. This isn't right. We can work something out."

McCracken smiled. Something almost genuine. "We already have."

J.C.'s gaze moved from McCracken's right hand, which held the Glock, to his left hand, which held a flashlight . . . and the aluminum attaché case.

Lynne stepped around J.C. and went to McCracken.

"Good work, babe," McCracken said. He pecked her on the cheek, then handed her the Glock.

"Are you okay, Cave?" she asked.

"Hurtin' a little bit." He patted the side where he'd taken the trooper's bullet. "But we gotta keep moving. Griz has probably figured out by now what's happened."

J.C. wished he had.

"Hey," McCracken said. "Where's the shotgun?"

"Lost it in the snow," Lynne said. "I took a fall, dropped it, and we couldn't find it." She spread her hands in a gesture of helplessness.

"Shit. Well, try to hang onto the Glock."

"Mind telling me what's going on here?" J.C. said.

"Later," McCracken answered. "Right now we got someone on our tail who's gonna shoot first and not bother to ask any questions at all. Let's go." He swept his flashlight beam over the snow, looking for the virtually obliterated trail he and J.C. had left earlier.

"It's in the attaché case, isn't it?" J.C. said.

"What?"

"Whatever Grizzly is after."

McCracken ignored the question and stepped off into the snow, the cold, the darkness, the knife-edged wind, and surged forward, Lynne and J.C. following. Their flashlight beams occasionally cut through the slanting snowfall and illuminated, ever so briefly, the dark Appalachian forest that stood guard around them like a shadow-army of giants.

J.C. wondered if the trees still sheltered the wolves, or had they continued their foray elsewhere?

Despite having his parka zipped to his chin and his hood cinched tightly around his neck, the icy fingers of the wind clawed at his skin. He shivered lightly, but pressed on, taking long strides and lifting his legs in an exaggerated manner, hoping to generate more body heat. The pain in his head waxed and waned. Once, feeling nauseous, he paused and knelt in the snow, but the sensation passed. He concluded the blow to his head from the shotgun stock had given him at least a minor concussion.

After ten minutes or so, McCracken halted. They seemed to have reached a level area in the woods. He swung his flashlight to the right and moved the beam slowly over the snow cover, back and forth, up and down, searching. "I think this is where we turn."

"Think?" J.C. said.

The distant bark of a big-engined motorcycle tumbled out of the darkness, sounding, in some ways, more ominous than the cry of the hunting wolves had earlier.

"Griz," Lynne said.

"On a bike?" J.C. said. "You can't ride a bike in snow."

"Griz can," McCracken said. "I once saw him ford the Chattahoochee on his Fat Bob. And he claims to have ridden from Clayton to Blue Ridge in Superstorm, that blizzard we had back in '93."

The sound faded. "Come on," McCracken ordered. "We don't have much time." He turned and moved off on a course perpendicular to the one they'd been following.

If anything, the snow fell more heavily now. What remnant of the track J.C. and McCracken had carved out the previous evening now lay buried beneath fresh drifts.

"You're sure this is the right way?" J.C. asked. He shivered more vigorously now.

"If it isn't, we're screwed."

"Thanks for boosting my confidence."

"Look, Mr. Mouth, you were on point when we came up this way. You wanna lead the way back?"

"No," J.C. mumbled.

McCracken plowed ahead, albeit more slowly now it seemed. Perhaps his wound, despite being patched up, still bothered him, still seeped blood.

The growl of the motorcycle faded in and out, but seemed to draw inexorably louder each time the wind lulled. J.C. guessed Grizzly would be upon them in a matter of minutes.

"Is that it?" Lynne yelled. She pointed her beam at a heaped up pile of snow a dozen yards ahead of them.

J.C. looked. *Yes!* The *Geländewagen*, buried in snow. He kicked through the drifts, pushed past McCracken, and reached the vehicle. Snow had pyramided to the top of the SUV and filled its interior, at least the front where the shattered window had provided access.

Using his hands, he knocked the drifts away from the driver's-side door, tugged it open, then pawed at the snow filling the inside of the G-Wagen. He found the work exhausting and paused to rest, but not for long. The throaty roar of Grizzly's bike came steadily now as he closed the gap on the fleeing trio.

"Don't stop," Lynne screamed at J.C. "Griz is almost here."

McCracken busied himself knocking snow away from the dual exhausts that emptied just forward of the rear wheels on either side of the vehicle.

J.C., deciding he had enough snow cleared away, fumbled for the keys in his parka and flung himself into the driver's seat. McCracken piled into the passenger seat, and Lynne, into the rear.

"Hey," she exclaimed, "there's a shot-to-shit bear back here."

"That's Teddy," J.C. said, inserting the key into the ignition. "Your boyfriend killed him."

"This thing gonna start?" McCracken said, ignoring the exchange between J.C. and Lynne.

"It's a Mercedes." J.C. turned the key. The engine ground and groaned but didn't catch.

"Maybe you should have borrowed a Chevy." McCracken turned to look out the rear window. "Crap." Snow coated the glass.

J.C. cranked the engine again. This time it burst to life. He put the G-Wagen in gear and stepped on the accelerator. The vehicle lurched forward, snow from the hood splattering against the windshield, blotting out whatever lay in front of the SUV. He tried the wipers—frozen in place.

"I gotta clear the windshield," he said. He bounded out, landing in a deep drift. Frantically, he brushed snow from the windshield and hood. Behind the vehicle, a light emerged from the forest and stopped, pointing in the direction of the G-Wagen. The hearty growl of Griz's bike filled the night. J.C. dove back into the SUV and punched the accelerator. The rear window blew out, glass flying through the interior in a crystalline blizzard.

"Jesus!" J.C. exclaimed.

"Griz," McCracken said, ducking. "He's got an AR-15."

"What'n the hell's that?" The G-Wagen plunged forward, snaking down the narrow track toward the main road, such as it was.

"A semi-automatic rifle."

Lynne handed the Glock back to McCracken.

It took only a matter of seconds for the vehicle, zigging and zagging, to reach the road. Or at least what appeared to be the road. Only the absence of trees suggested that pavement lay beneath a carpet of deep snow extending left and right. J.C. recalled they had come from the right. He cocked the steering wheel in that direction.

"Other way," McCracken snapped.

J.C. stopped the vehicle. "Deeper into the mountains?"

"Go."

"No."

"No? What the hell do you mean, no?"

"I mean it's my vehicle, I'm the driver, and I decide where we go." J.C. understood he'd reached a seminal moment. He hadn't forgotten his mission, to get the proposal to Durham by the end of the day. There weren't many flips of the hourglass left. Maybe it already was too late, given the ferocity of the storm, but he refused to surrender, refused to let McCracken continue calling the shots. The guy was wounded, hurting, and probably, like himself, more than a little frightened. J.C.'s conclusion: McCracken still needed him as a getaway driver.

McCracken pointed the Glock at J.C.'s head. "That blow from Griz must have scrambled what few brains you've got left, dipshit."

"Cave!" Lynne shouted from the rear seat. Vigorous admonishment.

"Your call, Cave Man," J.C. said evenly. "I'm heading for Durham. You're welcome to come along if you'd like. If not, pull the damn trigger and get this over with."

The headlight from Grizzly's bike hove into view, boring through the shot-out rear window of the Mercedes and bathing its interior in supernova brightness.

"It's Griz," Lynne screamed.

Grizzly's bike halted.

Lynne ducked. "He's gonna shoot again."

J.C. didn't wait to be blasted by either Grizzly or McCracken. He spun the steering wheel all the way to the right, hammered the accelerator. The vehicle fishtailed down the road.

Grizzly's shot pinged off the roof.

J.C. eased off on the accelerator and got control of the G-Wagen. Ahead of him, the SUV's headlights illuminated a family of white-tailed deer crossing the road, wading single file through the deep white mantle. Embedded in the thick, swirling snowfall, they appeared almost ethereal, as if floating in and out of a dream.

McCracken lowered his pistol. "Well, I gotta admit, dipshit, you've got balls."

"Nothing to do with me. It's for my son. You'd understand if you had kids."

McCracken issued a derisive snort. "All I know about kids is they make good punching bags for their dads."

J.C. glanced at McCracken.

"Yeah," McCracken continued, "any time I didn't get the firewood chopped on time, forgot to feed the chickens, or maybe just because I was there, *wham*. My nickname should have been Everlast."

"Sorry," J.C. said softly. He meant it. He'd never understood parents who abused their kids. Never got over the feeling that such children began life in the realm of the damned.

"I kinda figured it out after I left home," McCracken said. "My old man was unemployed most of the time, didn't have a pot to piss in, buried his troubles in cheap whiskey. Mom split from him, went to Vegas. So I was the only thing left he could exercise control over, and he did that with his fists." He paused, then added softly, "Douche bag."

Behind the G-Wagen, Grizzly's headlight appeared once more, closing fast. Not surprising. All Grizzly had to do was set his Fat Bob, as McCracken had called it, in one of the SUV's tire tracks and twist the throttle.

Chapter Twenty-six

Bogeyman

Northeast Georgia
Early Friday morning, December 30

J.C. HELD TO THE center of the road, or at least what he assumed was the center. He certainly didn't need to worry about encountering oncoming traffic, and he wanted to remain as far from the presumed edge of the road as he could. Only bad things could happen if the SUV plunged into a drainage ditch.

He maintained a slow but steady speed—in truth, a crawl—as the G-Wagen bulldozed through what must have been two feet of snow, and did so with the aplomb of a tracked vehicle on an arctic expedition. Blasts of wind, with a fury born of the tundra, hurled blinding shrouds of snow over and into the vehicle. Even with the heater on full blast, the interior of the Mercedes felt like a meat locker. J.C. and his passengers might as well have been riding in a convertible with the top down.

The visibility, if not zero, seemed only a matter of yards. J.C. had the sensation of moving through a white universe where there was no beyond, only the here and now, nothing else.

Nothing else except for the bright comet that hung doggedly on their tail. Grizzly. He made no move to pass them and apparently didn't wish to attempt firing the AR while concentrating on keeping his bike upright.

"Gotta lose that bastard," McCracken said.

"Yeah, like we can outrun him," J.C. retorted.

McCracken grunted and turned in his seat. "Get down," he said to Lynne. "Cover your ears." He rested his forearms on the back of the seat, took a two-handed grip on the Glock, and pointed it out the virtually glassless rear window.

Grizzly must have seen McCracken's actions and switched to high beam, throwing a blinding shaft of light into the SUV.

McCracken, startled, jerked the trigger as the brightness flooded into the vehicle. His shot blew through the roof of the G-Wagen instead of flying out the rear window.

"Shit," he shouted. He steadied himself and squeezed off two more rounds, the empty shell casings arcing into J.C.'s lap.

J.C., deafened by the Glock's firing, watched through the rearview mirror as the headlight tipped into the snow, spun, and disappeared.

"You got him!" he yelled but couldn't hear himself. Instantly, regret surged through him. It didn't seem right to rejoice over the shooting of another human, but his emotional pendulum swung quickly back. He realized if it hadn't been Grizzly, it probably would have been one, or all, of them.

McCracken turned, settled back into his seat, and clutched at his side. "I don't think I hit him. I think he just laid the bike down and slid off the road."

"Maybe that's enough," Lynne said, sitting up again. "Maybe he'll quit."

"Not Grizzly," McCracken answered. "He's like the bogeyman. You can't kill him. He'll be back."

J.C. glanced at McCracken. "You okay?"

McCracken stared back but didn't answer, which was answer enough.

They arrived at what appeared to be an intersection. Snow had plastered over the road signs so J.C. had no idea which direction might lead to Clayton. He turned to McCracken. "Okay, Sacajawea."

McCracken raised his head, scowled, and looked slowly around. "Sacajawea? The Indian chick who helped Lewis and Clark? Hell, I don't recognize anything." He sounded slightly out of breath. "Everything looks the same. White."

J.C. acknowledged their dilemma. They inhabited a featureless world; no shades of color; no perception of depth; no sense of direction. They might as well be prisoners in a sack of flour.

He sat for a moment, head resting on the steering wheel, as snow danced and darted through the G-Wagen's interior in a mocking ballet. "Hey," he said softly and turned to Lynne. "Keep an eye out for Griz."

He'd almost forgotten; like his own car, the G-Wagen had something called a COMAND® system that included GPS navigation. He activated it, entered Clayton as a destination.

McCracken watched. He shook his head. "No, not Clayton. You

got a 'message' to your wife, remember? She undoubtedly called the cops. So they're on the lookout for a Mercedes SUV with Georgia dealer plates. Let's stay out of towns, especially ones in Georgia. Otherwise, this ends badly for both of us. I get caught. You don't make it to North Carolina."

J.C. had to agree with McCracken. Cops wouldn't be out patrolling in a blizzard, they'd be hunkered down close to their home bases. And a G-Wagen, especially one with shot-out windows and a bullet hole or two, would stand out like a rabbi in a mosque.

"So what do we do?" J.C. asked.

"Scan down on the map toward South Carolina."

J.C. did. McCracken leaned close to the navigation screen. "There," he said. He pointed at a dot labeled Westminster. "Program that in. We'll follow the back roads into South Carolina, then toward I-85."

"So you're on my side now?"

"As long as it keeps me and Lynne alive."

With the visibility nil in the swirling, wind-whipped snow, and road signs caked in white, the navigation system proved its worth, highlighting intersections and turns that remained otherwise invisible.

J.C. held the G-Wagen at a steady yet snail-like pace as it wallowed through the storm like a land-bound ice breaker. In truth, he couldn't see a thing except for the shimmering brightness of the headlight beams reflecting off the thick, relentless snowfall.

He hunched forward, leaning against the steering wheel, almost willing his vision to see things that couldn't be seen. Futile, he realized. He gave up, sat back, and let the GPS guide him.

"Like flying by instruments," he said, though he had never flown a plane. "And it doesn't help I've got snow spinning around in the cockpit." He looked pointedly at McCracken.

"Only because you acted like an asshole," McCracken said.

"I didn't shoot it out, you did, Cave," J.C. countered.

"Okay," McCracken growled, "next time I'll blow your brains out instead of a window."

"That's comfort—oh, shit!" J.C. hammered the brakes, but too late. The G-Wagen slid forward, nosing into the boughs of a massive pine lying prone across the road. A victim of the storm.

"What happened?" Lynne asked.

"Tree," J.C. said. "Guess I'd better get out and take a look."

He opened the door, hopped out into knee-deep snow, and struggled to the front of the vehicle. A built-in brush-guard seemed to have absorbed the brunt of the encounter with the tree, with bent and scratched grillwork the only visible damage.

He climbed back into the G-Wagen. "Looks okay," he said.

"Now what?" Lynne asked.

"We backtrack."

"And maybe run into Griz?"

"Or we could just sit here and wait for him."

McCracken, who appeared to have been half asleep, joined the conversation. "Not much of an option. Turn this thing around and head back to the last intersection."

"Then what?" Lynne said.

"Sacajawea's digital daughter," J.C. answered and patted the navigation screen.

He performed a three-point turn, set the SUV into the tire tracks he'd just made, and drove off, moving a bit faster now that he had a readymade trail to follow. Lynne did have a point. What about Grizzly? McCracken seemed doubtful he'd put him out of the game, so he likely was still on their trail. If they encountered him head on, it could be an ugly scene. On the other hand, if they could get back to the previous intersection before Griz caught up with them, it could work out well: diverging tire tracks might confuse him.

They reached the intersection in a matter of minutes without meeting Grizzly. J.C. stopped and programed an alternate route into the navigation system, one he hoped would carry them east and south in the direction of South Carolina and the interstate. But that didn't happen. They'd been on the only road in the tiny arrowhead of North-east Georgia that crossed the Chattooga River into South Carolina. Now the GPS system vectored them southwest, back toward Clayton.

J.C. studied the proposed route. It eventually moved them off the road to Clayton and southward through virtually uninhabited terrain with switchbacks, ridges, and hollows. It would be an arduous trip, slow and dangerous. But unless they encountered more fallen trees, the G-Wagen should be up to the job. They should be able to reach another highway that would carry them across the Chattooga into South Carolina.

"Lynne," J.C. said, "there's a picnic cooler back there with some sandwiches and cookies and stuff. You wanna see if you can fish something out for us to eat? I'm starving. If you and Cave want something, help yourselves."

"I think Cave's asleep," she said.

Soft snores from McCracken confirmed her assessment.

"Well, grab a bite for yourself then. I'll take a roast beef if you can find it."

Lynne dug through the basket.

"Oh, Jesus," J.C. said.

"What?"

"The navigation screen just went blank. No satellite signal." He thumped the screen with his forefinger as though that might restore it to life. Nothing. Truly driving blind now, he slowed the G-Wagen to a creep.

"What's the matter? Can you fix it?"

Another eddy of snow curled through the vehicle's interior, a slap in the face emphasizing just how bad off their situation had suddenly become. Lost in the middle of nowhere, in a blizzard, with a pissed-off outlaw biker likely still on their tail.

"I don't know what's wrong with it. Might be something electrical. Maybe a loose connection." He slapped the unit with the palm of his hand. The screen continued to display NO SATELLITE SIGNAL.

McCracken awoke. "What the hell?"

"The nav unit is kaput," J.C. said.

McCracken mumbled something, sat up, and stared at the screen. "It still has power."

J.C. shrugged. "So?"

"So there's nothing wrong with it."

"Why'd it stop working?"

"Because it lost the sat signal."

"I know that."

"Why do think that happened?"

J.C. stopped the SUV. "Do you want to play a game, or do you have an idea?"

"I'm just a *dumb* biker and a *wanted* felon. How could I possibly have an idea?"

"I never said you were dumb. You told me you did well in college."

"But you had to be thinking 'What a moron,' right?" McCracken winced and leaned back against the headrest.

J.C. didn't answer.

"Where's the antenna?" McCracken said, his voice low. He seemed to have to force the words from his mouth.

For a moment, the question seemed a non sequitur to J.C. Then he got it. "Oh."

He opened the door, stepped out onto the narrow running board of the vehicle, and scanned the roof. He spotted a small, solid mound of ice and snow, the size of several generous scoops of ice cream, just above the center of the windshield. He stretched out and knocked the crusty pile away from a stubby black antenna. He ducked his head back into the interior.

"We got a signal," Lynne announced.

McCracken looked up, smiled, then leaned back in his seat and closed his eyes.

"Here's your roast beef," Lynne said. She tossed a sandwich onto J.C.'s seat. "Looks like your wife thought she was packing for a picnic." She pulled out a red and white checkered tablecloth, an apparent fugitive from an Italian restaurant, and displayed it for J.C.

"Let me see that," he said.

Lynne handed it to him. He folded it into fours, then held it up against the shattered window next to his seat. *It might work.*

"There's a roll of duct tape behind the rear seat," he said. "And a utility knife. See if you can find them."

Lynne hesitated. "Knife?"

"So I can cut the tape. I'm gonna secure the tablecloth over the window. At least it'll keep the snow out of my face."

From the front seat, without opening his eyes, McCracken said, "It's okay, babe. He's not a commando."

Unfortunately, J.C. thought.

Lynne handed him the tape and knife. In short order he had a jury-rigged shield over the window. He didn't know if it would hold, but at the low speeds they'd been traveling, it should do just fine. He surveyed his work.

"People will think we're Appalachian hillbillies driving a hundred thousand dollar beater," he said. He handed the tape and knife back to Lynne.

"Not likely," she responded, "because there's nobody around to see us."

J.C. stepped out onto the running board one last time to make certain the antenna remained clear. That's when he heard it. The snarl of an engine riding the wind, fading in and out. Not a truck. Something smaller . . . and that could be only one thing, one person.

J.C. looked back up the road. No headlight beam, at least not yet.

McCracken heard it, too, and moved the Glock onto his lap. "Go," he commanded.

Chapter Twenty-seven

Encounter

Northeast Georgia
Early Friday morning, December 30

J.C. TORE INTO his sandwich while steering with one hand, probably not the safest way to maneuver an SUV on a twisting, snow-encrusted road, but his hunger trumped the risk. Besides, at ten to fifteen miles per hour, he wasn't exactly moving at NASCAR speeds. The snow, driven by a saber-toothed wind, showed no sign of relenting.

Lynne nibbled on a ham and cheese sandwich and kept watch out the rear window for Grizzly. McCracken continued to doze.

At some point close to 5 a.m., they crossed the Chattooga into South Carolina. And still no Grizzly.

"Think we lost him?" J.C. said.

McCracken snapped an eye open. "Grizzly? Not a chance. He's still back there. Just being careful. Remember, he's on a bike. That's pretty damn treacherous even though he's using our tracks. Plus, his face is getting plastered with snow. That'll slow him, but not stop him. He's highly motivated."

"What have you got he wants so badly?"

"My . . . our retirement," McCracken said. He glanced toward Lynne.

"You wanna be more specific?"

"No. Let's just say, whatever it is, you don't wanna get stopped by the cops. By the time things got sorted out, your deadline for getting to Durham would be nothing but a sweet remembrance."

J.C. fit the pieces together. "So now I'm a drug runner?"

McCracken didn't respond.

J.C. drew a deep breath. How much worse could things get? As if the blizzard weren't enough, he had a cop-shooter beside him, an angry outlaw biker behind him, and a case full of illegal drugs inside his vehicle. *All I wanted to do was deliver a proposal.*

The terrain became less severe, more rolling as they pressed southeastward. J.C. picked up a little speed. The road remained unplowed, but at least straightened out. The G-Wagen's headlights, cutting through the storm, bounced off an abandoned pickup stuffed into a snow drift on the side of the road.

"Hold it," McCracken said. "Stop. Lynne, give me your flashlight." He pointed the beam at the truck's rear license plate. "We could use that."

"What?" J.C. said.

"The plate. We may stand out because we're a Gee-wagon, or whatever this thing is, but a Carolina license instead of a Georgia dealer's plate might help our cause, might make folks a bit less curious."

"You mean aside from the fact we've got a red-and-white diaper taped over a window, no glass in the rear window, and a couple of holes not made by woodpeckers?"

McCracken smiled. "Don't be such a Gloomy Gus. Grab a screwdriver and get out there."

J.C. pulled a screwdriver and pair of pliers from a tool kit in the rear of the Mercedes, tromped through the snow to the pickup, unscrewed the plate, and had it on the Mercedes in less than five minutes.

After mounting the plate, he stood and listened. Nothing but the low-pitched roar of the wind through the pines reached his ears. Perhaps they'd pulled out a bigger lead on Grizzly than he'd thought, or maybe the guy had given up the chase. He climbed back into the G-Wagen.

"I didn't hear Griz out there," he announced.

"He's out there, trust me," McCracken said. "He won't give up until he's dead . . . or we are."

"Wonderful," J.C. muttered and drove off.

They reached the outskirts of the tiny town of Westminster around six.

McCracken, seemingly more alert than earlier, called for another stop. "Let's assume they've got at least a small police force here," he said. "Someone might be up and about, so we probably should stay off the main drag." He fiddled with the navigation system and zoomed in on the town. "I'm thinking we go this way." He pointed at a complex of narrow, crisscrossing roads on the south side of Westminster.

J.C. eased the G-Wagen forward. "Looks like someone *is* up and about." Fresh tracks seamed the snow-covered highway they'd been following.

McCracken examined them. "Might be a police cruiser."

"Or a farmer."

McCracken shrugged. "Whatever. We'd better take to the secondary roads now, just in case." He studied the map more closely. "Take a right at the next intersection. We can weave our way around without having to go through the center of town and reach another highway that leads to the interstate."

J.C. turned into a warren of semi-rural, semi-suburban lanes—dark, white, and silent. He moved slowly, trying to guess where the center of the streets lay, buried as they were under a thick blanket of snow. If someone had just plopped him down here without the benefit of a GPS, he would have guessed he was slipping through a small New England village in the dead of winter, not through a laid-back whistle-stop in the Deep South.

To J.C., the snow appeared to have slackened, but maybe his imagination had kicked in, or wishful thinking had taken over. Achy and tired, he realized the toll the trip had already taken, though they had traveled less than forty miles. The slick roads, the near-zero visibility, the pursuit by Grizzly, the gunfire, all had served to bind his muscles and nerves into rock-solid knots.

"I think there's a thermos of coffee back there," he said to Lynne. "Maybe it's still warm."

She rustled around and came up with it. "It's still steaming," she said as she poured him a cup. She leaned forward to hand it to him.

He turned to say thanks. That's when he felt McCracken's hand tap his thigh.

"Don't stop," McCracken said, his gaze fixed on something out the windshield, dead ahead. "Just keep going."

J.C. saw it, too. A police car, blue lights strobing through the snow, sitting crosswise in the road, blocking it. J.C. glanced at McCracken.

"Don't stop. Don't turn around," McCracken said. "That would really draw his interest. Just ease up to him like anyone else would and ask what's going on."

"You don't think he's waiting for us?"

"Think about it. How in the hell would he know we're coming?" McCracken slipped the Glock into his parka.

"For God's sake, don't use that thing," J.C. said, his heart suddenly banging like a string of firecrackers going off.

McCracken kept his right hand on the weapon and with his left took the coffee from Lynne and sipped it. "Be cool," he said. "Just be cool." He turned to Lynne. "Put the attaché case on floor. Cover it with something."

"There's some blankets behind the seat," J.C. said, his voice wobbly.

The G-Wagen rolled up to the cruiser and stopped.

"Just remember," McCracken said, "we both want the same thing here—not to arouse suspicion."

Sure. With a rag over the window and a .45-caliber hole in the roof.

A police officer, slightly overweight, a black watch cap tugged down over his ears and eyebrows, wriggled from the cruiser and waded through the snow toward the G-Wagen. He flicked on his flashlight and aimed the beam through the SUV's windshield.

McCracken's right hand moved slightly, adjusting the position of his pistol.

J.C. swallowed hard. If he had to, he'd yell a warning or disrupt McCracken's aim. But he didn't want it to come to that. He cracked open the door and stuck his head out.

"Hey," he said, mustering more confidence than he had, "what's going on?"

Windy Hill Towers
Friday morning, December 30

TOM'S ALARM BUZZED at six thirty. He pushed out of bed, shuffled to the bathroom, then wandered toward the living room. He didn't get far before he remembered he had a house guest and retreated to his bedroom to get fully dressed.

Once clothed, he headed down the hallway toward the living room again. He stopped when he reached the door of the guest bedroom. Open. He rapped on the doorframe. "Sophie? You up?" No response. He called again. Silence. He leaned through the doorway cautiously and peered into the room. The bed, rumpled, sat empty. No Sophie.

The door to the bathroom had been open when he passed it. She hadn't been in there. Deciding she'd dressed and gone to the kitchen or living room, he continued down the hall.

"Hey, Sophie," he called out. "Good morning." No response.

In the kitchen, he found a hand-scrawled note on the counter.

Tom,

Thanks for your hospitality. I truly appreciated it. See you at work.
Sophie (The Lyoness) ☺

The note, terse and impersonal—except for the Lyoness touch and smiley face—took Tom aback. But then, what had he expected? A message signed *xoxo*? No, not from Sophie, ever the professional, ever the boss concerned with propriety . . . sans one little slip.

He wondered how long ago she'd taken off. Perhaps he could still spot her. He trotted to the living room window and looked out and down. But there was no out and down, only an opaque void of dimensionless grayness. No street lights. No traffic lights. No headlights. No building lights. For all Tom knew, the city of Atlanta had ceased to exist.

A brilliant flash of blue-white light sent him stumbling back from the window in surprise. For a millisecond, the darkness outside transformed into a shimmering fabric of streaked whiteness.

He remembered now. The upper-air disturbance. Instability. Lightning. As if seconding his assessment, a rumble of thunder shook the air with teeth-rattling vibrations. The condo plunged into total blackness. He wondered how much of the metro area had been rendered powerless by the storm, either by snow and wind bringing down power lines and trees, or by lightning taking out transformers. If ever a city had been rendered helpless, Atlanta had to be it.

New York City had been body-slammed by Sandy, but vehicular traffic and emergency services had continued to function, at least on a reduced level. New Orleans had been devastated by Katrina, but even there rescues by boat and helicopters had been carried out. But Atlanta? Atlanta had suffered a traumatic amputation of its transportation and emergency capabilities. For a city that struggled to deal with two inches of snow, two feet became hopeless. Even the plows had run up a white flag.

If structures caught fire, they would burn to the ground. Medical emergencies would go un-aided. Crimes, un-responded to. At least until the blizzard abated, a metropolitan area with a population of more than half the states in the country would teeter on the edge of anarchy.

And Sophie? What the hell was she thinking, taking off in the dark, in the middle of a historic storm, through snow-blocked streets?

Tom scrambled to retrieve his flashlight, feeling his way through a maze of tables and chairs and jutting counters to the kitchen drawer where he stored it. Not there. Sophie must have found it. At least she had light. But he didn't. *No, wait.* He remembered one stowed in his nightstand.

He performed his blind-man routine down the hall to the bedroom. He fished around in the nightstand and found a fist-sized flashlight that probably didn't pump out any more brightness than a votive candle. Following its anemic beam, he rushed to the front closet, dug out his parka, gloves, and Timberland hiking shoes, and bundled up. He still couldn't believe Sophie had left for work in these conditions. If she'd gotten lost or fallen . . .

"Like this should be my problem," he muttered as he worked his way down seventeen flights of stairs to the condo's lobby. He stepped outside into a world devoid of tangible reference points. The wind tore at him; the snow slashed the exposed parts of face. He cinched the parka's hood even tighter.

He aimed the virtually useless flashlight at the surface of the snow, trying to pick up Sophie's trail. A faint gully in the snow, already drifted over, gave the only hint to the direction she had gone. He stepped off, following her tracks, her *presumed* tracks.

After a couple of minutes, he stopped and lifted his head. A stab of panic surged through him. He realized he had no idea where he was. Somewhere between the condo and the NE-TV building, yes, but he could have been on Alaska's North Slope, too. He was that alone, that isolated. He gulped a lungful of icy, snow-filled air and calmed himself. He swung the light in a slow circle, searching for something, anything, that might offer a clue as to whether he was standing in the middle of a street or in a vacant lot.

The beam caught the base of a light standard, a utility pole, a row of tall bushes buried in snow. Somehow, perhaps with the help of a more powerful flashlight, Sophie had managed to stay oriented, moving toward NE-TV.

He pushed on, following the faint depression left by his boss. He sank deep into the snow with each step and shortly found himself gasping for breath. At last, he reached the entrance to the corporate parking lot, marked, ironically, by a hillock of snow under which slumbered Sophie's Lexus.

Exhausted, he stumbled into the lobby. He bent forward, hands on his knees, and wheezed like a steam locomotive from a bygone era.

Manfred, the security officer on duty, sat behind his lobby desk. "Didn't expect to see anybody this morning," he said, his voice thick with congestion and lack of sleep. "But first Miss Sophie, she come in, now you. Who-eee. Ba-a-a-d time to be out and about." He drew out the word *bad*.

"Only mad dogs and Eskimos," Tom said and wobbled off toward the forecast center.

"What?" Manfred called after him.

Tom entered the production area, pleased to see the auxiliary power units had kicked in, supplying light and heat to the space. In the forecast center, he spotted Al and Sophie deep in conversation. Al had undoubtedly spent the night at NE-TV, catching a catnap here and there, but remaining on top of things.

Tom pushed into the center and uttered his good mornings.

"Hey, junior," Al responded, his clothes looking as wrinkled as his face.

Sophie, in contrast, ignored Tom's greeting. Her coolness unsettled him, suggesting any apparent thaw in their professional relationship had been superficial and temporary, at least on her part; any ceasefire in their workplace cold war had been voided. Then again, maybe he'd read too much into their evening together. *Whatever.* The thought came with a wisp of disappointment.

Sophie, her discussion with Al complete, crooked a finger at Tom. "My office," she said and strode off.

Al squinted at Tom. "You just can't stay off her shit list, can you?"

Chapter Twenty-eight

The Ladies

Western South Carolina
Friday morning, December 30

"DIDN'T EXPECT anybody out in this weather." The police officer approached the G-Wagen. Clouds of vapor puffed from his nose and mouth into the cold snowfall. "Where ya'll comin' from?" He obviously knew they weren't locals.

J.C. turned to McCracken, wanting to key off him. McCracken knew this area, or at least J.C. hoped he did, and could probably come up with a convincing lie. With time running out to make it to Durham, he had to admit his captor was right. They both wanted, as bizarre as it seemed, the same thing: not to be stopped.

Instead of McCracken, Lynne responded. She leaned over J.C.'s shoulder. "Wahalla," she said through the opened door. "My husband"—she inclined her head toward McCracken—"has an appointment at the Toccoa Cancer Center this morning. We didn't want to miss it."

The cop reached the SUV's door and stopped. He examined the thin checkered tablecloth taped over the window. "Not what I'd expect on a Mercedes."

"Had a nasty encounter with a downed pine tree," J.C. said, working hard to keep his voice steady. "Visibility's crap in this snow."

"Yeah, I know," the officer responded. "Lots of radio chatter about fallen trees and blocked roads." He took a step back from the G-Wagen and ran his gaze over it.

J.C.'s gut knotted. He knew the bullet hole in the roof would stand out like a peach in a pickle barrel.

"Hey, sir," Lynne chirped, "I'll bet you know my friend, Tanya Gibson. She's lived in Westminster like forever."

The cop moved his gaze to Lynne and smiled. "Can't say I do, miss. I don't necessarily know everybody in town."

"You must be cold out here, Officer," Lynne said, keeping her patter going. She reached for the thermos. "We've got an extra cup, and the coffee's hot. Be glad to pour some for you."

"That's okay, I've got—"

"So what are you doing out here anyway? Waiting for bad guys or something? You should be home, snug in your little beddy." Lynne laughed lightly, the touch of a Southern belle.

She had her charm offensive turned on high, but J.C. wished she hadn't mentioned bad guys. It didn't seem, well, appropriate. His heart skipped a beat.

But the officer appeared socially disarmed. "No, not waiting for bad guys," he said. "There's a water main break on the Toccoa Highway. Road's a solid sheet of ice. I'm just sitting here to keep people off it. Didn't really expect anybody coming from this direction, though. You folks get lost? This isn't exactly the main road."

J.C. studied the officer's face, what little was visible below his watch cap. The guy may be a small town cop, but he was good at not accepting things at face value. *Think fast.*

"We were using the GPS," J.C. said, "but it went kaflooey, and we got kind of lost coming into Westminster."

"Maybe your antenna got snow covered, and you lost your signal," the officer said. He reached over the roof toward the front of the G-Wagen. "Looks okay now, though."

"Yeah, it is," J.C. said. "I think that was the problem."

Again, Lynne piped up from the back seat. "We've got some sandwiches, sir," she said. "If you're hungry, we'd be more than glad to share. Let's see"—she opened the picnic hamper—"there's roast beef and—"

J.C. broke into her chatter, afraid she might be overdoing it with the Southern hospitality schtick. "Look, I'm afraid we have to get going, Officer, if we're going to make our appointment. Any suggestions on how to get around the iced-over section?"

"Yeah, you're going to have to head back to the main drag and look for West King Street. Follow that out of town. It'll bring you back to the Toccoa Highway. Good thing ya'll got this German half-track. It's probably the only thing that can get around in this mess."

"Thanks, we appreciate your help," Lynne said. "Sure you don't want some—"

J.C., wishing she'd shut up, interrupted her again, added his thanks, shut the door, and backed down the street away from the cop, not wanting to give him a chance to realize the rear window was missing, too, if he hadn't already.

J.C. retraced their tracks to the main street and turned south.

"How'd he miss the bullet hole in the roof?" he asked.

"Maybe he got distracted by Chatty Cathy back there." McCracken looked at Lynne. "Or more likely, he just didn't see it because the roof was covered with snow."

"You think he was suspicious?"

"Sure, just because he's a small-town cop doesn't mean he's Barney Fife."

"Why didn't he hold us there if he was suspicious?"

McCracken shrugged and grimaced.

"Still hurting?" J.C. asked.

"No, I just enjoy scrunching up my face for the amusement of others." McCracken leaned his head against the window.

"You need a doctor."

"Sure I do, but we both know that's not gonna happen. Doctors have to report gunshot wounds. Oh, and to answer your question about why we weren't detained, maybe the cop wasn't sure. Maybe our bullshit story rang just true enough that he bought into it." He flashed a smile at Lynne.

"Or roadblocks could be going up all over the place," J.C. said, taking a dimmer view of their circumstances.

"Even if that's happening," McCracken said, "and it wouldn't be easy in these conditions, we've still got the advantage with, as the officer called it, our 'German half-track.'"

"So where to?"

"I-85." McCracken sat up and programmed a route into the GPS. "There," he said when he'd finished. "Follow Route 24 to the interstate, just northwest of Anderson."

J.C., back on an unplowed and untracked road, pushed southeastward through flat Carolina farmland, dark and silent under a deep snow cover. The snowfall had indeed diminished, but the incessant wind continued to whip streamers of snow over the landscape in a choreography worthy of the arctic tundra.

McCracken sipped the coffee Lynne had handed him earlier. "Were you scared back there, when we encountered the cop?" he asked J.C.

"Of course."

"Did you pray?"

"I—"

"Forgot?"

"No, I was . . . it just didn't enter my mind." J.C. knew where McCracken was headed with his question and didn't want to openly concede the point: that his motivations had been fear-driven, not divinely inspired. He elected to change the topic.

"Lynne," J.C. asked, "how'd you come up with your little spiel for the cop? That was pretty good."

"It wasn't hard," she answered. "I was raised around here, in Pickens, so I know the area well."

"And you have a girlfriend in Westminster?"

"No, in Easley. I just transplanted her."

"What about the cancer center?"

"My daddy died of lung cancer when I was twelve. I remember making trips to Toccoa."

"I'm sorry," J.C. said. "I know about cancer." He told her about Cole, about why he was out here in the middle of a blizzard, about how he ended up with McCracken in his vehicle. Ulterior motive, of course: It wouldn't hurt to have some sympathy on his side if it helped him stay alive.

He finished, then let the conversation lay fallow briefly before asking Lynne, "How'd you and Cave Man get hooked up?"

"After Daddy passed, I helped my mother raise my three younger sisters. It was hard. Daddy didn't have any life insurance. Mother didn't have a job, or any skills for that matter. We managed to survive, subsist really, on government and church handouts. But I wanted more out of life than being a nanny to my sisters, living in a leaky shotgun shack, and wearing hand-me-down rags from church."

"Good ol' Southern Baptists," McCracken interjected.

"Yeah, as if my life weren't tedious and boring enough, there I was stuck in a no-drinking, no-dancing, no-fooling-around-with-boys zone. I got damn tired of hearing God had a plan for me and that everything would work out fine in the end. All I had to do was be a good little girl, pray, and go to church. Tell ya what, if God had a plan for me, He must have shredded it by mistake. My life sucked, and there was no way I was getting out of it by staying where I was, or praying." Latent anger threaded her words.

"So along came your white knight on a motorcycle," J.C. said.

"No, not quite. As soon as I was out of high school, I bailed out of Pickens and headed to Panama City Beach. Got a job at a dive called Beer, Boobs and Bikinis. Tells you what kind of a joint that was, but it turned out to be a place where knights in shining armor hung out." She ran her fingers through McCracken's hair.

J.C. smiled. *A match made in heaven.*

"So, I rode off into the sunset on the back of a Harley," Lynne said. "Fun. Adventure. Thrills. Cave's really just a big ol' teddy bear, ya know. He's a good guy."

Sure he is, aside from shooting a cop, sporting a rap sheet, and teaming up with outlaw bikers. J.C. turned his head toward McCracken. "Yeah, we'll have to knock back a few beers together sometime after this is all over."

McCracken, through pain-riddled, half-shut eyes, returned his gaze. "Your sarcasm aside, maybe you're a bit more optimistic about how this works out in the end than I am." He took another swallow of coffee, then went on. "I mean, really, what are the odds you make it to Durham in time? The blizzard is bad enough, but we've got a pissed-off biker and maybe the cops looking for us, too. I know Griz and the cops really aren't *your* problem. But as far as Griz is concerned, you're helping me, so you're the enemy. And if the cops catch us, you're suddenly my hostage. See what I mean? Bad juju all around."

The Natural Environment Television Network
Friday morning, December 30

WITH SOPHIE'S office door already open, Tom rapped on the frame to announce his presence. She motioned him in while fixing her attention on a large, wall-mounted, flat-screen TV monitor.

With at least a modicum of trepidation—for he never really knew how to read her moods—he stepped into her office. She looked remarkably fresh for having spent the night at his place without the benefit of toiletries, cosmetics, or a change of clothes, and then risen at oh-dark-thirty to hike to work through a snowstorm. She appeared to be one of those rare women who looked better without makeup than with.

"Have a seat," she said, her gaze still on the monitor. "Let's watch this."

One of NE-TV's old-timers, Art Iccarino, who bore a mop of hair like a Kansas wheat field, faced the camera and tried to look grim. Tom knew otherwise. Like most meteorologists, when it came to "big weather," Art's gut response would fall more into the teenager-with-a-new-Corvette category.

"If you're one of the lucky ones in the Southeast who still has power this morning," Art said, "allow me to apprise you you're waking up to a historic weather event." He smiled. He couldn't help it. "Metro Atlanta, for instance, is being pounded by true blizzard conditions with the visibility near zero and winds gusting to forty-five miles per hour." A video from Hartsfield-Jackson popped onto the screen. In the background, the International Terminal loomed out of the gray gloom like a deserted warehouse. In the foreground, a snow-covered automobile, a taxi or police car perhaps, sat buried like some prehistoric animal trapped by a sudden ice age. If someone had told Tom it's really a video from Moscow's Domodedovo International Airport, he would have believed it.

"Officially," Art voiced-over, a more serious timbre to his voice, "nineteen inches of snow have fallen on Atlanta, though some northern suburbs report as much as two feet. Drifts to five and six feet are common. Virtually all roads are impassable. At least a dozen structure fires have gone unchecked with firefighters unable to reach them. Medical emergencies are not being responded to with EMTs stranded. At least three deaths have resulted, and, sadly, authorities expect many more. The National Guard is employing Humvees in attempts to reach the direst emergencies, but even those vehicles are struggling.

"Outside of the Atlanta metro area," Art went on, "reports are flooding in of people trapped on secondary roads, stuck in their cars with no way for help to reach them. Around the Southeast, the number of people stranded at airports, including Hartsfield-Jackson, is estimated at ten thousand. Locations affected include Charlotte, Columbia, and Raleigh-Durham.

"Among the more urgent situations we've heard of are several nursing homes, in and around Atlanta, whose auxiliary power generators have failed. National Guard troops, including medics, are making valiant efforts to reach these facilities, but so far have not been successful."

"Damn," Sophie muttered, "I didn't think it would be this bad."

"Gandalf was right," Tom added softly, referring to Al. "All along, he was right."

"Geezers rule," Sophie said. "Never discount the 'been-there-seen-that' factor."

"Yeah."

On television, Art continued speaking. "The Governor has declared a state of emergency for North Georgia including Atlanta. He has also initiated action to make the state eligible for disaster aid under federal law."

The on-screen image morphed into a weather map. "Here's the current situation," Art said. "The surface low or storm center is crawling northeastward, still strengthening, just off the South Carolina coast. Meanwhile, the upper-level storm center, packing intense snowfall rates and even thunder and lightning, is trundling across northern Georgia. Just ahead of that low aloft, a tongue of dry air has swept northwestward into South Carolina. So, ironically, at that same time Atlanta is getting blitzed by whiteout conditions, much of Upstate South Carolina is catching a break. That will change significantly as the day goes on, it seems." A more ominous tone wrapped Art's words. "Here's what we expect to happen."

The map image switched to an afternoon forecast. "The upper-low, or what meteorologists sometimes refer to as a comma-head cloud because of its appearance on satellite images, will pivot over the Carolinas as the day goes on. That means that while the snow will taper off in North Georgia, it will return with a vengeance over the western Carolinas. By late morning, heavy snow will be falling in Upstate South Carolina and by late afternoon in the Charlotte-Greensboro-Raleigh corridor in North Carolina. That area, by the way, has already been dumped on by a foot or more of snow that has fallen in advance of the surface low."

"What a mess," Sophie said and muted the TV, "but at least we were on top of it."

Tom knew the "we" was meant as a poke in the eye with a sharp stick at him. Al and Sophie had led the charge; he'd been dragged along like a recalcitrant child, kicking and screaming. In ninety-nine out of a hundred similar situations he would have been right, but the only one that counted was this one.

Now he understood why he'd been summoned to the Lyoness's Lair. The network didn't need a chief of meteorology who had more the qualities of a leader of the Fuckowie Indians than, say, the Comanches.

Sophie, clad in her jeans, sweater, and Uggs from the previous day, stood and walked to where Tom sat. She pursed her lips.

Tom recognized the warning sign. *Here it comes.* As Al had said, "You just can't stay off her shit list, can you?" He stood and faced her.

"I'd like to resign rather than get the axe," he said, "if that's okay with you. Looks better on the résumé." But maybe she liked the taste of blood.

Chapter Twenty-nine

Trapped

The Natural Environment Television Network
Friday Morning, December 30

"WHY ON EARTH would you think I want to fire you?" Sophie asked. As usual, she stood in violation of Tom's personal space. As usual, he found it simultaneously uncomfortable and titillating.

"We didn't exactly see eye-to-eye on the storm," he said.

"I don't necessarily need 'yes-men' around me. Just because you get my dander up at times doesn't mean I don't appreciate independent thinking." She stepped around Tom and shut the door.

"Then why am I here, summoned to the boss's office?" he asked.

"Because you scared me." She walked back to him.

"*I* scared *you?*" he exclaimed. "I thought I was going to find your body in a snowdrift this morning."

"That's sweet. You were worried about me."

He lowered his head. "Yeah," he muttered. In impeccable Sophie-style, she'd pushed him off-balance. But this time, he realized, he had a counterpunch. He looked up. "You said I scared you. How?"

She stared at him for a long time without responding, as though deep in thought, perhaps grappling with a reluctance to continue down the path she'd taken an initial step on several days ago. Finally, she allowed a gentleness to creep into her eyes and leaned even closer to him. "Because," she whispered, "when I saw you this morning, I wanted to embrace you, kiss you. And I was terrified I'd do something in front of others that might prove, well, embarrassing to both of us." She reached out, stroked his face, then pivoted and returned to her chair.

Tom, a little wobbly, sat. He waited for Sophie to continue.

A faint blush tinted her cheeks, a complementing contrast to the dark whiteness outside the window behind her. She suddenly looked more like a woman and less like a boss.

"Thank you for last night," she said. "I know you could have left me stuck in that snowdrift out there. But you were a gentleman and stopped. Even though I'm pretty sure you didn't want to, that you wanted to see 'Her Highness' brought low, passive-aggressive retaliation for the verbal slings and arrows I've let fly at you."

She paused and fingered a gold chain around her neck, perhaps hoping Tom would join with her in a conversation about . . . what? Them? But since he had no idea where Sophie's soliloquy was bound, he elected to remain silent and let her go wherever her thoughts and words carried her. *Never pass up an opportunity to keep your mouth shut.*

She bit her lip, an expression he hadn't seen before, then resumed speaking. "I suspect I've been a little too hard on you at times in the office. Overreacted. I apologize for that. It was, I suppose, a defensive action on my part. Because . . ." She paused again.

He waited.

"Jesus, Tom. Will you help me out here? Say something? This isn't easy for me."

"What isn't easy? Where are you going with this? What do you want me to say?"

Sophie sighed audibly and tilted her head toward the ceiling. "You know I'm attracted to you. A boss isn't supposed to let that happen. I probably put too much effort into keeping you at arm's length, but I'm not sure I want to do that any longer."

Choose. Words. Carefully. He drew a deep breath and let it out. "Then we have to figure out a way to make this work."

She smiled. "We're on common ground then. May I tell you something else?"

He waited.

"True confessions," she said. "I'm standoffish when it comes to men, ever since my divorce. Phillip, my ex, was a five-star shit. He was the neighborhood gunslinger, and I, wrapped up in my career, was the last to find out. And then only after he'd notched about half a dozen 'kills,' and one of his previous conquests called it to my attention—one of those 'Hell hath no fury' things. Talk about getting body-slammed."

"I'm sorry," Tom said.

"Nothing to be sorry about. Shit happens. But now, ironically, as a 'free agent,' I find myself on the other side of the playing field, so to speak. Instead of the innocent wife, now *I'm* the target of wannabe gunslingers. I'm even an outcast in my own country club because the wives shun me, each absolutely sure I'm a threat to her marriage. So I guess I go overboard attempting to keep men at arm's length."

"I know it's not fair, Sophie, but if I may offer a male perspective, because of your success, you've become a triple threat."

She cocked her head.

"You're a woman of some fame, at least within the broadcast industry. You're well off, maybe even wealthy, and you're, well, physically attractive. In essence, you're a natural target for a certain group of guys, I suppose you would say type-A, testosterone-fueled males. And you're probably the subject of fantasies for a whole bunch of others."

"Yourself included?"

Tom felt a surge of blood rushing to his cheeks. "Yes, since we're playing truth or dare."

"I'm relieved. I was worried I'd lost my female sixth sense. I kinda thought you were, well, hiding something last night. You know, under the covers." A shadow of a smile crept across her face and she waited.

The warmth in Tom's cheeks reached egg-frying levels. *Evil woman.* He loved it.

"It's okay. I'm not trying to embarrass you. If it will help level the playing field, I had the same urges last night. In your guest bed, I had to, uh, 'service' myself. Women do that, too, you know." She stared at her desk, then looked up. "Too much information, I suppose. Anyhow, my 'thank you' for last night is genuine. You were a gentleman. No hinting around about a sexual playtime. No double entendres. No leers. You didn't hit on me, didn't make a pass. I was almost," she chuckled, "disappointed."

"So last night was a test?"

"I guess it turned out that way." She gazed directly at him, a soft stare, not a hard one. Disconcerting.

"I passed?"

She nodded.

"So now what?"

She shrugged.

"Come on, Sophie. You're the boss."

"Get back to work," she said softly, "or I'll chew your ass out again."

Tom returned to the forecast center. Al looked up as he entered. "You've still got all of your body parts?"

"She's in love with me." Tom made it sound like a throwaway line.

"Sure she is, junior. Watch out. I'll bet she's a black widow. A sexual cannibal. Mates and kills. Anyhow, you should be so lucky." He snorted a laugh and wheezed.

"Might not be a bad way for you to go out."

Al tugged at his scraggly beard. "You know, it might not be. Only one problem."

"What's that?"

"The last time I got it up, Franklin Roosevelt was in office. Your kids got an Erector Set I could borrow?"

Western South Carolina
Friday morning, December 30

UNDERCUTTING THE pewter overcast, a thin sliver of bronze, a harbinger of dawn, threaded the southeastern horizon. The snowfall had ceased, but the landscape remained white and windswept. J.C. held a steady speed on the snow-buried road. He checked the time, a little after seven. A surge of optimism rippled through him. If the weather held, even at his current plodding pace, he should be able to reach Durham by 5 p.m. A little less than ten hours.

"When we hit the interstate," he said aloud, "we'll be able to make better time, if the snow doesn't start again."

McCracken grunted and raised his head. He'd been dozing on and off. "You're assuming the interstate is open."

"They ought to be plowing. The snow's stopped."

"This is South Carolina, not South Dakota."

"My, aren't you the bluebird of happiness."

McCracken sat up and placed the Glock in the foot well. "The bluebird of happiness died of exposure, dipshit. Look, I want to put as much distance as I can between me and Georgia. But I gotta be realistic. As my old granny used to say, 'If ya think ya got it made, ya done miscalculated the sityation.'"

"Granny may have had a point," Lynne chimed in, a note of concern resonating in her words. "I caught a flash of light behind us a few seconds ago."

J.C. glanced in the rearview mirror. Nothing. "Could be a farmer up early. Was it a single beam or a pair?"

"Couldn't tell. It was just there for an instant."

McCracken retrieved the pistol. "Put your foot in it a little harder," he said to J.C. "I'll guarandamntee you it's Griz."

"It's not going to do us any good if I try to go faster, and we slide off the road. Besides, we aren't sure it's Grizzly."

"I am. I know that son of a bitch."

"There it is again," Lynne said.

J.C. saw it. Twin beams, bright, boring through the leaden dawn. Not a Harley. A car or truck. Maybe three-quarters of a mile behind them. Closing fast. Following their tracks. J.C. pressed down on the accelerator with just a little more force.

"Better go," McCracken urged. "He's comin' hard."

"It's not Griz," J.C. said. "I'll bet it's that cop."

"Don't be so sure," McCracken said. "Cops use radios. I don't see any blue strobes, either."

The G-Wagen fishtailed, but the deep snow prevented it from careening off the road. J.C. kept his foot on the accelerator, the muscles in his shoulders and hands tightening into knots of fiber pulled taut.

"Get down," McCracken said to Lynne, "just in case." He rested the Glock on the back of his seat and pointed it out the glassless rear window.

"Interstate coming up," J.C. shouted.

He reached the interchange. The road went up and over the interstate. He braked as he brought the SUV down the opposite side of the overpass, then whipped a sharp right onto the looping entrance ramp to the highway. No signs or barricades indicated the interstate was closed.

In fact, there appeared to be a single lane that had been recently plowed. A sparse and widely-spaced line of traffic, mostly eighteen-wheelers, many with chains, trundled along in the "cleared" lane, probably moving at thirty-five or forty miles per hour over packed snow and ice. The unplowed portion of the freeway remained interred beneath at least a foot and a half of powder.

J.C., feeling more confident in his driving, accelerated onto I-85. He maneuvered in between two big rigs and joined the loose parade of traffic slogging northeastward.

"It's that cop from Westminster. He just went over the overpass," Lynne said, looking out the rear window.

"It's Griz. I know it's Griz," McCracken said. "A hick-town cop ain't gonna chase us down. He'd call the staties and let them handle it."

"Whoever it is," J.C. said, "by the time he's on the interstate, we'll have a buffer of three or four eighteen-wheelers between him and us." He couldn't come to grips with which would be worse: having the cops or Grizzly on their tail.

"That's great until we have to exit," McCracken said. "Then he'll be right behind us."

"Maybe he'll run out of gas," Lynne offered.

"Oh, shit," J.C. said.

"What?" McCracken whipped his head around to look behind them.

"No, not that," J.C. answered. "I'd forgotten about gas." He pointed at the gas gauge. It indicated less than half a tank left, and they were nowhere near halfway to Durham. He ran a quick calculation on the COMAND system. "About a hundred forty miles to empty."

"Sign back there said one-thirty-five to Charlotte," McCracken responded. "So we've got a little over three hours to figure something out." He paused, then suggested: "Or maybe we'll just have to wrap things up in Charlotte."

"Not gonna happen," J.C. snapped. "I'm going to Durham."

"Sure ya are," McCracken said, "just like the *Titanic* was going to New York."

J.C. settled the G-Wagen into a steady cruise between two tractor-trailers, knowing that whoever was in the car wouldn't risk trying to intercept them by charging into the snow-covered passing lane. He'd merely sit back and await an opportunity. So, in essence, they'd blundered into a trap, albeit one that wouldn't snap shut until they attempted to exit the interstate. That's when they'd lose the protection of the big rigs, and the cop, or Grizzly, would pounce.

"Got any ideas how to shake whoever is back there?" J.C. asked. Diesel fumes from the big rig directly ahead of them filled the interior of the Mercedes, swirling in through the flimsily-covered window next to J.C. He toyed with the idea of trying to pass the truck—a dangerous maneuver—but even if he could, they'd only get stuck behind another one.

McCracken, looking pale and sounding weak, tapped J.C. on the arm. "Let's get something straight, dipshit. That's not a cop back there. If it was, he'd have lit us up by now. It's Griz. And you don't shake Griz, you kill him."

"No wonder people call you Cave Man. Killing seems to be your solution to everything."

"Jesus, man. *My* solution? How do you think Griz got that police cruiser? You think he let Deputy Dawg live to broadcast an alert?" McCracken, his pupils narrowed to black BBs, glared at J.C. "Besides, I don't think I killed the trooper in Georgia. I was just trying to . . . discourage him."

"I suspect that's a distinction without a difference. Juries don't embrace people who shoot law enforcement officers."

"Juries? How did juries get into this conversation?"

"Sooner or later, you'll get caught."

"Whoa, whoa, whoa. Caught for what?"

"Self-evident, don't you think?"

"Really? The only person who can place me at the scene is sitting next to me. Helping me flee. Maybe you'd better think that over before you start babbling about the legal system. Ever hear of aiding and abetting?"

The truck ahead of them downshifted, and J.C. tapped his brakes.

"I don't think it's aiding and abetting," J.C. snapped, "when there's a .45-caliber pistol pointed at my head."

McCracken scratched his chin and didn't respond immediately. "Well," he said after several moments, "you may have a point." He turned to Lynne. "You think he has a point?"

Lynne nodded.

McCracken turned back to J.C. "That doesn't leave many options for me then, does it?"

"What do you mean?" J.C. asked.

McCracken addressed Lynne again. "You could drive this thing if you had to, couldn't you?"

"Sure."

"Does that answer your question, Mr. Corporate America?" McCracken asked, his words tinged with implicit threat.

J.C., his throat tight and dry, swallowed hard.

Chapter Thirty

Rolling Prison

Western South Carolina
Friday morning, December 30

THEY CONTINUED northeastward in their incarceration between two semis. A buffer of four eighteen-wheelers separated the police car from the G-Wagen. J.C. had decided McCracken had made his case: that Grizzly manned the police vehicle and had probably shot the Westminster officer. So that put him, J.C., at the mercy of two guys who had little compunction about offing cops. He acknowledged his survival odds had just slipped another notch. He struggled to stay focused and decided to address his situation as best he knew how, one step at a time.

"At least the snow has quit," Lynne said. She poured another cup of coffee and offered it to J.C. The odor of the still-warm brew mingled with the frigid air funneling into the vehicle through the driver's-side window and the heat blasting out of the dashboard vents.

They rode in silence. J.C. sipped his coffee and tried not to think about how things might end. Although he'd developed an uneasy alliance with McCracken, he'd almost forgotten the guy wasn't exactly a friend, that theirs was a partnership formed under duress. He understood that when all was said and done, he was nothing more than a disposable liability to the man seated next to him.

About Grizzly, he harbored no illusions. Grizzly would blow out his candles.

He finished the coffee and handed the cup back to Lynne, then addressed McCracken. "Cave, promise me one thing."

McCracken grunted.

"Promise you'll let me deliver the proposal before you . . . you know . . . do anything."

"Do anything?"

"Like terminate me." A tightness, like a python crushing its prey, wrapped around J.C.'s chest as he spoke the words.

McCracken snorted, a derisive response. "You want promises, go to church or visit a used car salesman."

"I'm asking for my son." J.C. hoped his voice sounded assertive, not desperate, but he knew otherwise. He glanced at Lynne. Would he have an ally there, female sympathy? Apparently not. She sat staring out the side window at the alabaster landscape.

To occupy his mind, J.C. ran some calculations in his head. He estimated they were 260 miles from Durham. At thirty-five to forty miles per hour, it would take roughly seven hours to get there. Plus whatever time would be eaten up stopping for gas. He realized the estimate harbored two huge assumptions: that Grizzly wouldn't catch them and that the snowfall wouldn't resume.

He switched the Mercedes' radio on and selected the weather band. He heard what he didn't want to, a prediction that slammed into him as though he'd been flung to the floor and kicked in the gut by someone wearing work boots. Blizzard conditions were forecast to return to the western Carolinas within a matter of hours.

"What's the deal?" McCracken asked. Apparently he'd been only half listening.

"We're in some sort of lull right now," J.C. said. "I didn't understand it all, but I guess there's a surface storm and an upper-air storm, and in between there's a dry pocket or slot or something like that."

"So we're in that dry pocket?"

"I guess. The trouble is the upper-air storm, the second storm, is headed this way. That means—"

"We're screwed, right?"

J.C. clenched his jaw. *At least I am. If the snow and wind return, I might as well be trying to reach Denmark as Durham.*

They drove on, continuing up I-85 in their little prisoner's parade, tracking along the single plowed lane through a gray dawn and a bleak, snow-covered Southern landscape—a scene so out of place it seemed to J.C. it could have been a photograph from another time and another venue, not something he was part of.

McCracken dozed off, his fitful sleep punctuated by involuntary groans, soft but audible. Lynne leaned forward from the rear seat, close to J.C.'s ear. "He's really more bark than bite, you know," she whispered.

"I wouldn't want to stake my life on that," J.C. said, even though he guessed he had.

"No, really. He's not, as they say, bad to the bone. He's always treated me with nothing but respect. The thing is, I think he wants to be a tough guy without being a bad guy. Trouble is, he's never figured out how to do that. He always comes off looking like a bad guy."

"That generally happens when you shoot a cop and cart coke around."

Lynne sighed. "I know, but he's got reason to change."

"What might that be?"

"He knows," she said, a slight catch in her voice. She sat back in her seat.

J.C. nodded but didn't respond. *Knowing and doing are two different things.*

The caravan slowed and compressed as it neared Greenville. As the column rounded a sweeping curve, J.C. spotted a pair of plows about a quarter-mile ahead, working in tandem to clear the interstate. Behind them, the line of traffic, mostly big rigs, compacted and decelerated.

They passed a maze of exits, and J.C. considered the possibility of attempting to execute some sort of maneuver that would shake Grizzly. But he knew whatever he tried, Grizzly would follow and likely not hesitate to stop them with his AR-something-or-other, his semi-automatic rifle. J.C. pressed on.

He studied the median as they plodded northeastward, wondering if he could make a break into the cleared southbound lane of I-85. Grizzly might not be able to follow them through the deep snow that separated the north and southbound sides of the interstate. Of course, the G-Wagen might not make it either. In which case, they'd be dead meat.

"Not a good idea," McCracken said, awakening from his snooze and seeming to read J.C.'s thoughts.

"What?"

"Trying to cross the median here. Where they don't have concrete crash barriers, they have cable barriers, and those are buried in the snow. You'd never see them. We'd get stopped dead."

"So what do we do?"

"Continue on."

"I'd kinda figured that out on my own. Don't you have any other ideas, aside from some crazy shootout?"

"You mean like a real plan?"

At the slower speed, the fresh air flow through the Mercedes' broken window ebbed. A stale odor filled the vehicle, an amalgam of McCracken's rancid breath, his body odor, and dried blood.

"Yeah, like actually trying to save ourselves."

"We'll make it up as we go along."

"That seems to be working well," J.C. muttered.

"You ever see *Animal House?*"

"The movie? Yes."

"There's a line in the film, I think John Belushi's character said it. 'This calls for a stupid and totally futile gesture, and we're just the guys who can do it!'"

J.C. didn't respond. He got the point.

They crawled through the I-26 interchange near Spartanburg. The morning had turned strangely darker, and light snow again sifted from a low, scudding overcast. Behind them, a blue-white flash of light arced across the horizon, filling it like summer heat lightning.

"It's coming again," Lynne said, her voice tight with apprehension.

Ahead, on the left, a water tower in the shape of a giant peach loomed out of the grayness. In the misplaced snow-cloaked landscape, it looked like an immense scoop of orange ice cream topped with marshmallow crème.

"The Peachoid," Lynne said. "We're near Gaffney."

"Almost in North Carolina," McCracken said.

J.C. checked the gas gauge. Down to less than a quarter. He turned to McCracken. "I think it's time to start making it up."

McCracken stared out the windshield, as if studying the lay of the land.

Immediately ahead of the SUV, a mud-and salt-encrusted eighteen-wheeler limited the forward visibility to nothing more distant than the rear of its trailer.

"Drop back a bit so I can see more of what's coming up," McCracken said.

"Why? You got an idea?" J.C. slowed and opened more distance between the G-Wagen and the semi.

"Maybe." McCracken grunted, winced.

J.C. waited.

"Shortly after we cross the border," McCracken said, his words pinched in pain, "there are a couple of places where the north-and south-bound lanes separate. I mean by quite a bit. The median is filled with trees, but in a few spots there're dirt roads that cross the median. For emergency vehicles."

J.C. thought about it and decided to play devil's advocate. "Here's my concern. Even if we made it across, wouldn't Griz be able to, too?"

"Maybe. Maybe not. Two feet of snow. I don't think that cruiser has snow tires. It certainly doesn't have four-wheel drive. Good chance it'll get stuck."

"And if *we* get bogged down?"

McCracken held up the Glock.

"Really? Against a semi-automatic rifle?"

"If we run out of gas or try an exit, it ends up that way anyhow."

The snow fell harder, encasing them again in a constrained, white world. J.C. gripped the steering wheel and pushed doggedly ahead, wondering how long the plows would be able to keep the road open. He ran through his priorities, significantly altered over the past twenty-four hours. His number one objective, getting to Durham by 5 p.m., had slipped down the list a few notches.

Number one now: getting away from Grizzly. Number two: finding gas. Number three: maintaining a tenuous alliance with McCracken, that is, staying alive, at least until priority number four could be attained: reaching Durham. *But,* he reminded himself, *one step at a time.* The only thing important at the moment: losing Grizzly.

They crossed into North Carolina.

"Can't be far now," McCracken said. "Keep your eyes peeled."

"I can't see more than a hundred yards," J.C. grumbled.

"Well, we're going slow enough; you'll have time to react. Just remember, when we see what we think is the crossover road, commit to it. Balls to the wall. No second thoughts. We'll make it."

J.C. wished he were as certain as McCracken.

"Here comes the median," McCracken said.

The north-and south-bound lanes pulled apart, separated by a park-like island covered in pines and the winter skeletons of deciduous trees.

J.C. craned his neck forward, searching for an opening through the trees that might suggest a road. Nothing. The island disappeared to their rear, swallowed in the whipping snowfall.

"Damn it," J.C. said, "I didn't see anything that looked like a road."

"We'll have another shot in a few miles," McCracken said. "Slow down even more next time. It might be our last chance."

The checkered tablecloth guarding the Mercedes' side window rippled in the slipstream of the big rig just ahead. The huge tires of the semi kicked up fresh powder from the highway as the blizzard continued to re-intensify, gaining its second wind.

What daylight there had been disappeared into the maw of the storm, replaced by incongruous flashes of lightning accompanied by the dull, dead thump of thunder.

"Damn it," J.C. said. "I can't see anything."

Lynne leaned over his shoulder, staring out into the storm. McCracken inclined forward, his eyes searching.

"Trees," McCracken said, pointing.

Another median loomed out of the gloom.

"There, there," Lynne yelled.

A gap through the trees.

"Go," McCracken screamed.

Without braking, J.C. flung the G-Wagen to the left and charged headlong into an opening through a copse of pine and oak.

McCracken turned to look for Grizzly.

The SUV hit the deeper snow in the passing lane, slowed, then surged into the median. Abruptly it sank and ground to a stop with its tires spinning, losing traction in a thick, fluffy quicksand of snow.

Grizzly's first shot blew off the side-view mirror next to J.C.

Lynne screamed and ducked.

McCracken fumbled for his .45.

Chapter Thirty-one

Waffle House

The Natural Environment Television Network
Friday morning, December 30

SOPHIE ENTERED the forecast center just after eleven. Al, plotting and analyzing the latest surface chart by hand—"old school" as Tom called it—looked up and nodded. Tom, leaning over the shoulder of a forecaster seated at one of the computerized workstations, turned and walked toward her.

"Are we in trouble again, boss?" he asked, feeling, after their tête-à-tête in her office, a bit freer and more comfortable in her presence.

"You tell me," she answered, her face expressionless, her gaze somewhat hardened, more like that of a superior again than a would-be lover; perhaps her way of reminding him that this was a work environment, not a bedroom. Or that this was her domain, not his.

"A few of the networks," she continued, "are starting to hype the blizzard as a threat to Washington and Baltimore. You guys have been telling me it's not. What's the story? We did a great job for Atlanta. Let's not blow it for other cities."

Tom glanced at Al who looked up from his work with a dead-eyed stare, a hard-to-read expression.

"No, I'm asking you," Sophie said, "not Al. You're my chief of meteorology."

"Who didn't get it right the first time around," Tom said.

Sophie blinked; her gaze softened. "It wasn't because of incompetence or negligence. We had this conversation earlier. You just had a different philosophy than me. Look, don't wallow in defeatism. If it will make you feel better, I can send you packing if you screw up again."

"Ever the boss," Tom countered, regretting the words even as he spoke them.

"Yes, I am. You probably shouldn't forget that." Her words came out like a hammer hitting iron.

"Sophie—"

She raised her forefinger to her lips: *Shut up.* "Just give me an answer, Tom."

Without immediately responding to Sophie, Tom walked back to the workstation he'd been at when she'd entered. He looked again at the computer monitors, conferred with the forecaster there, and returned to where Sophie waited.

"A couple of the models continue moving the storm up the coast," he said, "threatening DC and Philly. A couple don't."

"Make the call," she said. She stood with her hands on her hips.

"There's a strong core of jet stream winds rounding the base of the trough now—"

"No gobbledygook," she said, "is DC gonna get dumped on or not?"

"Do me the courtesy of at least listening to my explanation," he snapped, peeved at the return of her imperialism. The intimacy of the conversation a short time ago seemed to have evaporated like morning mist in the heat of the sun. "I don't pull this stuff out of my ass." *Wonderful to be back in our adversarial relationship.*

Hands remaining on her hips, Sophie fell silent.

"The jet," Tom continued, "will kick the storm out to sea and not carry it up the Eastern Seaboard. Northern North Carolina and Tidewater Virginia will catch the brunt of it. Washington will get maybe six inches or so. A moderate snowfall, not a shut-down blizzard. Does that answer your question?"

Sophie didn't answer. She wheeled and stalked from the forecast center.

Al leaned back in his chair and placed his hands behind his head. "Lover's spat?" His words seemed the verbal equivalent of a smirk.

"Do I detect a note of jealousy coming from your testosterone-starved existence, old man?"

Al laughed, a watery chortle bubbling up from deep within him. He bent back to his work. "Remember my words, junior. Black Widow."

Western North Carolina
Friday morning, December 30

J.C. EASED OFF on the accelerator, not wanting to dig the stalled Mercedes deeper into the layered snow and ice that held it captive. He ducked down in his seat until his nose touched the hub of the steering wheel. He expected Grizzly's next volley to come through the already-missing rear window. He chanced a glance to his right, hoping McCracken would return fire and disrupt Grizzly's aim.

Instead, he found McCracken staring at him.

"Lock the differentials," McCracken screamed. "Get us out of here."

J.C. punched the button to lock all three differentials.

"It's stuck," yelled Lynne.

For a moment, J.C. feared she meant the G-Wagen. But no, Lynne stared rearward, toward the edge of the freeway. He tracked her gaze. The police cruiser had slewed sideways and cemented itself into a deep drift. Grizzly, out of the car and using it as a shield, struggled to level the AR-15 at the Mercedes. His first shot had apparently been fired from the moving vehicle.

"Go, go, go," McCracken yelled at J.C.

J.C. eased down on the gas pedal, willing the G-Wagen to find traction. It did, lurching forward like a walrus freeing itself from polar ice. The vehicle plowed through snow headlight-deep and bulled across the median as J.C. struggled to steer it along what he could only assume marked the track through the trees.

He glanced in the rearview mirror and saw several muzzle flashes as Grizzly fired wildly at them. The shots kicked up tiny geysers of snow, but missed the G-Wagen.

The Mercedes reached the edge of the southbound lanes. J.C. unlocked the differentials and eased the SUV into a loose line of traffic between two eighteen-wheelers, apparently startling the driver of the big rig immediately behind them. The driver gave them a blast of his air horn, flashed his headlights, and hammered his brakes. The semi fishtailed but didn't jackknife. J.C. gave the driver a dismissive wave and accelerated.

"Watch for Griz, Lynne," McCracken said.

"He looked pretty damn stuck to me," J.C. responded.

"Don't discount his resourcefulness. If truckers think he's a cop, they could help get him unstuck real fast."

"So what's our next move?"

"There'll be an exit coming up shortly. We can bail out there and get back to the northbound side."

They reached the exit, and J.C. steered the G-Wagen down an unplowed ramp to a road running perpendicular to the interstate. He stopped at the foot of the ramp and studied the situation.

"The road goes underneath the interstate," he said. "If Griz happens to be passing over at the same time we're going under, he could spot us from there and get back on our tail."

"Maybe not," McCracken said. "The visibility's so damn poor it's hard to see much of anything."

"Let's not chance it. Let's make a right here, pull down the road a hundred yards or so, turn around, and wait a few minutes. We'll be able to see Griz if he comes down the ramp, and we'll be able to see him if he stays on the interstate."

"Okay," McCracken said. "Kill the headlights when we stop. There's no traffic down here to run into us, and I sure as shit don't wanna give Griz a beacon."

J.C. turned right, turned around, stopped, and doused the lights. They waited, the thick snow swirling around them as if they were a dog sled team running the Iditarod in a whiteout.

A minute passed. Two minutes. Three. A string of vehicles crawled across the overpass, their lights looming out of the gloom as if they were sea creatures suspended in a gray-white ocean. The five-minute mark passed and still no police car.

"Where is he?" J.C. said.

McCracken shrugged. "Beats me. Maybe he's well and truly stuck. But let's not wait any longer."

J.C. agreed, switched on the G-Wagen's lights, and headed toward the entrance ramp. Once again they merged into the northbound flow, now barely moving because of the renewed snowfall. In spots, deep snow had drifted across the single plowed lane, making it almost impassable save for the constant battering by the parade of eighteen-wheelers. J.C. doubted the road would remain open much longer.

He thought about what McCracken had said earlier, about Grizzly being the bogeyman. The guy wouldn't just give up. He had to still be on their tail. Somehow. Some way.

They passed the spot where they'd made their dash into southbound I-85 earlier. J.C. half expected to find Grizzly lying in wait for them there, but he wasn't. The police car was gone.

Punctuated by flashes of lightning, the snowfall slanted through the gray morning in thick, rippling sheets. It appeared wetter now, accumulating in great, soggy clumps on the windshield, coating road signs in a white frosting, and morphing into an icy sheen on the highway as the semis, acting like Zambonis, packed it into a hard rime.

On the instrument panel of the G-Wagen, the low-fuel warning light flickered on.

"We're done," J.C. said.

McCracken looked at him.

"We're almost out of gas," J.C. said.

"How much we got left?"

"A couple of gallons. Maybe enough to get us twenty miles. After that, we become a six thousand-pound paperweight."

"Hard to see what's coming up," McCracken said. He craned forward, peering into the storm. "All the signs are covered in snow. And besides, I'm not sure there's much of anything open."

"Then you'd better come up with Plan B real fast."

"You're the one who wants to get to Durham. Why don't you come up with a Plan B?"

The low-fuel light stopped flickering and settled into a steady glow. J.C. had to concede McCracken was right. He, J.C., had a lot more incentive to get to Durham than McCracken. McCracken just wanted to get away. It didn't matter whether it was to Durham or Denver.

They appeared to be on the outskirts of Charlotte. The thick, blowing snow made it virtually impossible to tell for sure. Regardless, J.C. knew he had to get off the interstate and had to find fuel.

A sign for a Pilot Travel Center, a truck stop, loomed out of the grayness. At least J.C. thought it was for a Pilot Travel Center. All he caught was __LOT TRAV__ ___TER, the missing letters covered in a stucco of snow.

He eased the G-Wagen down the exit, turned right, and plowed through the rapidly accumulating snow toward the center.

He pulled into the parking lot. Snow-laden eighteen-wheelers, SUVs, and automobiles littered the lot, vehicles of travelers who'd surrendered to the storm. It looked like an igloo city in an arctic whiteout. The gas pumps sat dark and idle.

"Wonderful," McCracken exclaimed. "They're probably out of gas."

"Or there's no power," Lynne suggested.

"There's a Waffle House next door," McCracken said, pointing.

"At least we can get coffee and something to eat."

"We don't need coffee, we need gas." J.C.'s words came out tinged in frustration.

"*You* need gas," McCracken responded. "I need coffee."

"I need to pee," Lynne added.

"We win," McCracken said. "Park by the Waffle House. Lynne, grab the attaché case."

They entered the Waffle House. The place brimmed with people, exhausted travelers, yet a single booth near the rear of the restaurant remained open. A waitress, a large black woman with arms as thick as J.C.'s thighs and wearing a seemingly perpetual smile, steered J.C., McCracken, and Lynne toward it. Odors of freshly brewed coffee, sizzling bacon, biscuits and gravy, steak and eggs, and a variety of waffles mingled with a chilly dampness that seem to cling to the walls of the establishment. Puddles of water, melted snow and ice from patrons' coats and boots, spotted the floor.

J.C. and McCracken, weary and red-eyed, sank into their seats while Lynne scurried to the restroom. McCracken placed the attaché case, his "retirement," beneath the table and draped his legs over it.

"The Pilot station is out of gas?" J.C. asked the waitress, inclining his head toward the idle fuel islands.

"Nope. Outta power. No 'lectricity ever since the storm picked up again. Pumps don't work."

J.C. felt hope flee from his being, almost palpably, as if someone had slammed him in the gut with a hockey stick.

"How come you guys have power?" McCracken asked, seemingly oblivious to, or at least unconcerned over, J.C.'s dismay. "And food? It looks like everything else is shut down."

The waitress leaned toward McCracken, holding her coffee pot in a precarious hover over the table. "Honey, ain't you never heard of the Waffle House Index?"

He shook his head. "You're pullin' my leg, right?"

"Red, yellow, green," the waitress said. "After Katrina, when over a hundred Waffle Houses had to shut down, the boss man, he decided he didn't want that to happen again, no. So he made a plan to get ready for 'sasters so's we can stay open or get open quick after t'ings like hurricanes and tornadoes." She looked out the window. "And I guess t'ings like blizzards, too, though I ain't never seed one before."

"So red, yellow, green, what's that mean?"

"Green, everyt'ing okay. Not much damage. Yellow, backup generator, maybe a limited menu. Red, t'ings really bad, unsafe. Maybe we closed. Today, yellow. We ready. That government outfit, Feemee or somet'ing, they use the Waffle House Index to gauge how bad a 'saster be."

"You mean FEMA? Really?"

"Yeah, FEMA. That's it."

"So it's like the Saffir-Simpson Scale?" J.C. asked, struggling out of his funk. "Like for hurricanes. Category one, cat two, cat three, and so on?"

"I guess," the waitress said, obviously not sure of Saffir-Simpson. "Take a look at the menu. I'll be right back. Oh, we outta grits and only gotta couple a eggs left." She lumbered away.

Lynne returned from the restroom and plopped down beside McCracken. She stared at J.C. "Why the long face?"

"Looks like this is the end of the road. The gas pumps aren't working."

A shadow fell across the table. J.C. sensed a cold, damp, malodorous presence looming over him. Slowly, he lifted his gaze.

McCracken sensed something, too, and jerked upright. Lynne gasped.

Grizzly, his face scratched and bloodied, one eye swollen shut, stood by their booth, the muzzle of his AR-15 peeking from beneath a soggy Hudson's Bay blanket draped over his forearm. Clumps of snow from an ill-fitting, lightweight Westminster Police parka slid onto the floor.

Chapter Thirty-two

Grizzly

Western North Carolina
Friday midday, December 30

GRIZZLY'S FOUL breath and body odor gave rise to the sense a garbage truck had just rolled into the Waffle House. More than a few customers ceased eating and stared at the new arrival.

McCracken eased his hand inside his parka.

Grizzly leaned toward him, the barely visible nose of his semiautomatic rifle only inches from McCracken's head. "Bad idea, old friend." Grizzly's voice, gravelly and rough, resonated with low-frequency menace. "Let's not get a bunch of people hurt in here. We can do this so we all walk away in one piece." He paused, then added, "Much as I'd like to blow your sleazy ass to kingdom come."

McCracken twitched. J.C. shook his head. *Don't do anything stupid.* McCracken slowly removed his hand from his parka, leaving the Glock tucked in the waistband of his pants.

"Good," Grizzly said. "Now, sweetie"—he looked at Lynne—"take the pistol from your boyfriend's pants, nice and easy, just like you were going to give him a hand job—you're good at that, right?—eject the clip, then rack the slide. Let the gun slide to the floor as quietly as you can. Easy does it. Then give me the clip. Do things nice and easy so we don't upset any of the fine folks in here."

J.C. wondered if any of the *fine folks* had dialed 911. Probably not. Other than stinking up the place, Grizzly hadn't done anything to warrant a call to law enforcement. He'd kept his weapon concealed and his voice low.

Lynne, her eyes wide in fear, her hand trembling, followed Grizzly's instructions. She removed the clip and racked the slide, ejecting a chambered round onto her lap. She covered the clip and loose round with a paper napkin and slid them to Grizzly. Using the noise in the restaurant as a cover, she allowed the Glock to clatter to the floor beneath the table, then using her foot, pushed the pistol toward the wall, out of sight.

The waitress arrived on scene, sidling up to Grizzly. "Hi there, 'hon. You be joinin' your friends?"

"No. I'm not staying."

Whether she caught a whiff of his body odor, was put off by his glare, or sensed an implicit threat in the growl of his voice, J.C. couldn't tell. Whatever she perceived, she beat a hasty retreat, waddling toward the kitchen with a speed J.C. thought her incapable of.

Lynne sat back in her seat and wrapped her arms across her chest. McCracken glared at Grizzly with unmistakable hatred.

"Let's finish this up," Grizzly said. "I saw you bring the case in here and put it under the table. Keep it there and push it with your feet to where I can reach it. Then I'm outta here. And you can finish your breakfast."

McCracken didn't respond, sitting still. A cigar store Indian.

"For shit sake," Grizzly said, his voice a harsh whisper. "If I start shooting, things will get really messy. I'll still get the case, but your brains'll be splattered all over the pecan waffles the kid behind you is eating."

McCracken still didn't move.

Lynne looked at him askance.

"You can't win this," J.C. hissed. "Let him have the case, damn it."

"It's not *your* retirement," McCracken said, his voice a snarl.

"Actually, it's not yours, either, dickhead," Grizzly said, keeping his volume low. "Three seconds, and you won't be able to tell your blood from the strawberry syrup, or maybe your girlfriend's blood from the syrup." He altered the position of his arm so the muzzle of the AR-15 pointed at Lynne. "Her first, then you. One. Two—"

The case scraped along the floor, a raspy sound lost in the din of the busy restaurant, as first McCracken and then Lynne slid it toward Grizzly with their feet.

When the case, still beneath the table, reached the end of the booth, Grizzly retrieved it with his free hand. "Bon appétit," he growled and backed away, down the aisle toward the door. He exited into the storm, disappearing once he was only a few feet from the Waffle House.

McCracken didn't have a play. Even though the Glock lay at his feet, J.C. knew he had no ammo. The only clip he'd had was the one in the weapon when he'd taken it off the Georgia State Patrol officer. Now Grizzly had it.

McCracken slumped in his seat. "Fuck, fuck, fuck," he muttered.

"How in the hell did he find us?" J.C. asked.

"He never followed us once we crossed the median," McCracken said, defeatism wrapping his words. "He obviously got the police car dug out, probably with the help of 'good citizens.' Then he gambled. He was pretty sure I wouldn't head south, back toward Georgia. So he hunkered down at an interchange someplace along I-85 north and just waited for us to pass by. Once we did, he got on our tail again."

Outside, the ghostly image of a police cruiser flashed by the snow-splattered windows of the Waffle House.

"Damn it to hell," McCracken said. He folded his arms on the table and lay his head on them. He turned toward Lynne and muttered something.

"What?" she said.

"Sorry, babe."

She laughed.

He raised his head, malice glistening in his eyes. "You think it's funny?"

She placed a hand on his arm. "Yes," she said softly.

"Because?"

"Because all Griz has is an aluminum briefcase with a stale ham and cheese sandwich."

McCracken stared at her.

"And some dry cookies, a tow rope, a flashlight, a first aid kit, and a roll of duct tape for weight."

McCracken's laughter started deep within his belly, rose like a geyser, and burst into the restaurant like a hydrothermal explosion. He ceased laughing abruptly and grabbed his side, the bullet wound grabbing him in a fit of pain.

"So where's my . . . where's *our* retirement?" he asked.

"In the picnic basket," Lynne said. "While you snoozed and J.C. drove, I had a feeling—call it female intuition, I guess—that it might not be a good idea to keep the stuff where we had it. You know, just in case."

"You're the greatest, babe." He leaned over and kissed her, grimacing as he did so.

"So what's in my picnic basket?" J.C. asked.

McCracken smiled and shrugged. "You probably don't want to know."

"I'm kinda in this up to my ass. What's in the picnic basket?"

"Okay, man. You asked." He leaned forward and whispered to J.C. "About eight hundred thousand dollars' worth of crack cocaine."

J.C. hadn't believed things could get any worse, but they just did. It was bad enough his mission to salvage his son's medical care, his job, and the future of the corporation he worked for seemed ready to end in failure. Worse, he'd aided and abetted a cop shooter! But now illegal drugs, almost a million dollars' worth? Catastrophic seemed the only word that fit.

McCracken leaned even closer to J.C. "God damn the pusher man," he sang softly, an incipient grin on his face.

J.C. felt his breath sucked away, his world suddenly depressurized. A tsunami of dread swept over him. *Don't people do hard time for transporting drugs?*

McCracken sat back, smiling. "Well, I suggest we hightail it before Griz discovers his load is a little light." He leaned forward, retrieved the impotent Glock from beneath his feet, surreptitiously slipped it under his parka, tossed a ten-dollar tip onto the table, and stood. "We can catch breakfast later."

"Where the hell do you think we're going?" J.C. said. "All we've got out there is a *Gelande-brick*. In case you forgot, we're out of gas, and the pumps are dead."

"Oh, stop with the woe-is-me crap. I'm a criminal, remember?"

Outside, they entered a dim, flannel-hued world of swirling snow and razor-edged wind. J.C. found it difficult to discern objects more than a dozen yards from him.

"I need to pick up a few things in the service station," McCracken said. "Get the G-Wagen and bring it around."

J.C. with Lynne's help brushed several inches of fresh snow from the Mercedes. But as fast as they dusted the vehicle, new snow frosted it over.

"Come on," J.C. said, "let's go. This is a losing battle." He drove to the front door of the Pilot station. A portable gasoline generator hammering away near the entrance seemed to be the sole source of power for the facility.

McCracken, carrying a large plastic bag, exited the store. He clambered into the G-Wagen's passenger seat. "Okay, find me a nice, big SUV somewhere in the lot, preferably in a far corner."

J.C. eyed the bag. He had a pretty good idea what it contained. "You're gonna steal gas?"

"*We're* gonna steal gas," McCracken said. "We're in this together, remember? Of course, if you'd rather wait for Griz to show up again, or the cops to check out our coke-mobile, that's your choice."

J.C. put the G-Wagen in gear and guided it toward the rear of the lot in a sedate slalom, weaving through a maze of snow-heaped semis, SUVs, and automobiles. "How's this?" He pulled in behind a massive pyramid of snow harboring an SUV of some sort.

"Good." From the bag, McCracken fished out a large screwdriver, several different diameter plastic hoses, a couple of hose-adapter fittings, and a battery-operated siphon pump. "Let's hope its tank is almost full."

He pried open the filler flap with the screwdriver and twisted off the gas cap. He studied the situation for a moment. He climbed back into the G-Wagen and went to work with the hoses and fittings. He stopped from time to time to draw a deep breath, clutch at his side, and wince.

"It's not easy to siphon gas from newer vehicles," he said, his voice wavering a bit. "There's a siphon-block, a little ball, at the base of the filler neck, so you need a relatively stiff, small-diameter hose to work past it."

Fifteen minutes later he had his jury-rigged siphoning system ready to go. "Give a holler if anyone comes wandering by. Although in this weather, I don't know why anyone would." He slipped from the Mercedes and went to work. He forced the smaller diameter hose into the target vehicle's gas tank and ran the larger hose into the G-Wagen's. Even though he stood only a few feet from where J.C. sat, he virtually disappeared once or twice, swallowed by intense squalls of snow.

He ran the pump for about ten minutes before the siphoning process sputtered to a stop. "Drained the tank," he yelled, challenging the wind.

J.C. checked the gas gauge. "Not enough," he yelled back. "We're gonna need more."

McCracken, breathing heavily, staggered back into the G-Wagen. "Your turn," he gasped. "Find an older model minivan. It'll have a big tank and won't have one of those stupid siphon-blocks."

"I don't think I can—"

"Sure you can, man. You're a hardened criminal now. Forget the corporate executive shit. This is real-life survivor stuff. We're scrambling for our lives here."

J.C. herded the Mercedes through the drifting and blowing snow until he found a beat-up Dodge Caravan, a refugee from the late '80s.

"Go on," McCracken said. "You can do it. I'll keep a sharp lookout and warn you if I spot anyone coming."

"You can't see three feet out there," J.C. said, mounting a weak argument; stalling.

"It works both ways. *You're* basically invisible, too. Get your ass out there."

"For your son," Lynne chimed in.

She had a point. Getting only part way to Durham wouldn't be a victory. They needed more gas.

He climbed out of the SUV, struggled through snow heaped almost to his knees, and bent to the task of stealing gasoline. *This one's for you, Cole.* Even with the hood of his parka cinched tightly around his face, the wind sliced into him like frigid ice picks, seeming to find ways to wriggle beneath his outer garments and flail his skin with tiny, icy cuts.

The siphoning took forever. J.C. wondered if time and luck weren't about to run out on them. Once, two figures, hunched over against the storm, passed within a car length of where he stood. But with their heads down and the visibility verging on zero, they never spotted him.

After several minutes, the siphoning ceased, the tank of the Caravan sucked dry. He tapped on the Mercedes' window, alerting McCracken. "How much we got?"

McCracken switched on the ignition, checked the gauge. "Just over half."

J.C. ran a quick calculation in his head. "Should get us there."

"If it's good enough for you, it's good enough for me. Let's get going."

J.C., accompanied by a strange sense of exhilaration, scrambled back into the G-Wagen. In the past it seemed he'd never been able to get away with anything, no matter how innocent or insignificant. If he'd dared exceed the speed limit by five miles per hour, made a rolling stop, or failed to signal a turn, there'd always been a traffic cop lurking nearby to nab him. But now? *Holy shit.* He'd just stolen third base, tied the bell on the cat, slipped behind enemy lines, and hadn't gotten caught. He grinned like a court jester.

"We're all crooks at heart," McCracken said, reacting to J.C.'s expression.

"You believe that?"

"Sure, but some of us are just better at it."

Chapter Thirty-three

Out of Time

Western North Carolina
Friday midday, December 30

ON THE INTERSTATE, they fell into a column of eighteen-wheelers once again—a procession of mechanical mastodons plodding through a modern-day snowscape.

The line of semis had carved deep ruts in the snow, and the diehard truckers, those who dared challenge the storm, held a steady pace near thirty miles per hour. J.C. guessed most of them were probably from Snow Belt states, used to driving in extreme winter conditions. A lot of them had mounted chains on their tires.

"I'm surprised it's still open," Lynne said from the rear seat.

"The interstate?" J.C. said. "Me, too. Maybe officials figured blizzard warnings would be enough to keep most people off the highways."

"Highway departments around here," McCracken said, "are a lot more used to dealing with ice and snow than ones in Georgia. They've probably brought in snow removal equipment from the Smokies to help out. They've done that before."

"How far to Durham?" Lynne asked.

J.C. checked the navigation unit. "About a hundred sixty-five miles."

"What time do you have to be there?"

"No later than five."

Lynne leaned forward and rested her arms on the back of his seat. "Think we'll make it?"

He looked again at the nav system. "If we can maintain this speed, we'll be there at 4:47 p.m."

"Cuttin' it thin."

She didn't need to tell him that.

"Think your wife is worried?" Lynne continued. "You haven't been able to call her, have you?"

"Not since yesterday. Sure, she's probably worried sick." *I am, too.*

"How long have you been married?"

"Eleven years."

"Good for you. A lot of people don't make it that far."

On the right shoulder of the highway, out of the grayness, a mound of snow, higher than the surrounding accumulation, materialized. J.C. stared hard at it as they approached, wondering if beneath it there might be a stolen police vehicle. But no. Closer inspection suggested something bigger than that, likely a step van or large SUV abandoned to the storm.

Lynne continued to chatter. "Your son, what did you say his name is?"

J.C. couldn't recall if he'd mentioned the name to her previously. "Cole."

"You love him to death, don't you?"

The metaphor cut a tiny slice from J.C.'s soul. Lynne no doubt hadn't intended it that way.

"Sure."

"Does he know you're on sort of a quest to help him?"

"Probably not. He's only six."

"But still, you're his hero. Dads can do anything, right?"

Can they? A lump formed in J.C.'s throat, and he didn't answer.

They continued to crawl through the blinding snowstorm. In spots, fender-high drifts had blown across the "open" lane, but the constant battering by the big trucks kept the road passable.

J.C., his shoulders aching, his back stiff, his fingers bordering on arthritic from doggedly gripping the steering wheel, watched the towns reel by. Kannapolis. Salisbury. Lexington. And finally Greensboro where I-85 turned east and merged with I-40. He began to think, maybe, just maybe, he had a chance. The ETA now indicated 4:44 p.m. They'd actually picked up a few minutes. But the needle on the fuel gauge had nudged down to less than a quarter of a tank. *Enough to make it to Durham?* J.C. didn't know. But he did know the option of making another siphoning raid was out. It came down to do-or-die—perhaps another poor choice of metaphors—with the fuel he had.

He glanced at McCracken. At least the guy didn't have any more bullets for the Glock. If McCracken were hell-bent on getting rid of him as a "witness," he'd have to beat him to death with an empty pistol, not shoot him. Given the biker's weakened state, J.C. felt for the first time since picking the guy up, he had the upper hand.

Things are gonna be okay.

They passed Burlington. In a few miles I-40 would split off from I-85 and vector them southeast toward Durham, or more particularly toward Research Triangle Park on the southeast side of Durham where Rampart Aerospace maintained its headquarters.

Traffic slowed as they approached the split.

McCracken sat up and peered forward. "Something's happening. Lots of flashing blue lights ahead." He reached into the right-hand pocket of his parka and extracted an ammo clip. He rammed it into the Glock.

J.C.'s heart sank. "Jesus, where'd that come from?"

"Where do you think, dipshit, the cop. You don't think I'd run around with just a single clip, do you?"

They neared the exit where I-40 split from I-85. A mobile electronic sign indicated I-40 CLOSED DUE TO ACCIDENT. Several highway patrol cars blocked the ramp. A trooper stood in the storm, apparently answering any questions travelers had.

J.C. opted not to stop and ask about alternate routes into Durham. Given the "battle damage" to the G-Wagen, it seemed prudent not to heighten the curiosity of law enforcement.

They continued on, tracking a mud-and-salt-caked moving van out of Denver, Colorado, as it crept through the frigid gray maelstrom of the blizzard into the growing dusk of a short winter day. The snow, tracing horizontal trajectories, seemed to be as much flying as falling.

Using the navigation system, J.C. expanded the view of the area's road system. It indicated another way to approach Durham and Research Triangle: the Durham Freeway off I-85. But when they reached the exit to the freeway, they found it closed as well. No police cars this time, just a barricade of orange-and-white striped construction barrels. J.C. looked over at McCracken. McCracken merely shrugged, and J.C. rammed the G-Wagen through the blockade, taking out one of the barrels in an explosion of plastic and sand.

The G-Wagen hit a rampart of unplowed snow and bogged down, clawing for traction. J.C. locked the differentials and got the Mercedes moving forward again, but at an agonizingly slow pace. Still, he had time, maybe fifteen minutes, to spare. He could make it. He could still deliver the proposal to Rampart before the deadline.

J.C. pushed the SUV through the deep snow, guiding it down a gentle incline off an overpass. Near the bottom of the overpass, a small sedan sat crossways in the expressway, its front end imprisoned in a roof-high drift, its left rear tire flat. A man, waving frantically, waded through the storm toward the G-Wagen. In its headlights, his face reflected desperation.

J.C. braked. Not that he had a choice. The man stood directly in the Mercedes' path. The G-Wagen slid to a stop, and J.C. removed the tablecloth from the driver's-side window. Riding a blast of icy air, a whirl of snow punched into the vehicle's interior.

"Christ on a crutch," McCracken said and yanked his parka tighter around himself.

Outside, the man slogged through the snow to the Mercedes' side. Seemingly oblivious to the odd window covering, he extended a pleading hand toward J.C. "I need help," he said, his voice wavering, strained, as though he were on the verge of tears.

"What is it?" J.C. asked. He checked the time. He couldn't afford another delay. Not now.

"My wife," the man said. "She's having a baby. She's bleeding bad. She needs to get to the hospital. Help me. Please, please."

"Call 911."

"I did. They're backed up with emergencies. Said they couldn't reach me for another hour, maybe not even then, the roads are so bad. Please."

J.C. understood the man's desperation, but did the man understand his, J.C.'s? He had less than fifteen minutes to reach Rampart. And he had no clue how many minutes a side trip to a hospital might waste.

"Look, I'm sorry," he said. "I have to be someplace by five o'clock. It's really important. I'm sure the paramedics will get here as fast as they can."

"The hospital's only a couple of miles, sir. It wouldn't take long." The man placed his palms together, a prayerful, pleading gesture.

A couple of miles? Under the circumstances, it might as well be a couple of hundred. "I can get to where I'm going," J.C. said, "and come back for you." He tried to sound compassionate, but his own angst engulfed him.

"No, no. It'll be too late. She's bleeding. I'll pay you, I'll pay you a lot. Whatever I have, whatever you want." His eyes brimmed with tears.

"I can't, I just can't," J.C. said. "I have to go. I'm sorry. I'll be right back." *Maybe.* He took his foot off the brake.

McCracken leaned toward J.C. "Like I said, fear rules," he whispered.

A strong gust of wind shot another stinging volley of snow into the SUV.

Lynne entered the conversation. "What if it was your wife, J.C., your baby?" Her words came out sharp and accusatory, instinctive maternal defensiveness.

Fear? Love? What does rule our decisions, our actions? Is McCracken right? And what's with Lynne? Is she . . . ? J.C.'s thoughts evaporated as the man grasped the window frame, a vain effort to waylay the vehicle's departure.

"Everything we do is driven by fear," McCracken continued, his mouth close to J.C.'s ear, his voice remaining low. "Love is theoretical, a mere concept. A word used to describe our deeds at times when our fears temporarily relent, and we poke our head out of our self-centered, foxhole existence to pretend we're concerned about others." He grinned and leaned back in his seat.

J.C. slammed the G-Wagen to a stop and pushed open the door. "Damn you to hell, McCracken," he muttered and bounded from the vehicle toward the crippled automobile. He yanked open the door to the back seat and found a woman prone, moaning, her face pale, her dress blotched with dark stains.

"I'll grab her arms," J.C. said to the woman's husband, "you grab her feet. We'll carry her to the back seat of the Mercedes. Come on."

In an awkward effort, slipping and sliding, they transported the woman to the SUV where Lynne helped pull her into the vehicle. She slipped a blanket underneath the woman and rested her head on her lap. The woman seemed unaware of the turmoil around her and continued to moan, occasionally punctuating her groans with cries of pain. Her husband scrambled into the rear cargo area and knelt behind her, grasping her hand.

"Straight ahead," he said. "The turnoff to the Duke University Hospital is about a mile down the road, on the right."

J.C., hoping for more speed, unlocked the differentials and surged forward, the G-Wagen furrowing through the snow like a plow without a blade. Almost dark now, the headlight beams provided the only clear view of the relentless blizzard. Snowflakes danced and twirled through the conical illumination like ballerinas cavorting across a tiny, floodlit stage.

The turnoff proved to be *more* than a mile away, and at a top speed of twenty-five miles per hour, despite J.C.'s efforts to move faster, he knew he'd lost any hope of delivering the proposal by 5 p.m. Had he just sacrificed his own future, and perhaps his son's, in his endeavor to get this frantic couple, complete strangers, to a hospital? In all likelihood, the woman had lost her baby anyhow. With his fist, J.C. hammered the steering wheel in silent frustration.

He found the emergency entrance to the hospital and raced inside to summon help. It came quickly. As orderlies lifted the woman onto a gurney, her husband embraced J.C. in an awkward bear hug.

"I can't thank you enough," he said, tears flowing freely now.

J.C. broke from the man's grasp. *No, you can't.* "It's okay, don't worry about it. Look, I gotta run. I'm late for an appointment."

"I'm sorry," the man said, "but I thank you from the bottom of my heart." He fumbled for his wallet, but J.C. had already entered the Mercedes and started the engine.

The man extended some bills toward J.C. as he put the vehicle in gear. J.C. held up his hand, palm out, in declination.

"Maybe I can name my kid after you," the man said, raising his voice against the wind. "What is it?"

"Cave Man," J.C. yelled as he pulled away. *There won't be any kid. Your wife miscarried.*

The G-Wagen's clock read 4:54.

Chapter Thirty-four

End Game

**The Natural Environment Television Network
Late Friday afternoon, December 30**

SOPHIE SUMMONED Tom to her office just before closing time. Seated in her chair, she didn't rise to greet him. She merely smiled wanly. She appeared weary, her vitality sapped. "It's been a long week," she said, her words soft.

Outside, the snow had stopped. Through the window behind Sophie, Tom saw a scattering of cars and trucks back on the roads, crawling along like bears emerging cautiously from their dens after a long winter. Travel remained at best difficult, at worst, impossible.

"Final tallies?" Sophie asked.

"Twenty-three point four inches for Atlanta. That's not breaking a record, that's nuking it."

"Others?"

"Virtually every city from Birmingham to Charlotte set a snowfall record. Top of the list: twenty-six inches in Gainesville, Georgia. There aren't enough superlatives to describe this storm. Epic. Historic. Legendary."

"And now?"

"It's following the scenario I laid out earlier. It's lit its afterburners and is taking off for the Atlantic. It dumped about eighteen inches on Raleigh-Durham, will leave maybe twelve in Hampton Roads, but DC may get no more than three or four."

"Good call."

The two lapsed into an awkward silence.

Sophie broke it. "I'm sorry," she said. "I got a little too testy with you earlier today."

"Just like old times."

"Yes, but I'd like to think we're past that."

"So, where are we? Where are we going?"

Again, an uneasy silence permeated the office.

Sophie slid some papers across her desk toward Tom.

"What are these?" he said.

"Your termination papers. They're—"

"Sophie! What the hell *is this*? I thought . . ." He didn't know what he'd thought. He just knew he'd been sandbagged. Hammered on the head from behind with a Louisville Slugger. Al's warning words thundered in his head, *Black Widow*. He spun and strode from the office. He burned with both anger and embarrassment.

Sophie called after him. "Tom, wait. You didn't let me finish. This isn't what it seems. Come back here." Her voice sounded more pleading than commanding.

Tom ignored her. *Screw you.* The thought carried no sexual connotation. He knew unless he exited the building quickly, he'd say or do something he'd regret forever.

Durham, North Carolina
Late Friday afternoon, December 30

"Thank you, J.C.," Lynne said, "for helping those people."

J.C., suffocating under the misery of his impending defeat, didn't respond.

McCracken twisted in his seat to address Lynne. "He didn't do it out of the goodness of his heart, babe. He did it because we were all over his ass." He turned to face J.C. "Fear of repercussions from his peers, that's why he acted. Not love." He paused, then went to the coda, "Fear."

"Oh, shut up," J.C. said.

McCracken chuckled and fell silent.

J.C., clinging to the last desiccated vine of hope, pushed the G-Wagen to the point he feared losing control. He hurtled through the storm, the gathering dark, his own metastasizing ennui. Save for an ambulance passing them going the opposite direction, toward the hospital, no other vehicles appeared. J.C. wondered if anybody had even shown up for work at Rampart today. Maybe he'd catch a break by default, a one-day postponement of the delivery date. But his final, grim assessment: *Sure I will.*

The checkered tablecloth flapped in the wind, allowing the blizzard to continue extending its icy tentacles into the SUV's interior.

"Tape that damn thing back up, will you," McCracken commanded.

J.C. struggled to fasten it back in place while he drove.

"How far to the aerospace place?" McCracken asked. His interest seemed less than sincere.

J.C. studied the nav system. "Looks like eight or nine miles." A surge of nausea roiled his gut, a feeling identical to the one he'd experienced two days ago—had it been only two days?—when Billingsly had summarily given him the bum's rush. He bit back an urge to spray the contents of his stomach, mainly Waffle House coffee, all over McCracken.

Eight or nine miles? He didn't need an automated system to do the calculation. It would take a good twenty minutes to reach Rampart, barring encountering any more travelers in need of a Good Samaritan.

McCracken must have read the anguish in his face. "You didn't have to pick up those people, you know. I wouldn't have."

"I'm not you," J.C. snapped.

"Too bad." McCracken stared out into the snow flying through the last gasp of the day's light. "Well, press on, my friend. Our journey has to come to an end someplace." He pulled out the Glock and rested it on his lap.

J.C. held his gaze straight ahead and maintained his speed, ignoring the implied threat. If anything, the snow seemed to be relenting, but he couldn't be sure. It might be just the light of the dying day playing tricks on his tired eyes. He leaned over the steering wheel and hunched his shoulders, trying to relieve the steel-band tension that bound the muscles of his back and neck. Fatigue wrapped him like a death shroud. He'd been driving for over twelve hours.

"Hey," Lynne said, "that sign back there said Research Triangle Park."

"I know," J.C. responded, his words slurred with exhaustion. "It's a huge campus for high-tech R and D firms. It extends about eight miles north to south." He checked the nav screen. "We get off at the next exit." *Not that it makes any difference now.*

A minute later, he guided the Mercedes down an exit ramp and turned left. "Not far now," he said. The vehicle's clock indicated ten minutes after five. On unplowed roads, they passed Research Triangle Park headquarters—dark except for a well-lit and empty parking lot—and knifed under I-40. Ahead, on the left, a large illuminated sign indicated RAMPART PARK, HOME OF RAMPART AEROSPACE

AND DEFENSE CORPORATION.

J.C. turned into the park, a pine-covered sub-campus of Research Triangle, and steered the G-Wagen along the main road toward the middle building of three large four-story glass-and-steel structures that comprised Rampart headquarters.

The buildings, dark except for isolated, brightly-lit offices that appeared devoid of occupants, stood like silent palaces in a fairy-tale winter wonderland. That, coupled with the lack of vehicles and absence of tire tracks in the snow, suggested that Rampart had indeed been closed today. Deadlines aside, had the trip to deliver the proposal been for naught?

A single snow-enshrouded vehicle, apparently a midsize SUV, sat near the main entrance of the middle building. J.C. pulled in beside it. It was 5:18. A figure appeared near the glass-doored entrance and looked out. A frisson of hope shot through J.C., energizing him as if he'd just downed a triple espresso.

"Somebody," he said and pointed.

McCracken tucked the gun back inside his parka. "Well, let's go."

J.C. spoke to Lynne. "Hand me one of those boxes. Maybe there's still a chance."

Hoisting one of the three boxes containing the proposal, J.C. opened the door and stepped out into knee-deep snow. The snowfall, save for a wind-driven mist of tiny flakes, had virtually ceased. Spumes of snow slithered across the surface of the snow and snaked into drifts that in spots had piled as high as the building's first-story windows.

"Hold it," McCracken said. He stopped at the rear window of the snow-entombed SUV, the one parked near the entrance, and brushed the snow from it. He examined several decals pasted to the glass.

J.C. had wondered why McCracken and Lynne had stuck with him until now, until the end of his odyssey. Now he understood: transportation. The G-Wagen—being almost out of gas aside—would be a marked vehicle. Unique, expensive, shot-up, and bearing stolen plates. Too easy for law enforcement to spot. McCracken needed new wheels. He'd just found them. But where did that leave him, J.C., and whoever owned the SUV? J.C.'s temporary elation at spotting someone at work at Rampart deflated like a blown-out tire. He supposed this had been destined to end badly from the moment he'd picked up McCracken, but now someone else seemed about to be snared in the web.

"Okay," McCracken said and motioned him forward, toward the entrance to Rampart.

J.C. hesitated, mulling his options. He didn't have any. McCracken pushed him. "Go, damn it. Remember who has the gun."

Head down, J.C. trudged toward the entrance. He supposed he could just drop the box and refuse to go any farther. But that likely wouldn't solve anything. He'd get shot, then so would the guy standing by the door, which likely didn't contain bulletproof glass.

The door swung open for them as J.C. and McCracken approached.

"Holy cow," the man who opened the door said, "I didn't expect to see anybody else here today." Bleary-eyed, unshaven, and wearing a rumpled suit, he looked as though he'd had a rough day.

"I'm surprised to see *you*," J.C. said. "I thought Rampart might be shut down."

"Technically, it is," the man said. "The main workforce was dismissed yesterday at noon, but I was asked to stay until closing since we were expecting some document deliveries. I hung around until five, our nominal closing time, but by then the weather was so bad I didn't even try to make it home."

J.C. placed the box on the floor. "I'm J.C. Riggins from American-International Systems Solutions." He extended his hand to the man. "And this is . . . my associate, uh, Delvin Smith." McCracken nodded but didn't offer his hand to the man.

"I'm Ralph Gentry," the man said, shaking hands with J.C. "If you're from American-International, I assume you're delivering a proposal."

"Two more boxes in the vehicle," J.C. said.

"Wow, I don't know how you made it here. We had a couple of proposals straggle in yesterday via FedEx, but I figured that would be the end of it, with everything closed today."

"But here I am, and here you are." J.C., despite the ever-present threat of McCracken, felt a surge of elation. "Sign me in." *This one's for you, Cole. Your old man came through.*

Gentry, his eyes drooping with weariness, frowned. "Sorry. I can't do that."

J.C., incredulous, stepped forward. "Why not? Here's the proposal." He touched the box with the side of his boot. "I know it's a few minutes late, but come on. You don't know what I went through to get this here."

"I'm sure it was a heroic effort, but the deadline was 5 p.m. I don't make the rules, Mr. Riggins, but I do have to abide by them."

"Come on, man. Pencil whip the entry. Make it 4:58 or something.

This is all in good faith." J.C. felt desperation begin to rise within him once more, like a subterranean flow of molten rock wending its way toward the surface of the earth.

"No can do. It's a computerized log-in archival with an automated date-time stamp. I can't tweak it." Gentry's gaze moved from J.C. to McCracken and back and seemed to harden.

McCracken, one hand remaining tucked beneath his parka, addressed Gentry. "So log him in with the current time. Nobody's going to care."

Gentry shook his head slowly back and forth as though responding to the statement of a "slow" child. "How long have you been in this business, Mister . . . what was it?"

"Smith. Not long."

"Yes. Well, a late delivery, even by a few minutes, may be just a technicality to you, Mr. Smith, but to competitive bidders in a high-stakes game, it would be more than enough justification for disqualification of AISSI. And believe me, they'd have you disqualified in a heartbeat."

J.C., feeling gut shot, seated himself on the box, not trusting himself to remain standing.

"I apologize, gentlemen. I know you probably went through hell to get this here, but there's nothing I can do."

"Where's the log-in system?" McCracken asked, interrupting, his voice commanding.

"In my office," Gentry answered.

"Let's have a look."

"I'm sorry, I can't do that." Gentry backed off a step. "Look, I think our business here is concluded."

"Not by a long shot, dickhead." McCracken yanked the Glock from beneath his parka. "Your office. Now."

Gentry, wide-eyed, fixated on the gun. "Hey, come on. There's no need for this. This isn't professional. What in the hell's going on here? Is this how AISSI handles its business dealings?" He flicked his gaze to J.C.

"He isn't with AISSI," J.C. said. "We're both kinda in deep shit here. I suggest you do what he says." He didn't know what McCracken had in mind but figured it couldn't be good.

He moved next to McCracken. "Hey, Cave," he said, his voice just above a whisper. "This might be a good time to bail out. You know, don't make things worse than they are. It would be great if we could all leave here in one piece. Why not just ask the guy for his keys and—"

"What? And leave my good buddy in a lurch? After all we've been through together? Not gonna happen." McCracken waved the Glock at Gentry. "Go, Mr. By-The-Rules."

"Jesus, this guy's your friend?" Gentry said to J.C. and started down a semi-darkened hallway.

"Hardly," J.C. mumbled.

They reached Gentry's office after a short walk.

"Let's all have a seat," McCracken said.

Gentry sat behind his desk, J.C. and McCracken in front of it.

"Keep your hands where I can see them," McCracken said, nodding at Gentry.

"Okay, stay calm. I'll do whatever you want." Nascent fear flickered in the man's eyes.

"Let me tell you about my, well, let's just call him my acquaintance," McCracken said. "First of all, he's right. He isn't really my friend. I carjacked him. I'm a wanted felon. He's a good guy. He busted his butt to get here. I'm the reason he missed the deadline. He's got a son dying of leukemia, so he's highly motivated to win this proposal effort. But he can't win, his company can't win, unless the document is logged in on time, right?"

"This is all very heartrending, Mr. Smith, but I still can't override the system. Everything is automated and tightly controlled." He stared at the gun. "I'd help you if I could, really, but I'm powerless."

J.C., stunned by McCracken's "defense" of him and at a loss for words, remained silent.

McCracken, with remarkable quickness for a wounded man, lurched from his chair and, with two quick swings, smashed the computer monitor with the butt end of his pistol.

Gentry ducked as glass flew from the shattered screen and littered his desk in a crystalline shower.

"Now what?" McCracken growled. "System's broken. Maybe you'd better log in the proposal by hand."

Gentry nodded. "It might not stand up under close scrutiny and hard questioning, though."

"Mr. Gentry," McCracken said, his voice authoritative and even, "look at me."

Gentry did.

"You've got one son and one daughter, right?"

Gentry's eyes widened.

"A dog and a wife, too. Kids in St. Brigid's Prep School. Like to vacation on Cape Hatteras."

J.C. knew now why McCracken had examined the stickers on Gentry's van. A family caricature. A school logo. An iconic lighthouse. Strange how much intelligence can be gleaned from innocuous little decals.

Gentry sat with his mouth agape.

"A wonderful family, Mr. Gentry," McCracken continued. "You wouldn't want anything to ever happen to them, would you?"

Gentry shook his head in the negative, vigorously.

"Then you would of course make certain that your manual log-in of my friend's proposal stood up under close examination, wouldn't you?"

He nodded. Equally as vigorously.

"Okay, then. Let's conclude our business. Sign in the proposal. Then slide your car keys over to me."

Gentry complied.

"Good," McCracken said. "Things went well, don't you think, J.C.?"

J.C. looked at McCracken, searching his eyes for his intentions. What he saw sent a dagger of fear into the heart.

"Both of you," McCracken said, "step into the hall and kneel facing the wall."

Gentry babbled incoherently and then morphed into gasping sobs.

"You don't have to do this, Cave," J.C. said, struggling to get the words out, his mouth dry with terror.

"Sorry, buddy. Can't leave any witnesses. You know, the cop and everything." He gestured with the Glock. "Come on."

On legs so rubbery he could barely stand, he wobbled into the hall and knelt, Gentry beside him, sobbing loudly.

"Gentry wasn't a witness," J.C. choked out.

"He will be. However briefly."

J.C. wrapped his arms around himself, leaned forward, and rested his forehead against the wall. *Cole, I love you. Ginny, I love you.* He waited for the bullet.

He never heard the shot that delivered it. He merely tumbled into an abyss of blackness amidst a blizzard of stars, Cole and Ginny reaching helplessly after him.

Chapter Thirty-five

Conclusions

Windy Hill Towers
Friday evening, December 30

A GLASS OF JACK Daniel's in hand, Tom stood at the window of his condo and surveyed the vast snowscape below. He didn't bother sipping his whiskey, he gulped it. The scene with Sophie sliding his dismissal papers across her desk toward him played over and over in his head. Sophie dropping the guillotine; Sophie yanking open the gallows; Sophie throwing the switch on the electric chair.

How could he have been so fucking gullible? How could he have been so stupid as to believe Sophie had any real romantic interest in him? How could he have believed that there could be any other motive in his boss igniting an amorous spark between them besides the twisted thrill of notching another kill in her Black Widow's diary? What was the parallel word to misogynist for a female who hated men? He didn't know but supposed there must be one. Sophie's picture should appear in the dictionary next to its definition. Hard to believe she had only one divorce on her rap sheet. There had to have been others.

He tipped the glass to his lips, but only a cascade of crushed ice tumbled into his mouth. He walked to the bar, grasped the Jack Daniel's bottle, and raised it aloft, holding it at arm's length. "Jack," he said, "I have a feeling we're going to become good friends by the end of tonight."

Jack didn't respond.

"That's okay. I wouldn't know what to say in this circumstance either."

Jack didn't give any indication he'd heard Tom. Or even cared.

"Look, all you have to do is listen. Guys have a right to whine once in a while, don't they? Just like women? You know, bare their souls, confess their sins, damn the universe. Just like women?"

Jack remained perfectly quiet.

"It's all right. No need to acknowledge me. At least I know what to expect with you. Our 'friendship' is predictable, unlike some I thought I'd had. Tell you what, I'll blurt everything out, rend my garments, gnash my teeth. You extend some cold comfort, a little buzzy pat on my head. I'll tumble into bed, fall into a stupor, forget my pain, and wake up feeling like shit." He poured several ounces of the liquor into his glass. "Doesn't matter. Whether I hang out with you or not, I'll still wake up feeling like shit." He took a long swallow of the booze.

"No," he said to himself. He set the glass on the counter. "Before I stumble down the rabbit hole . . . Billy and Bonnie." He punched in Billy's number on his phone.

"Hey, kid," he said when Billy answered. "How was the sledding?"

"Awww, Dad, we didn't go. Too much snow. And then the electricity in the house went out. We've been stuck here for two days with nuthin' to do."

"I know the feeling. But here's the deal. As soon as the roads are open again, I'll come get you and Bonnie, and we'll hit the slopes. Spend all day there. Drink lots of hot chocolate, maybe grab a pizza. How's that sound?"

"Promise?"

"Promise."

"You're the greatest, Dad."

That's all he needed to hear. He said goodbye and toyed with the tumbler of booze while he watched TV with relative disinterest. An anchor, who sounded on the edge of exhaustion, rambled on about the "Storm of the Millennium." He hit the highlights: a state of emergency expected to remain in effect for North Georgia through the weekend; essential traffic only; everything closed except for hospitals.

Kind of academic, Tom thought. *There's no way to get to them.*

DOT crews, the anchor continued, will be working twenty-four seven to clear roads, interstates, and main thoroughfares first. If you live outside the metro area, forget it. Expect to remain snowbound for a week, maybe longer. Food? A major concern. Grocery store shelves, the anchor said, are "emptier than our governor's promises after the last storm."

Tom almost choked. *Did the guy really say that? Well, yes. He's probably loopy after being on the air for twenty-four hours straight.* Tom raised his glass of Jack to him. "Here's to you, my friend. Tell it like it is, but you'll probably be joining me in the unemployment line next week."

The dire wrap-up continued. The National Guard calling up more troops. *But how would they reach their mobilization points?* Emergency air drops of food and supplies being considered for hospitals, the Atlanta airport, municipal parks. *How in the hell could anyone get to a city park?* Over a half-million homes and businesses lacking heat and light with utility crews rushing in from Florida, Louisiana, Mississippi, Tennessee. *They won't be rushing once they hit the snow.*

And on and on. The ninth largest metropolitan area in the nation gasping for breath in the wake of an unprecedented natural disaster. At least twenty-six people dead—from house fires, traffic accidents, carbon monoxide poisoning, hypothermia, and the inability to reach medical care, or vice versa.

Tom shuffled back to the window. In the distance, small armadas of flashing orange lights crawled along the highways, the tedious process of clearing hundreds of miles of interstate in and around the city underway. In many spots, eight to twelve lanes would need to be scraped bare. On the twisted ribbon of road known as Spaghetti Junction, where I-285 and I-85 collide, a flyover eighteen lanes in breadth would need to be plowed. "And where do you put the snow?" Tom mouthed. "The Chattahoochee? Lake Lanier? Underground Atlanta?" He shrugged. *I don't really give a damn,* ran through his mind as he emptied the second glassful of whiskey.

Weighing the pros and cons of a third refill, a sharp rap on the door to his condo interrupted his contemplation. He debated responding to the knock. *Oh, leave me alone. . . . But it might be a neighbor in need of something: food, batteries, a flashlight.* He ambled to the door and put his eye to the peephole. *Shit.* Sophie. Come for the coup de grâce?

"Get the hell out of here, Sophie," he said through the closed door.

"Open up, asshole."

"Yeah, that's it. Turn on the charm. Huff and puff all you want to, Your Highness. No way you're stepping across my threshold."

Silence.

He jammed his eye to the peephole. No Sophie. But then she reappeared. She'd apparently stooped to retrieve something from her briefcase. Now she stood in front of the door holding up two pieces of paper for him to see, one in each hand.

"Tom," she said, "listen to me for a second. Pull your male ego out of your butt. Yeah"—she waggled the paper in her right hand—

"one of these is your termination agreement. The other is something else, something good. Now open the damn door so I don't have to stand out here blathering away like some sorry-assed Jehovah's Witness."

Tom hesitated.

Sophie waited.

Tom opened the door.

Sophie, briefcase in one hand, an oversize shoulder bag in the other, stormed past him into the condo. She slammed the items onto a table and, her mouth tightly clenched in what Tom knew well as a warning sign, whirled to confront him.

"If you ever walk out on me again, I swear to God I'll make sure you're a leper in the broadcast business," Sophie said, her words boiling in a seething broth of anger.

"How could I walk out on you *again?* I don't work for you anymore. Or have you fried all your brain cells?" His words came out knife-edged, as intended.

Sophie peeled off her parka and tossed it onto a chair. She drew a deep breath and looked away from Tom as though contemplating her next move. She sighed audibly, then reached into her briefcase and drew out the sheets of paper she'd held up earlier. She placed them on the table, facing Tom.

She tapped her forefinger on one. "Yes, it's your pink slip. Sign it." She tapped the other one. "Sign this one, too." She paused. "Please."

He stared at it. A contract of some sort.

"It's a consulting agreement," she said, "working for NE-TV full-time at roughly twice your previous salary."

"What's going on here, Sophie?"

"The corporation," she said, her words wrapped in the soft tones of appeasement now, "has a policy against fraternization. I think it's a stupid policy, but the mucky-mucks think it helps avoid sexual harassment suits, appearances of favoritism, and possible conflicts of interest. It's all bullshit, but it's the company code."

"I don't get it."

She rolled her eyes. "For an MIT grad, you're really dumb."

"Okay. I'm dumb." He had an inkling but wasn't about to verbalize it.

She blushed, actually blushed. Very un-Sophie-like. "It means if we're going to be lovers, we can't both be NE-TV employees."

"Are we going to be lovers?"

"As soon as you sign the damn papers." Her face continued to glow.

"Got a pen?"

She fumbled in her briefcase.

He signed. "Am I still going to be working under you?"

She grabbed her shoulder bag, turned, and strode down the hall toward the bedrooms. "Maybe. But it's going to be a long weekend with nothing else to do. I might discover I like working under you better."

Yes, Virginia, there is a Santa Claus. He drew a deep breath, sucking in Sophie's wake of perfume, and wobbled after her.

She stopped abruptly and pivoted toward him. "Before you come near me, though, use some mouthwash. Get that God-awful Jack Daniel's off your breath."

Magnolia Heights Subdivision
Saturday, January 7

"WATCH ME, DADDY." Cole took a running start with his plastic sled, something called Winter Lightning, belly-flopped onto it, and barreled down a long hill on the sixth fairway, still buried in several inches of crusty snow.

"Last one, son," J.C. yelled after him. He didn't want Cole to get excessively tired. Already, after just a couple of trips down the slope, Cole, rosy-cheeked and breathing hard, seemed on the edge of exhaustion. J.C. didn't want to push it any further. They were due back at MD Anderson the following week, and he didn't wish to return there with a sick child . . . well, at least any sicker than he was already.

The air filled with a swirl of tiny snowflakes riding a busy northwest wind, courtesy, according to the local TV weathercasters, of a fresh push of arctic air. The previous five days had brought a slow moderation of temperatures with the snow cover—record snow cover—surrendering, albeit at a grudging pace, to daytime readings climbing into the forties. Nighttime temperatures, however, continued to sink to subfreezing levels, spawning icy commuting conditions.

Little matter. The city had remained shuttered to all but essential businesses, whatever they were, by order of the mayor so that the cleanup of ice and snow could proceed uninhibited. Still, many roads, especially in the suburbs, remained all but impassable. J.C. knew it would have been a different story in many other areas of the country, places used to dealing with winter weather, but not here in the South where plows, chains, and snow tires are uncommon, not to mention winter driving skills.

J.C. rubbed the lump behind his ear where McCracken had pistol-whipped him. The double vision had relented, but not the soft, ringing echo that rattled around in his ears. A minor issue, really. He still didn't understand why he stood here at all, alive, playing with his son, looking forward to a pot roast dinner in the warmth and safety of his home, wrapped in the love of his family.

Why had McCracken let him live? He, J.C., was, ultimately, the only person who could place the biker at the scene of the shooting of the Georgia State Trooper. When asked by investigators if he'd picked McCracken up at the weigh station, J.C. had not hesitated. He said, "I picked him up on I-85."

He hadn't lied exactly. He'd just told a half-truth by broadening the definition of "on" to include things such as weigh stations. Why? He wasn't sure. McCracken had, after all, shanghaied him, threatened him with death, and thrown him into a den of crazy-assed outlaw bikers. The guy wore the black hat of a drug dealer and a cop shooter.

Yet he'd made sure, however self-serving his motives might have been, that J.C. got to Durham on time—almost on time—and that despite being technically late, that the proposal got logged in as being delivered prior to the deadline. After hearing J.C.'s story, Gentry, the Rampart employee, allowed the delivery time to stand despite the traumatic circumstances under which he had accepted it. Then again, maybe McCracken had just scared the crap out of him.

J.C. acknowledged that McCracken bore responsibility in the first place for the dire circumstances that had unfolded. On the other hand, even without the forced excursion into the mountains, the G-Wagen would have run out of fuel before reaching Durham. And he, J.C., would not have had a clue about how to steal gas. In truth, he wouldn't have had the balls.

"Hey, Dad, one more time. Okay?" Cole, tugging his sled, stood in front of J.C. Chest heaving, he puffed tiny clouds of steam into the wispy snowfall. His eyes danced in excitement as the shouts and whoops of other children cut through the fading light.

"Nope. You're done, kid."

"Awww, Dad. P-l-e-a-s-e." He dragged out the word "please" in the most pitiful manner.

"Maybe we can come back tomorrow," J.C. said, knowing full well that for Cole "maybe" amounted to a promise. At least it defused the possibility of an immediate conflict. He draped his arm over his son's shoulders, and they trudged toward home.

His thoughts, nevertheless, lingered on McCracken. The guy had gone to bat for him at Rampart, albeit in a thoroughly mafioso manner. J.C. knew *he* could never have been so, well, persuasive.

So how do you figure it? A guy with a "me-first," "people-are-motivated-by-fear" philosophy reaches out on behalf of someone other than himself. *Maybe I should have brought him along when I returned the G-Wagen to RQB.*

The authorities in North Carolina had impounded the Mercedes for several days, but allowed it to be returned to RQB on a flatbed truck on Thursday.

J.C. had been there when it arrived.

Carl stood beside him. "So grandma lived in Durham, not on top of Grandfather Mountain?" he said.

"You could think of that way," J.C. said.

The flatbed splashed through thick slush coating the dealership's lot and pulled up in front of J.C. and Carl. Carl ran his gaze over the battered SUV, its shot-out windows, crumpled fenders, and bullet-riddled exterior.

"I guess Grandma was pissed, huh? Late with her Christmas gifts?"

"Late with something, anyhow," J.C. said, wondering if Carl was bemused or angry.

The flatbed driver lowered the G-Wagen to the ground. Carl stepped closer to it and peeked into the windows. "There's a dead bear in the rear seat," he said.

"That's Teddy. Cole has been asking about him."

"Cole may turn out to be a more difficult lender than I am."

"I'm sorry about this, Carl. Really, I am."

"Well, there's gotta be a great story behind it," Carl said, a hint of a grin reflected in his voice.

"Three-beer story," J.C. said.

"Step into my office, then. Let's get started. I can't offer you a beer, but we've got coffee, and I might find something to add a bit of, shall we say, *body* to it."

Accompanied by the aroma of freshly brewed Gevalia, a splash of expensive cognac, and the alluring scent of $100,000 new cars, J.C. related his tale, leaving out, as he'd carefully rehearsed, any mention of the weigh station and the shot-up police cruiser.

Carl steepled his fingers together and rested them under his chin when J.C. had finished. He seemed lost in thought. J.C. waited.

"Well, I believe you've succeeded in establishing a new image, a fresh legend as it were, for the Mercedes G-Wagen," Carl finally said, keeping his voice low and sounding not at all upset. "Russian Mafia be damned." He chuckled. "Don't worry about it. I'm sure our insurance will cover it. And I was thinking, we could probably come up with a really good deal for you on a reconditioned G-550. . . . if you're interested."

Chapter Thirty-six

Questions

American-International Systems Solutions, Inc.
Friday, February 24

J.C. HAVING BEEN summoned to his boss's office, rapped on Cyrus Billingsly's door.

Billingsly responded with his usual curt command, "Enter."

J.C. did. Upon returning to work the second week of January, Billingsly had reinstated him as a corporate vice president, but their contact since then had been minimal.

Billingsly, as steely-faced as ever, but appearing relaxed and approachable, nodded for J.C. to take a seat.

"You know, I still don't know how you did it, how you got that proposal delivered through a historic storm, but you did," Billingsly said. "I'd call that a remarkable achievement."

"Thank you, sir, but it was my screwup in the first place that made it necessary."

Billingsly almost smiled. "Still . . ." He spread his hands as if to say, *Still, you did it.* He extracted a pair of reading glasses from his desk drawer, slipped them on, and studied a piece of paper on his desk. "We've been asked for our 'best and final' from Rampart." This time he did smile. "Rumor has it the finalists on the contract award have been whittled down to us and a team led by Boeing. Great job, Mr. Riggins." Billingsly stood and extended a congratulatory hand across his desk to J.C.

J.C. arose and accepted the kudos, but he knew any celebration would be premature. AISSI still had to *win* the contract.

"So, one more thing," Billingsly said. He gestured for J.C. to return to his seat.

"Yes, sir?"

"Well, a question before I continue: How's Cole doing? I understand he's back at MD Anderson."

"He is and seems to be doing well. His doctors believe he can avoid a stem cell transplant, but the jury's still out."

"You wife is with him?"

"She is, and both sets of grandparents, too."

"So you're comfortable with the situation?"

"I'm a lot less worried than I was a couple of months ago."

"Good. I'm happy for you."

J.C. studied Billingsly, his etched-in-stone features, his probing gaze. *He has a soul after all.* But J.C. sensed the man's expression of empathy went deeper than just that. He waited for Billingsly to continue.

"So, given that you're relatively free of outside distractions, and I understand that none of us ever is totally, I'd like you to coordinate the effort to put together our 'best and final.'"

"When is it due?" J.C. shuffled his feet in an uncomfortable reaction. He'd promised Cole he'd visit him in Houston this weekend, and he had a pretty good idea the 'best and final'—the last and most attractive bid to Rampart—would be on a tight schedule.

"A week from today," Billingsly said.

J.C. looked away from Billingsly and bit his lip. Next Friday. That meant working through the weekend.

"Problem?"

"I'm visiting Cole this weekend."

Billingsly looked thoughtful. "I understand. Family first. W-e-l-l"—he drew out the word—"I suspect if you appealed to our new COO, he'd understand. He's got overall responsibility for the final bid, and he's had first-hand experience with the damage that preoccupied employees can cause."

J.C. jerked into a more upright position in his chair. "New COO? Since when does AISSI have a chief operating officer?"

"He'll be easy to work with."

"Who is he?"

Billingsly brushed a hand through his bristly hair and, for the first time since J.C. had known him, actually laughed. "Congratulations," he said.

Five minutes later, J.C., boasting a grin as wide as I-285, returned to his desk.

He'd barely seated himself when his desk phone rang. He thought it might be Ginny, but, being unsure, he resisted the urge to answer it

"J.C. Riggins, Chief Operating Officer." Instead, he merely said, "J.C. Riggins."

"Hello, dipshit."

J.C., taken aback, hesitated. "Cave?"

"Yeah."

"You're alive."

"You should have been a detective."

"In jail?"

"No."

"Cops never caught you?"

"No. I guess I wasn't high priority enough to send a task force after. Seems I'm more of a person of interest than a suspect. I wonder how that happened?"

J.C. didn't answer. He set the new nameplate Billingsly had given him on his desk and centered it, waiting for McCracken to continue speaking.

"Perhaps," McCracken went on, "there was nothing, or nobody, to place me at the scene of the shooting? Whaddaya think?"

J.C. didn't know what he thought. He wanted to ask a particular question but couldn't quite frame it. Instead, he said, "How's Lynne?"

"She's fine. She's pregnant."

"Oh?" Something clicked into place for J.C. It didn't surprise him. It's a thought that had flitted across his mind in Durham. "That's why you made an issue of picking up that stranded couple, isn't it?"

"Well, it wasn't out of Christian love, if that's what you're driving at."

"I'm not driving at anything, Cave. It's just an observation. Anyhow, congratulations."

"Yeah. Hey, your boy okay? What was his name?"

"Yes, he's okay, and his name is Cole."

"Cole. Good name. Maybe I'll think about that for my kid."

"What if she's a girl?"

"Coleen."

"Nice. Say, I don't suppose it would do any good to ask where you are?" J.C. picked up a pen and placed a pad of paper in front of him, just in case.

"Nope."

J.C. set the pen back on the desk. "Just out of curiosity, did Griz ever track you down, you know, trying to get his . . . stuff back?"

"No. I'm a long way from the Appalachians. Besides, I heard Griz was caught and is awaiting trial in a South Carolina jail. Anyhow, I'm getting out of that business."

"Turning over a new leaf?"

"Probably not. Just discarding the previous one. Anyhow, it's funny how things work out, isn't it?"

"How so?" J.C. swiveled in his chair and gazed out at the bright sunlight flooding the late winter landscape. Already, in response to temperatures that had knocked on the door of seventy degrees, ornamental fruit trees had dared blossom, probably too early for their own good.

"I mean," McCracken continued, "if I'd shot you and that other dude in Durham—my version of eliminating witnesses—I really would have sealed my fate. The law would have been relentless in hunting me down. Instead, because you're still walking and talking, but apparently not talking all *that* much, I've been given some breathing room. Isn't there a foreign word for that? *Quad pro* something?"

"*Quid pro quo.* You scratch my back, I'll scratch yours."

"Yeah. You think that applies in our case?"

"Does it?"

"Probably not. I know you might like to think I didn't shoot you because I had an epiphany—I think that's the right word—and suddenly realized in a blinding flash of light that mankind really is driven by love, not fear. No, my friend. Fear rules, always will."

And that framed the question J.C. knew he had to ask. "So why didn't you shoot me? I mean, at that very moment, hindsight aside, what prevented you from pulling the trigger?"

McCracken didn't answer immediately. J.C. waited.

"Because," McCracken said after a long pause, "the clip was empty."

"You knew that all along?"

"Yeah. The whole deal with the Glock after the Waffle House was a bluff."

"You would have shot me, the other guy, too, if the clip had been loaded?"

"Yeah."

"You're sure?"

McCracken didn't answer. Instead, he said, "Hey, I almost forgot. I sent your kid a teddy bear."

J.C., taken aback, found himself unable to articulate a response.

McCracken kept talking. "I felt bad after I assassinated Teddy, especially when you told me your kid had sent him along as a guardian angel. Anyhow, I figured *Cole* could maybe use a guardian angel. You know, with all the shit he's facing. So I put a bear in a box and sent it to you at your company's address."

"Cave, I don't know what to—"

"You don't have to say anything. Life goes on without us trying to dissect it or figure it out. It is what it is. Look, I'm going to hang up now. I won't bother you again. Take care of your wife and kid, J.C." McCracken terminated the call.

J.C. sat at his desk for a long time, staring at nothing, digesting the conversation he'd just had. His question hadn't really been answered, and he knew it never would be. He'd never know if the reason he sat here at this moment, attempting to analyze *why* he sat here, was due to some sort of cosmic roll of the dice, or something more deliberate but still unfathomable: a numinous nudge of the chaos that seems endemic to the world.

He wondered how much of his life, if any, was dictated: influenced by powers unseen, unknowable, undefinable. Or was he—any of us—merely adrift in a universe ruled by randomness, accidents, and arbitrary conjunctions of events: a failed task, a historic blizzard, a crook on the lam, an empty .45-caliber ammunition clip?

How do you explain a guy who steals a car, shoots a cop, and deals drugs sending a guardian angel teddy bear to a kid fighting leukemia?

He couldn't have been motivated by fear.

J.C. wondered if Cave Man realized that.

The End

Author's Note

Blizzard, while a product of my imagination, has its roots in personal experiences. (No, not the part about the bikers.) I lived for twenty years in New England, near Hartford and Boston, so have been through dozens of snowstorms and several full-blown blizzards. The one that stands out in my memory is the Blizzard of '78 in Boston. That storm literally shut down the city for the better part of a week. Years later in Atlanta, I experienced Superstorm 1993, a blizzard that left portions of north Georgia snowbound.

My thirteen years as a Senior Meteorologist at The Weather Channel informs the scenes set in the fictional Natural Environment Television Network. The characters at NE-TV, however, in no way reflect the fine people I worked with at The Weather Channel. Prior to working at The Weather Channel, I spent some time in the defense industry, where I gained at least a handshaking knowledge of proposal efforts.

You may wonder where the scene with the wolves in north Georgia came from. (Yes, I know there are no wolves in the eastern U. S., but I think I explained away their presence satisfactorily.)

At any rate, the scene actually had its genesis in Germany. There's a castle, Burg Arras (constructed ca. 1100), near my wife's hometown, that overlooks the Mosel River Valley. During the forty years I've visited the area on and off, Burg Arras has become kind of a favorite of mine. It's more of a tourist spot for locals than for international visitors.

The castle sits atop a steep, forested hill several miles back from the river. I often imagined a scene, as I hiked up to the castle, in which a medieval peasant, pursued by a pack of wolves, struggled through deep snow seeking the safety of the burg. Knowing I'd probably never write a tale set in medieval Germany, I merely transplanted my musings to the modern-day southern Appalachians.

I received no remuneration from Mercedes for having my protagonist use a Geländewagen in his epic journey. It just seemed like the right vehicle for the job. Of course, the fact my wife is German and we have a good friend who's a former general manager of a large Mercedes dealership in Atlanta probably had something to do with the choice, too.

As usual, a lot of people helped make *Blizzard* a better book than it started out. First of all, there was my Books For Less/Barnes & Noble critique group that suffered through numerous iterations of various chapters. They always found ways to make my writing more readable. Next, my "first" readers, Jeanie Loiacono, who is also my agent, Gary Schwartz, Tom Howley and Dave Spiegler all labored through the first draft of the novel and pointed out where the characters and/or the story needed improvement.

Finally, many thanks to my editor at Bell Bridge Books, Pat Van Wie, for lending her boundless skill, wisdom, and insights to improve my feeble efforts.

I also wish to acknowledge Jeff Wright, Director of Security for Waffle House. Jeff called my attention to the "Waffle House Index" (it's for real) in addition to answering my questions about police procedures.

Glossary

AJC—Atlanta Journal-Constitution

BLOCKING HIGH (or BLOCK) high pressure area that remains nearly stationary or moves only slowly, thus effectively blocking the typical west-to-east progression of weather systems.

BLIZZARD—a condition characterized by high wind and reduced visibility due to falling or blowing snow (snow lifted from the surface). In the U. S., the definition of a blizzard is strict: sustained winds or frequent gusts of at least thirty-five miles per hour accompanied by falling or blowing snow frequently reducing visibility to less than a quarter-mile for three or more hours.

COMMA HEAD—a large-scale cloud pattern exhibiting a comma-like shape; often seen on satellite images associated with large, intense storm systems.

CUT-OFF—an upper-level, low pressure system that is completely displaced (cut off) from the basic westerly wind flow aloft and is thus moving independently of that flow.

DETERMINISTIC (or OPERATIONAL) MODEL RUN—the version of a numerical weather prediction model that is used on a regular, ongoing basis (i.e., for day-to-day operations).

DRY SLOT—a relatively narrow zone of dry air that wraps northward into the eastern portions of a mature storm system; generally best seen on satellite imagery.

ENSEMBLE—multiple, numerical weather predictions made by using slightly different initial conditions in each run or slightly different versions of the same model. The objective is to improve forecast accuracy by averaging the model outputs, thus smoothing out extremes and reducing uncertainties.

EURO—the short name for the European global forecast model, or more accurately the model run under the auspices of the European

Center for Medium-Range Weather Forecasting (ECMWF) in Reading, U. K.

FANTASYCAST—a slang term used by meteorologists to describe an unlikely weather event predicted by a numerical model in the longer range, usually beyond ten days.

FEMA—Federal Emergency Management Agency.

GFS—Global Forecast System; the name generally applied to the U. S. weather prediction model (which is part of the Global Forecast System).

HERO—Highway Emergency Response Operators (a Georgia Department of Transportation program).

ISENTROPIC LIFT—a technical term for lift created when warmer air is forced aloft by colder air at or near the surface.

NE-TV—the fictional Natural Environment Television Network.

PERIMETER—the Interstate (I-285) encircling Atlanta.

SUPERSTORM '93—a record-breaking storm also known as "The Storm of the Century": An exceptionally large and powerful storm system that spread heavy snow and high winds from the Deep South to eastern Canada (March 1993). The storm also triggered tornadoes in Florida and a significant storm surge on the northwest Florida coast.

WINTER STORM (or BLIZZARD) WATCH—an alert issued by the National Weather Service when conditions appear favorable for a winter storm (or blizzard) within the next twenty-four to seventy-two hours (winter storm criteria varies from location to location).

WINTER STORM (or BLIZZARD) WARNING—a warning issued by the National Weather Service when winter storm or blizzard conditions are expected within the next twelve to thirty-six hours.

EMERGENCY ITEMS FOR YOUR VEHICLE:
WHAT TO CARRY WHEN A WINTER STORM LOOMS
(just in case you get stuck)

HEAVY BLANKET—maybe two—one to keep you warm, another for a pillow.

WARM OUTERWEAR /EXTRA SOCKS AND UNDERWEAR—gloves, a heavy jacket, a warm hat; extra socks, boots and underwear.

BOTTLED WATER—it's important to stay hydrated.

FOOD—items that have a long shelf life: packages of nuts and crackers, granola bars, hard candy, maybe a few fresh fruits such as bananas or apples

PRESCRIPTION MEDICATIONS—in original pharmacy containers.

CAR CHARGER FOR YOUR CELL PHONE—plugs in cigarette lighter in your car (mine works on my cell phone *and* my e-reader).

FLASHLIGHT WITH FRESH BATTERIES—perhaps two flashlights; you can never have enough.

TOILETRIES—toothbrush, toothpaste, hand sanitizer, wet ones, paper towels, toilet paper, lip balm, etc.

PAPER OR PLASTIC CUPS/PLASTIC SEALABLE ONE-QUART CONTAINERS—some to drink from, the latter to act as a "waste" container for elimination.

TRASH BAGS AND TIES—you don't want garbage accumulating in your vehicle and you are not allowed to litter.

FIRST AID KIT—you should have one in your vehicle anyhow; check to make sure there is enough of everything (band aids, 4x4s, tape, aspirin, thermometer, alcohol swaps, several pairs of disposable gloves, handkerchief for tourniquet, AAA ointment, hydrocortisone cream, etc.)

JUMPER CABLES and FIRE EXTINGUISHER—again, these should be everyday items in your vehicle.

EMPTY GAS CAN—fill it only as needed to replenish your vehicle's fuel—NEVER CARRY A FULL GASOLINE CONTAINER IN YOUR VEHICLE!

BAG OF SAND OR KITTY LITTER—for emergency traction.

SMALL OR COLLAPSIBLE SNOW SHOVEL—can be purchased at any hardware store.

"OLD FASHIONED" PAPER MAPS—just in case your GPS malfunctions (as J.C.'s did in *Blizzard*).

SPRAY DE-ICER—can be purchased at any hardware store; may be a seasonal item.

ICE SCRAPER—keep in vehicle at all times; one with a brush on the opposite end is a plus.

A BOOK OR E-READER—to help pass the time.

EXTRA CASH—in case ATMs and card readers aren't working.

WHISTLE—might be helpful if you end up off the road; your voice may not carry or you may get tired or become hoarse from yelling.

About the Author

H. W. "Buzz" Bernard is the bestselling author of *EYEWALL*, *PLAGUE* and *SUPERCELL*.

EYEWALL-his debut novel, became a number-one best seller on Amazon's Kindle; nominated for Georgia Author of the Year 2012— Fiction Novel

PLAGUE-nominated for Georgia Author of the Year 2013—Novel; Winner 2014 EPIC eBook Award for Suspense/thriller!

SUPERCELL-climbed to number four on the Kindle best-seller list; finalist for 2015 EPIC eBook Award for Suspense/Thriller; semi-finalist for Georgia Author of the Year 2014—Fiction

Buzz is a native Oregonian and attended the University of Washington in Seattle where he earned a degree in atmospheric science and studied creative writing. He's currently Vice President of the Southeastern Writers Association. Bernard is represented by Loiacono Literary Agency www.loiaconoliteraryagency.com.

He and his wife, Christina, along with a fuzzy Shih-Tzu named Stormy, live in Roswell, Georgia, near Atlanta. To learn more about Buzz visit: buzzbernard.com or his author page on Facebook: H. W. "Buzz" Bernard.

CPSIA information can be obtained
at www.ICGtesting.com
Printed in the USA
FFOW04n1501270215